ORANGE MINT AND HONEY

ONE WORLD

BALLANTINE BOOKS

NEW YORK

Orange Mint and Honey

and

a novel

Carleen Brice

A One World Books Trade Paperback Original

Copyright © 2008 by Carleen Brice

Reading Group Guide Copyright © 2008
by Random House, Inc.

Published in the United States by One World Books,
an imprint of The Random House Publishing Group,
a division of Random House, Inc., New York.

ONE WORLD is a registered trademark
and the One World colophon is a trademark
of Random House, Inc.

RANDOM HOUSE READER'S CIRCLE and colophon are
trademarks of Random House, Inc.

Grateful acknowledgment is made to Alfred Publishing for permission to reprint an
excerpt from "Ain't No Use" by Rudy Stevenson, copyright © 1967 EMI GROVE
PARK and NINANDY MUSIC. All rights controlled by EMI GROVE PARK
(Publishing) and ALFRED PUBLISHING Co., Inc. (Print). All rights reserved.
Reprinted by permission of Alfred Publishing, Co., Inc.

LIBRARY OF CONGRESS CATALOGING-IN-PUBLICATION DATA
Brice, Carleen.
Orange mint and honey : a novel / Carleen Brice.
p.   cm.
"A One World Books Trade Paperback Original"—T.p. verso.
ISBN 978-0-345-49906-6 (pbk.)
1. African American women—Fiction. 2. Mothers and daughters—
Fiction. 3. Reconciliation—Fiction. 4. Domestic fiction. I. Title.
PS3602.R494073 2008
813'.6—dc22   2007030854

Printed in the United States of America

www.randomhousereaderscircle.com

2 4 6 8 9 7 5 3 1

Book design by Barbara M. Bachman

For Dirk

MORE GROWS IN THE GARDEN
THAN THE GARDENER SOWS.

—*Spanish proverb*

ORANGE MINT AND HONEY

What Would Nina Simone Do?

I SHOULD HAVE KNOWN THINGS WERE GETTING BAD when Nina Simone showed up. Don't get me wrong. I love Nina. I've been listening to her since History of Jazz sophomore year. The professor taught us to worship the great men of jazz, but it was the women who drew me in: Billie Holiday, Ella Fitzgerald, Sarah Vaughan, Dinah Washington, Bessie Smith, Mildred Bailey. They were queens, priestesses, goddesses—encouraging me, pointing me away from danger, schooling me in the ways of life. Especially Nina Simone.

I listened to Nina Simone a thousand times, and I always got something from her music. But the night she came to me for the first time she must have known I needed more than a song could offer. I knew a famous singer—and a dead one at that—shouldn't have been in my bedroom, but somehow I wasn't surprised to see her because I had been wishing she were there. Wishing she would tell me what to do.

Usually when I was down I could keep going. But this time I bumped up against something that I couldn't get over, a wall as hard and cold and impossible to see through as frosted glass. I had lost my job writing grant proposals for an indigent-care clinic, stopped going to class, and received an eviction notice from my landlord. But still all I could do was listen to music, hanging on to the life preserver of Nina Simone's eerie, regal voice.

That night, I was listening to the fast version of "House of the Rising Sun." It's a live recording, seven minutes long. Nina gets so into it, you can't make out what she's singing. Behind her, the band chants "rising sun, rising sun" over and over, and the audience claps to the fast beat. The piano, the clapping hands, and the tambourine sound like church and juke joints, like sweat and heat, free and *alive*. I started dancing. I hadn't had the energy to get out of my pajamas for a week, but "House of the Rising Sun" had me shaking my head back and forth, twirling in circles, and pumping my arms and legs up and down like I was performing a tribal ritual, like I was one of Alvin Ailey's dancers. I danced through the song three times until all thoughts of jobs and grad school and unpaid bills were erased from my mind, and I could sleep.

At 3:33 A.M. I opened my eyes and Nina Simone was there, as if I had conjured her, standing in front of my bedroom window, blue moonlight spotlighting her features—thick lips, proud nose, slanted eyes rimmed in kohl like Cleopatra's. I had been asking myself for days WWNSD

(What would Nina Simone do?) and now she had come to tell me. I didn't know if she was a ghost or a hallucination, and I didn't care. Eyes wide, heart thumping like the speakers in the car of a teenaged boy, I sat up and waited for Nina Simone to say something wise, to tell me how to fix the mess I'd made of my life, to comfort me, and convince me that I had everything I needed to move forward inside me.

"You've really screwed up now," she said.

"*What?*"

"You heard me."

That's how low I had sunk. Even the spirits of the dead or my own daydreams were turning on me. "I thought you were going to offer me some advice!"

"You're a grown woman. Why should I tell you what to do?"

It sounded bad when she said it. But I was tired. Tired of always having to figure things out, tired of always having to do everything myself. I'd been taking care of myself since I was eight years old. So for someone else to tell me what to do was exactly what I wanted. For once in my life, I wanted someone else to carry the load. "Because I need help!" I shouted. They were words I had never said before. But then again Nina Simone had never been in my apartment before. It was a night of firsts.

"You got that right," she said, taking in the mounds of dirty clothes, used Kleenexes, heaps of junk mail, textbooks, CDs, notebooks, and milk-crusted cereal bowls and teacups.

"What I need is . . . is just a break. A rest. A time-out."

Just the week before, Carl, my advisor, had convinced

me that time off was what I needed. Actually, he had "strongly suggested" that I take a year off.

"No!" I had yelled, the most intense emotion I had shown in forever. As exhausted and sick of everything as I was I couldn't just drop out. I couldn't be away from school for an entire year.

He stared at me, even more worried.

"I mean, I can't fall that far behind. I can take a semester off. You're right, a semester off will do me some good."

"Okay," he said, relief washing over his face.

I guess since that MIT student set herself on fire a few years ago—even *after* visiting the mental health service— the plan was to get depressed college students off campus ASAP. Let them be someone else's lawsuit in the making.

"What will you do with your time off?"

"I have no idea." What did people do with time off? I had never taken a day off in my life. If I didn't have to work, I still had papers to write or tests to study for. Even during the summers I took at least one class or put in extra hours at work. I'd never even skipped school before now. Playing hooky was something that bad kids, going-to-end-up-just-like-their-parents kids did.

"What about your family? Friends? Don't you have anybody who can help?"

You would think that since I was sitting in front of him in dirty, rumpled clothes and a bandanna on my head, looking like "Who shot John?" as my old hairdresser Belinda used to say, he would know the answer to that question.

Of course, being an academic, he wasn't much better dressed. Like me, he had on the requisite khakis and button-down shirt. We could have been twins except his clothes probably didn't come straight out of the hamper. He still thought I was like all his other students, who got care packages, plane tickets, and checks from home. But all I ever got from Nona were postcards from her new, allegedly sober, life. And friends? The last good friend I had was in high school. Stephanie was still back in Denver. I hadn't spoken to her since we graduated.

"I'll be fine," I said.

"I don't know what's going on, but you might want to see someone. You know? A professional. I want you to come back ready to finish your thesis."

My thesis was just one of many things that had stalled. I nodded, exhausted. All I wanted to do was go back home and turn on my music.

"Let's touch base in a month or so. Send me an e-mail, let me know how you're doing."

"I'll be fine," I repeated.

Though, clearly, I was far from fine. Things had only gotten worse. I had been "resting" for a week now, and look what happened: A dead woman was sitting in my bedroom talking to me.

"Go home, Shay," Nina Simone said.

She knew my name.

"You need to go home," she said.

She must have read my mind, which shouldn't have been too hard considering there was a good chance she was being generated from the same place. But like Carl, she didn't understand.

The last time I saw Nona I was in my junior year in college. She came to Iowa City when she reached the step where they make you apologize. She was very pregnant, and I couldn't believe how ugly she was. Her face was all broken out and she must have gained fifty, sixty pounds. Not just in her breasts and stomach, but in her face, arms, hands, back, butt, and thighs. The bags under her eyes were puffed up like pot stickers. Even her feet were fat.

When I saw her, saw how heavy and zitty she was, I was almost happy she had come. I kept my eyes on her bloated feet the whole time she read her apology. Her voice shook. I don't remember exactly what she said. Something about being sorry she let me down, sorry I learned I couldn't trust her. But I remember her saying something about us "being mother and daughter again" and, even though I was looking down at her feet, I saw her rest her hand on her stomach when she said the word mother.

That was too much. Acting like her pregnancy was a good thing, not a horrible, stupid mistake. I had actually been hopeful when she told me she was going to A.A. For the first few months I thought, *Wow, she's really going to do it this time*. Stupid me, I actually let myself believe her. Then she got pregnant. Knocked up by a guy she met in A.A., who promptly left her high and dry just like my own father had; and there she was expecting me to believe that things were different. She couldn't even do A.A. without going off with some guy! She was thirty-six years old and she had never heard of birth control? Never heard of AIDS or chlamydia or herpes?

She told me she hoped I would give her another chance. I think she wanted me to shout "I forgive you!" and throw myself into her arms. But I just stared at her feet, at the flesh rising like bread dough over the straps of her red sandals.

Nina Simone gingerly toed a pair of jeans out of her way, revealing the panties I had worn with them weeks ago tangled up inside, and walked toward me. I hoped she wouldn't get too close. It had been a while since I had seen soap and water. I was cloaked in a cloud of funk toxic enough to re-kill a dead woman.

She sat on the foot of my bed. "You could rest. Let your mother take care of you."

I snorted. "That's not how it worked. I took care of Nona. And I'm done."

"Maybe it would be different. Maybe you've got nothing to lose."

I doubted it would be very different, but she was right about my having nothing to lose. Spending the next few months in my old VW Bug didn't sound very appealing. But still I hesitated.

"Go home," Nina Simone urged, her long earrings swinging like chandeliers.

So I picked up the phone and called Nona for the first time in seven years.

Strands

A WEEK LATER, ON THE EIGHTH NIGHT OF THE EIGHTH month of the year, I arrived at the address Nona had given me, still questioning the visitation/fantasy/fever dream that had made me think coming back to Denver could ever be a good idea. The sun had just disappeared behind the mountains far to the west. It's eight hundred miles from Iowa City, and I had been driving in my unair-conditioned 1972 Volkswagen all day. I was exhausted, dirty, and sticky with sweat, but not at all ready to go in.

A cool Colorado night breeze, so unlike the fog that passes for air in Iowa, flowed through the windows and Nina Simone's voice floated out of the car speakers. Just as she was singing "A gal who's been forgotten may forgive, but never once forget" two figures, one big and one small, walked toward me out of the darkness into the light of the streetlamp. I turned the key to stop the cassette tape, but I could still hear Nina's voice telling me to go on, go on and do what you came to do. I got out of the car. A woman who I had to assume was Nona, though I barely recognized her, opened the gate and walked right up to me and hugged me as if there had never been hundreds of miles and years of bitterness between us.

She pulled away from me smiling, teary-eyed. "I'm so happy you're here."

I gaped at her, my eyes dry. At forty, she still looked more like my sister than my mother, especially now that the baby weight was gone. What was really strange, though, was that she had on glasses and, even more striking, she had cut her hair into a very short afro. Long straight hair used to be her thing. She always wore weaves and extensions that floated around her shoulders like feathers; and no matter how much she was drinking, she made it to the beauty shop every six weeks to get her relaxer retouched. She was probably always the best-looking drunk in the bar.

She rubbed her hand over her tight curls and said, "I look different, huh?"

I don't know why, but I answered no. Maybe it was because I didn't want to talk about looks. I was wearing old cutoffs, a t-shirt stained with truck-stop burrito sauce, and, to complete my ensemble, my bandanna. I had started pulling my hair again, something I hadn't done since the ninth grade, and had cleared three bald patches around my head. The scarf was to cover the carnage.

A little girl in ballet flats, pink tutu, and a Colorado State University sweatshirt hugged Nona's leg.

"Hey, this is Sunshine." Nona picked up the little girl and beamed at her like she was the cinnamon on her cappuccino.

I'd seen her before, but only in pictures. She could have been anybody's baby sitting in a bathtub with soap bubbles on her head or smiling like a Buddha in the middle of a patch of orange and blue flowers. She could have been one of those child models they display in picture frames for sale at Target. But right here in front of me, in Nona's arms, looking like Nona, looking like me, with the same thick eyebrows, bags under her eyes, and a chin like the sharp tip of a heart, there was no getting around it: She was Nona's daughter. She was my sister.

"Sunny, this is your big sister. Say hi."

Sunny mumbled hi.

"Hi?" I responded as if to ask: Do you know how it came to be that I have a little sister and Nona has cut off all her hair and I'm back in Denver?

Not surprisingly, Sunny didn't have any answers.

"Come on in," Nona said.

I got my things out of the car and followed them through the gate and up a path of small river rocks to the house. In the living room, there was music playing, men singing a cappella, something gospelly and soulful.

"Have a seat."

Nona left and Sunny sat on the couch staring at me with her head cocked to the side like a puppy. Nona's daughter. My sister. *Half* sister, actually, but it still was never going to sound right to me. I looked away.

Three votive candles flickered on the coffee table. The

air smelled like lemons and flowers. There were Barbies and stuffed animals everywhere and soft pillows on the couch. The window across from the couch was surrounded by plants: big trees in pots, ferns and vines hanging from the ceiling, and flowers sitting on the windowsill. I stared at an orchid plant, thinking that if I concentrated hard enough on its red flowers, shaped like exploding stars or poisonous spiders, I might be able to focus myself and regain my equilibrium.

"Come on, sit down," Nona repeated when she returned.

She put a bamboo serving tray—*a serving tray!*—with sliced green apples, cheese, crackers, a small plate of sugar cookies, and two glasses of iced tea on the coffee table.

I sat on the couch next to Sunny, who immediately scooted over to the other side.

"Don't try to play shy now," Nona said, tickling her. "She's been driving me crazy all day. 'When's my sister coming? When's my sister coming?' " She handed me a glass of tea with a slice of orange in it. "I made it with orange mint from my yard. The cookies too. My sponsor calls me the chocolate Martha Stewart."

I made a halfhearted laugh at her joke.

"What?" She smiled.

She was serious. Nona, who used to think she was really doing something when she chopped up some hot dogs on top of a pot of pork and beans, thought she was Martha Stewart!

Clearly, I had lost my mind, somehow smoked some crack I didn't know about, but now I could see that letting a dead singer's ghost or a figment of my imagination talk me into moving in with Nona, even temporarily, was a mistake of epic proportion. Nina Simone had put a spell on me, and I needed to sleep it off, then I'd be able to think better, figure out where to go from here. I put down my glass. "I just want to go to bed."

Nona murmured something to herself, then stood. "Okay. Let's show you to your room."

I followed her and Sunny through a short narrow hallway and turned right into a large room that was half kitchen and half sitting room, like something out of *Little House on the Prairie.*

"This is the everything-but-the-shouting room," Nona said.

The prairie room looked like it was from a time when one main room was enough for a whole family and all their belongings, when people darned their own socks and told stories and sang songs after dinner. On one side of the room were the stove, refrigerator, sink and table, and on the other side were bookshelves (Nona *reads* now?), a toy stove and refrigerator, a red wagon filled with dolls, a wicker rocking chair, and more plants.

We walked through the prairie room and Nona went to the doorway on the left. "This is your room. Sunny's going to sleep with me."

At first all I saw was yellow, as if all the butter, lemons, canaries, rubber ducks, and Easter bonnets in the world as well as the sun itself had been collected into one room to please a little girl. Yellow walls, yellow comforter, yellow rug, and yellow curtains.

Nona pointed to a vase of flowers on the nightstand.

"The daisies are to bring you joy, the lavender will help you sleep, and the roses are because . . . well, who doesn't like roses?" she said. "You sure you don't want anything to eat? Or something to drink? A glass of water? I like to keep one by the side of my bed. You know the altitude dries you out. It'll take you a while to get used to it again."

I just wanted to go to bed. "That's okay."

She sighed and her eyes dimmed like headlights going out when you turn off a car. I knew that look. The same look she'd have when she came home from the bars earlier than intended. But she didn't chew her lip, so she wasn't too upset.

"Then, I guess this girl and I will get ready for bed too." She picked Sunny up. "Got the clinic and preschool tomorrow."

"The clinic?"

"I work over at Eastside. I'm an admin assistant."

Eastside was part of Denver Health, the county hospital system. I was studying epidemiology. I wanted to be a hospital administrator or a disease surveillance officer, and Denver Health was the kind of place I hoped to work in myself one day. Mi Casa de Salud, the clinic that fired me, was a lot like Eastside, except they provided care mostly for migrant farmworkers from Mexico. I never in a trillion years would have guessed that Nona and I would end up even remotely in the same line of work.

"We'll be right next door if you need anything. Your towels are in the bathroom—the pink ones. Help yourself to anything. Lord, listen to me." She put Sunny back down, took a deep breath, and put her hands on my shoulders. I couldn't tell if she meant to brace me or herself. She looked at me, her eyes so clear and bright behind her lenses. "LaShay, you're home—"

"You know I hate it when you call me that. It's just Shay."

"I'm sorry. I forgot. But, anyway, you're home. *Home.* So, just . . . act like it, okay? Claim it."

She looked like she wanted to say more, a lot more, but, luckily, she made herself stop because I was stunned enough by what I had already heard. *Claim it?*

After they left, I closed the door and sat on the bed. In my Nina-induced haze, I had agreed to stay through Christmas, but now I could see there was no way I was going to last that long. A week or two max. However long it took for me to come up with a plan B. But that was it.

As grimy as I was, I was too tired to shower and brush my teeth. I turned off the light and a glow-in-the-dark constellation of stars and moons appeared on the ceiling. I kicked off my shoes, pushed the toys off the bed, and lay down. Just as the galaxy above me dimmed, I heard Nona and Sunny go in the other bedroom. Then I heard running water, like there was a broken pipe in the wall between this room and Nona's bedroom. It threatened to drive me crazier than I already was. I got my iPod out of my backpack, took the bandanna off my head, and put in my earphones.

In the darkness, I touched my hair. The inches of new growth near the scalp were soft and fuzzy and the straightened hair beyond the new growth was dry and rough. My hand traveled to an egg-shaped bald spot above my right ear. One of these days I was really going to have to stop doing this, but today wasn't it. I separated out one strand of hair and pulled it gently until it lengthened and flattened and all the curl in the new part was gone, then I slowly wrapped it around my index finger and yanked hard. In my hand, the nappy part of the freed hair curled back up, twisting around until it was back as nature wanted it. I separated out another strand and did the same thing. I pulled three more hairs and one by one my muscles unclenched, the spaces between my bones opened, and my blood flowed more freely. I felt my lungs expand. I closed my eyes and went to sleep with Nina Simone in my ear and five black strands of hair in my hand.

I WOKE UP, MY FACE pressed into the pillow, earphone cords around my neck. At first I didn't know where I was, then I smelled the roses on the bedside table and heard the running water and remembered. I heard Nona's bedroom door close and footsteps through the prairie room. I tensed and looked at the digital clock on the nightstand: 12:32. Between midnight and six A.M. were the itchy hours, when Nona would be on the prowl. I watched the red glowing numbers change to 12:33 then 12:34. One, two, three, four. Finding patterns in time was a game I invented when I was little. For example, there's sequential, like now. There are repetitions: 11:11, 2:22, etc. There are combinations that add up to each other, such as 11:56 and 5:23, and then symbolic times like 2:14, my birthday, and 9:11, which in 2001 became infinitely sad.

My time game helped me get through the nights when

Nona was gone. She would start to get ready after she thought I was asleep. I would hear her taking a shower and getting dressed. It doesn't seem possible, but I used to think I could hear her in the next room brushing her hair, lining her eyes, and coloring her lips even with the TV on in the background. When she was ready, she'd come and stand in the doorway and watch me lying there pretending to sleep. Then she'd whisper "Be good" and leave.

At 12:38 she wasn't back yet. When I called her from Iowa, she cried on the phone about how she had prayed for this, prayed so hard for me to come home, but on the very first night I was back she was leaving to go drink! I jumped out of bed and ran into the living room. The door was open, and I was even more pissed. She didn't even have the decency to close the door, let alone lock it behind her! Was she *that* desperate for a drink that she didn't even think about what might happen to me alone in bed in the middle of the night? I went to the door to lock it and saw her through the screen door. She was squatting down in the yard with her back to me, her long white nightgown glowing in the moonlight. Obviously, she wasn't heading out to a bar. I couldn't see what she was doing. Was she having some kind of midnight gardening emergency or did she keep a bottle stashed in the yard? After a couple of minutes, she stood up and brushed dirt off her hands and knees. I hurried back to bed. For some reason, I didn't want her to know that I'd seen her. I waited until I heard her come back in, at 12:44, and put my iPod back on.

—

A CLOSED DOOR DOESN'T HIDE much in a small house. My earphones had come out again, and soft gospel music and the sounds of Nona and Sunny singing, talking, and getting ready for their day slipped under the door and tapped on my ears. Nona sounded less raspy than she used to in the mornings. She didn't cough or clear her throat once. Her voice was filled with exclamation points, like an elementary-school teacher's. Yay! There were oatmeal and bananas to eat! Faces to wash! Teeth to brush! Sunny was all question marks. Why do I have to be quiet? Why is my sister still sleep? How come my sister don't have to go to school? Can my sister have some oatmeal?

Blinding sunlight streamed through the curtains and landed yellow everywhere. I had a room cheery and bright like this once, only mine was pink. Bubble-gum-pink carpet, flowered Barbie-pink wallpaper, My Little Pony bedspread. When I was nine, Nona hooked up with a guy named Bill and we moved into his house. I liked Bill. While we lived with him, we were like a real family. We had dinner together every night and on Saturday mornings after cartoons I had to clean my room and dust and vacuum the living room. But the best thing about living there was that someone else was in charge of Nona.

It didn't last long though. The first time she stayed out all night, I knew it the minute I walked into the kitchen that morning. Bill made pancakes and bacon, and he was trying so hard to act normal that I could tell he was afraid Nona was never coming back. I wanted to tell him she would, but I didn't know how without letting him know this wasn't the first time she had left home at night. That afternoon, Nona came home, took a shower, changed clothes, and started cooking dinner. When Bill got home, we all sat down and ate like nothing had happened. But after I went to bed, they fought. I couldn't hear what they were saying, but I could tell by the tone of their voices he was angry. I was so scared Nona would say she was leaving, I almost vomited. I wished he would hit her. I wanted him to make her stay home and stop drinking, and I didn't care if he had to knock her out to do it. I thought all she needed was somebody stronger than she was to make her do right. The next morning, I was both disappointed and relieved to see that Nona's lip wasn't busted and her eyes weren't blackened.

Three months went by before it happened again; then just when I had started to relax, I woke up early in the morning to hear them yelling. After that, it happened a couple of times a week. One time, they were so loud I could hear every word. Bill called Nona a slut and a bitch. She screamed at him to shut the hell up, then started crying and whimpering that he was hurting her. I don't remember making a decision to get up, but I guess I couldn't take him hitting her after all. I walked into their bedroom, and when I opened the door, Bill had Nona by the shoulders. He was a big man and Nona is small. Except for the dark expression on his face, he looked like a father about to toss his daughter into the air. I didn't know what to do, so I sat on the edge of the bed and stared at them. They were both so startled they just stood there. After a minute, Bill let her go, rushed out of the room without looking at me, and left the house. I asked Nona if she was okay and when she whispered yes, I went back to my bedroom. Later that day, while Bill was at work, we moved out.

I waited until Nona and Sunny left, then got up to use the bathroom. There was a collection of rubber ducks and damp brown-skinned Barbies on the side of the tub. I used the toilet and washed my hands. On the mirror above the sink orange sticky notes read:

Let go and let God.
There is a reason and a season for everything.
Be the change in your life.
Expect a miracle.

It was the same stuff Nona had been writing in her letters to me, but I still wasn't convinced about her great transformation. I opened the medicine chest. SpongeBob SquarePants Band-Aids, dental floss, Vaseline, saline tears, Tums, ibuprofen, Children's Tylenol, and kids' alcohol-free cough syrup. Perfectly respectable contents, but that didn't mean anything. In the cabinet beneath the sink I found toilet paper, tampons, and cleaning supplies.

Back in the prairie room, light bounced off crystals and pieces of stained glass hanging in front of the windows, making rainbows on the walls and hardwood floors. The bookshelves held self-help books, knickknacks, and pictures: several of Sunny; one of me when I was little, with a white flower tucked behind my ear; and one of Nona with a younger black woman and a very tall, white woman who looked to be in her fifties.

I ran my hand over the round oak kitchen table and wondered how old it was. It had a few good nicks on it and what looked like Magic Marker, but otherwise it was a nice table. I liked old things, antiques, vintage clothes. Things that last. My table was stained dark mahogany and had carved feet and two high-backed chairs with red satin seats. I bought it at a garage sale for a hundred dollars. I missed it already. All my stuff was in storage.

When I looked inside the refrigerator I almost fell over. Fish oil caplets? St. John's Wort? Ground buffalo? Bean sprouts? Just as weird: eggs, bread, cheese, fruits, and vegetables. Nona never kept food in the house. I was the one who went to the store and kept the kitchen stocked. I drank a glass of orange juice, and kept looking. In the freezer, there were fruit bars, fish sticks, frozen vegetables, chicken breasts, and two loaves of wheat bread. A heart-shaped wooden plaque above the stove read "May God's love warm our home." I looked inside the oven. Empty.

The cabinets were covered with headlines from magazines: *Live fully. Life begins at 40. Choose happiness.* There were also typewritten quotes: *Without struggle, there is no progress.— Frederick Douglass* and *God writes the gospel not in the Bible alone, but on trees and flowers and clouds and stars.—Martin Luther.*

I opened every cabinet. There were more bizarre things: green tea, unsalted peanut butter, spices, roasted almonds, brown rice, and cans of soup lined up in their red-and-white suits like a college marching band. I looked under the sink. Only cleansers and sponges.

I went into Nona's room and discovered the source of the rushing water: a CD player and a CD of "soothing water sounds" were on the nightstand next to a stack of books, including a small navy-blue paperback with the words *Alcoholics Anonymous* etched into the cover. You'd never see the words unless you were looking for them. I ran my thumb over the ridges and dents of the letters.

I checked under the bed and in the dresser drawers. In the closet, I looked in the hamper and opened all the shoe boxes. Nothing but clothes and shoes. She could have gotten rid of her bottles before I arrived, but it also dawned on me that, as unbelievable as it sounded, it was possible that she really had stopped drinking.

I sat down on the bed, which was covered with a blue-and-red star quilt. I noticed a needlepoint pillow that said, *Live the life you love, love the life you live.* The house was a living self-help book. Everywhere I turned it seemed to be yelling "Be happy, damn it!" Like those guys who always insist on telling you to smile. Total strangers! Well, what if I didn't feel like smiling? What if I didn't have a good goddamn thing to be happy about?

I had to get out of the oppressive cheerfulness. I went back through the house, out the front door, and stood squinting in the bright sun. I had forgotten the sky here. In Iowa, I had grown used to sunlight filtered through a moist, hazy screen. This sun was unchecked except for a few whipped-cream clouds. The air was as clear as glass. There seemed to be no atmosphere, no gases, no water between earth and sky.

I hadn't been able to see much in the dark last night. The house was an L-shaped, honest-to-God cottage sitting behind a picket fence at the back of a large lot. The house and fence were periwinkle blue, and clouds of white roses bloomed in an arch over the orange front door. In front of the house, there was a small expanse of shaggy, pea-green lawn dotted with clover in bloom. The rest of the yard had beds of brightly colored flowers exploding over the ground like fireworks. A small flagstone patio sat in the "L" of the house.

Nona always managed to grow a few scraggly plants, even when things got really bad. But never anything like this before. This took work and commitments of energy, money, and time. This took digging deep into herself to make what she wanted to happen come to pass.

I paced barefoot through the soft, warm grass.

Well, if Nona could make a garden oasis, she could pay for me to have power, water, food, and shelter for a few months. That's the least she owed me. I had said I needed a break, but I didn't even know what people did on a break. However, I was going to find out. I would turn the yellow room into *my* oasis. I'd read, sleep, and listen to music until the fog lifted and I became myself again or until it was time to go back to school.

I stopped. I was breathing hard. At my feet was a dandelion, a lone globe of a hundred almost-translucent white parachutes ready to carry this weed's babies across the winds. I plucked it.

Nona wasn't fooling me. Even if she had stopped drinking, what did that really change? The nights I spent alone, all the times we moved, the roaches, and evictions didn't just disappear because of a bunch of flowers.

I lifted the dandelion to my lips and blew on it until hundreds of seeds spun into the air and flew across the yard.

The God Box

NINA SIMONE WAS WRONG ABOUT MY HAVING NOTHING
to lose. As it turned out, I had a lot to lose. Privacy. Brain
cells. The slim remains of my sanity.

As planned, I was sequestering myself. Every evening
after dinner, I'd go to my room. But Nona had her own
ideas about what I should be doing. Not an hour would go
by before she would have some excuse to knock on the
door: Did I have any darks that needed to be washed?
Could she come in and strip the bed and put on clean
sheets? Did I need anything from the store? Did I want to
join her and Sunny for a walk? For some lemonade? Some
ice cream?

Dinner was on the table by 6:30 every evening, except
for Thursday nights when she went to an A.A. meeting
right after work.

Tonight, it was burgers and sweet potato fries. Stranger
even than Nona cooking dinner every night, she and Sunny

said grace. With every meal! And I even heard them saying prayers before Sunny went to bed.

Nona and Sunny bowed their heads and reached for my hands. They did this every night, but I still found it shocking and jumped again when Nona touched my hand.

"All right, Sunny," she prodded.

"God is great. God is good. Letusthankhimforthisfood. A'mam!"

"Amen," Nona said and slowly let go of my hand. "Eat up. It's buffalo. Very lean. And sweet potatoes are healthier than white potatoes, lots of Vitamin A."

Now all of a sudden Nona cared about nutrition? There were entire weeks when I ate nothing but Cap'n Crunch and fried chicken with biscuits. She never said a word, just gave me the money I needed to go to the corner store for milk or down the street to KFC for a two-piece dinner. I started babysitting and making my own money when I was ten, and starting cooking for myself. I used to call her Momo instead of Mama when I was little. The first time I came in the house with a sack full of groceries I'd paid for, I dropped Momo and started calling her Nona.

"I don't like buffalo," I said.

"You've had it before?"

"I don't want none either," Sunny said, frowning and poking at her orange fries. Her hair was in two French braids, and she was wearing a blue-and-white flowered cotton pajama top, a necklace of large red beads, yellow denim shorts, yellow–and–mint green argyle socks, and pink flip-flops.

"Eat them anyway. They'll make you grow up big and strong and smart like your sister."

I wasn't sure that was going to be much of a selling point. Sunny still wasn't talking to me. She kept her distance, watching everything I did like I was a scary animal at the zoo. Which was fine with me. She was cute enough, but being around her for over an hour was plenty advertisement for birth control for me, not that I needed it, considering I wasn't having sex. But I had decided a long time ago I didn't want kids, and moving here just confirmed my decision.

"But I don't love 'em," Sunny whined.

"How old are you?" Nona asked her.

"Three."

"Well, then, you have to eat at least three bites. It's the law."

Nona looked at me. "What'd you do this afternoon?"

"Nothing."

"Surely, you did *something*."

"Listened to music." I lifted the burger to my nose; it smelled just like beef. I took a bite, and it tasted like beef too.

"What kind of music do you like?"

Oh God, she wanted to "talk." I hadn't told Nona why I left Iowa. When I called her, I made up a story about my landlord evicting me so he could turn my apartment into a condo, and told her that since it was right before the fall semester, I couldn't find another place to rent.

"Nina Simone. She was a jazz singer and a civil rights activist, among other things," I said. She was the original

Warrior Princess, before Xena, before Angela Davis. Trying to describe Nina Simone would take all day. "You wouldn't know her."

"I've heard of Nina Simone. She did that song 'To Be Young, Gifted and Black.' So you like jazz?"

"It would appear so." I wondered what she would say if I told her Nina Simone spoke to me. Bet that would end the conversation!

"When did you get into jazz?"

"Few years ago."

She waited for me to say more, but I was done. I took a bite of an orange fry. It was good: crunchy on the outside and creamy and slightly sweet on the inside.

"Like it?" she asked.

"It's okay," I grudgingly admitted.

"Mama, I don't like it." Sunny puckered her face like she was eating a lemon. Her face showed her every emotion. At first I thought she hadn't yet learned to hide her feelings, then I thought maybe she didn't need to. Maybe she had never experienced anything so awful she would want to hide it from people.

I was still shocked by how alike we looked. The only way you could tell we had different fathers was that her skin was a few shades darker than mine. Our personalities were very different though. I was the kind of kid who separated the M&M's by color and didn't like my food touching. I liked my clothes to match and hated having sticky hands. For as long as I could remember, I needed things a certain way to feel okay, which seemed like going out of my way to add to my pain, since Nona barely covered the essentials (shelter, food, clothes). There was no way she was going to give much attention to my little quirks. Sunny, though, seemed like an easygoing child. Completely carefree.

Nona held up three fingers. "How many is this?"

"Three."

"Okay, Miss Frowny Frowness, that's how many bites you have to eat. Ooh Lord, I'll be glad when the terrible twos that became the terrible threes are over."

Sunny crossed her little arms and frowned deeper. "I want a knuckle sandwich!"

Nona curled her right hand into a fist and held it up to Sunny's face. Sunny softly bit her hand and pretended to chew.

Nona cracked up. "I told her one day I was gonna give her a knuckle sandwich and she said she wanted it. She thought it sounded good. So what else do you like to do for fun?"

I rubbed my forehead, wishing I could snatch just one hair from under my scarf. "Fun?"

"Pleasure? Joy? Entertainment? You have any hobbies?"

With her wide eyes and dimpled cheeks, Nona had a cheeriness about her. Even when she smelled of stale smoke and liquor, even after hours of crying or vomiting her guts out and there clearly wasn't a damn thing funny, she always looked like she was just about to laugh. People used to eat it up.

I shrugged. Fun was for slackers, losers, deadbeats, and drunks. The closest I came to fun was going to school. From my very first day at Head Start, when I was four, I loved school. It wasn't home.

"Be cool, stay in school" is what they used to say on After School Specials, and I believed them. I breathed school into my bones. School was the only religion I had. Schoolwork saved me on all those nights Nona was out doing whatever it was she did. Staying in school was not the problem. It was leaving school I was afraid of. Maybe that's why I dragged my feet on my thesis. Maybe I didn't want to be thrown out into the grown-up world without my religion. What would I do without school? Who would I be?

"Isn't there something you've always wanted to try? Now that you have a little time on your hands you can try some new things."

Ignoring Nona's nosy butt was starting to sound like a good hobby to me. I decided to take that up, but I didn't think she wanted to hear about it. I was done with my food, so I took my plate to the sink and headed for my room.

"Come on. Don't hide out again tonight. Hang out with us for a while."

My shoulders sagged. "Nona . . ."

"Just for a little while. Pleeeze."

We went into the living room. Sunny popped a video into the VCR. A few minutes later, Nona brought out some cookies.

We ate our cookies without speaking. They watched the video and I picked up a magazine. All of the books in the house were either self-help or children's stories so I had taken to flipping through the cooking and gardening magazines Nona subscribed to.

"You want to tell me what happened?" she asked.

"I told you. I couldn't find a place to rent for the fall."

Doubt filled her eyes. "What about a dorm room?"

"It was the last minute. They were full. Besides, I'm twenty-five. I'm not living in a dorm," I snapped.

"I'm just asking because you seem kind of . . . blue."

"I was going to grad school and working. I'm tired."

She nodded like she understood, all *Now we're getting somewhere.* "In A.A., we say HALT. Never get too hungry, angry, lonely, or tired. That's when people slip. And as black women, we're especially vulnerable. That strong-black-woman-die-before-you-admit-weakness thing is foolish and deadly. That's why so many of us have heart attacks and strokes, and why so many of us are overweight. There's no shame in needing to rest from time to time. It's healthy."

Nona was one to talk. She stayed busy until her head hit the pillow, as if she thought her empty hands would immediately start searching for a bottle. She should have had *Idle hands are the devil's workshop* embroidered on a pillow instead of the happy-talk.

I had been afraid Nona was going to be her same drunk, basket-case self, but it was much, much worse. She was born again. Like somebody who just lost fifty pounds and couldn't wait to tell you the calories in every bite you were about to eat, she couldn't shut up about the Glorious Experience of Sobriety. It was only the third week into this experiment in torture and I thought I was going to scream if I heard the words "in A.A. we say" ever again. And she was sounding amazingly feminist and power-to-the-people for somebody who used to dress up and go trolling bars at

night. I looked at the TV. Cinderella was singing and waiting for her prince to come. "Why do you let her watch this
bullshit?"

Sunny turned from the TV and stared at me, her eyes as
big and round as the cookie she was no longer shoving in
her face.

"Watch your mouth please," Nona said, eyebrows raised
in Sunny's direction.

"You of all people should know better than anybody
there's no such thing as Prince Charming. How can you let
her watch garbage that's going to tell her that one day a prince
will come and rescue her, when you know it's not true?"

Sunny looked at Nona.

Nona took one of the many deep breaths she seemed to
be taking these days. I could almost hear her counting to
ten or saying a prayer in her mind. "Because we need miracles and magic in our lives. Life is bleak and boring without
the possibility that something amazing and completely un-
expected just might happen. We need to believe in something bigger and more powerful than ourselves, something
mysterious and beyond our understanding. It creates hope.
It's why I go to A.A. It's why we go to church. And it's why
we *occasionally* watch fairy tales."

Sunny looked at me.

Magic and miracles were a crock of shit. The best chance
we have in life is to be prepared so that when the rug is
pulled out from under us, we don't land any harder than
necessary. "Well, I don't need make-believe, thanks." I
stood up, telling myself that having conversations with the
late Nina Simone was very different.

"Don't be that way, La— I mean, Shay. Please. I'm sorry. Let's go outside. Come on, I want to show you something."

I slumped again and sighed loudly so she would know that I really, really didn't want to go outside.

"Surely a few minutes of fresh air and sunshine will not kill you."

"Me, Mommy?" Sunny asked.

"Not *you,* Sunshine. Outside sunshine," Nona answered, then said to me, "Well?"

"Whatever." I hated that I was starting to talk like a surly teenager around her. There was a time when our roles were as completely reversed as if we'd switched bodies like the mother and daughter in *Freaky Friday.* But somehow, she had started acting suspiciously like an adult, and I seemed to be left with nothing to do but turn into a child.

She handed me a notebook and pen, and put on a battered straw hat. We both put on sunglasses, and went outside. The air was hot and dry, and all the flowers looked wilted. The sun is ninety-three million miles away from Earth. I looked it up once. It seems impossible that being only one mile closer to it would make a difference, but it does. The sun shines three hundred days a year here, and in July and August everything gets fried.

"This is *my* hobby," Nona said, bending down to run her fingers over the wilting leaves of a lavender bush and breaking off a stem. She put it to her nose and took a deep breath, then handed it to me. "Smell."

I inhaled. It was lavender just like you'd find in bubble bath at the drugstore. I didn't see the big deal.

"I sure do have a lot more dandelions coming up all of a sudden," she said, and bent down and pulled a sprout.

I looked up at the sky.

She went to the side of the house and turned on the garden hose, and started watering from plant to plant. We walked along the path, the small blue, gray, and pink stones dredged from some river warm beneath my bare feet.

As she watered, she called the plants' names: African marigolds, lamb's ears, lemon thyme, basil, tomatoes, California poppies, zucchini, lilacs, roses, coneflowers, ponytail grass, black-eyed Susans, columbines, chives, rosemary, yarrow, yucca, spirea, orange mint, sneezeweed.

For all I cared she could have been showing me the hangers in her closet or pulling tissues out of the box one at a time for me to look at.

Sunny came outside and climbed on her tricycle.

"Did you turn off the video?" Nona asked.

She nodded and started riding in circles around the patio. A slight wind blew and wooden chimes clinked, making music in the breeze.

"I come from a long line of drunks and gardeners," Nona said. "People better at taking care of roses and willow trees than of themselves. My great-grandparents had a farm in St. Marys, Kansas, did you know that? Elsie and Max Dixon. I always think about them when I'm out here. It's like they're calling to me, trying to make themselves known to their only grandchild."

The odds are good that if you're raised by an alcoholic, you'll become an alcoholic, but I never understood how. That would be like spending your whole life watching someone burn themselves on a hot stove, then walking up and plunking your own hand down on the burner.

Nona's parents were dead and she had no siblings and hadn't been close to any extended family, so I didn't know anything about the Dixons. Was I supposed to be taking notes on this little history lesson? Is that what the notebook was for?

"They were the only black family in town. In high school my grandmother was the only girl in her class not invited to a big party. Later, the mother of the girl who was throwing the party came over and talked to Elsie. She hired my grandmother to wash dishes at the party. All the other kids were in the living room laughing and eating and my grandmother was in the kitchen washing dishes. Sometimes I wonder if being a black girl in that place at that time is what made her so mean and so mad, if that's why she drank and kept company with plants."

Jeez. How far back does this go? All the way to slavery?

Nona looked around. "This is nothing compared to my father's garden. Daddy grew everything: all kinds of flowers and vegetables like I haven't seen since. Corn, and big, juicy tomatoes, peppers, greens, radishes, cucumbers, you name it. And we had cherry trees and plum trees. He used to make his own jam, and his own booze for that matter. He and his mother both drank themselves to death." She stooped to pull another weed, and the only sounds were the water running out of the hose and the chimes. "God willing, I'm going to be the first one to make it."

"It's too hot out here," I said.

"I'm sorry." She took her hat off. "Want my hat?"

"I want to go back inside."

"Just stay with me for a little while."

We walked across thick grass to a raised bed of cherry tomatoes, herbs, peppers, and red and yellow flowers growing on low vines. "This is what I wanted to show you." She squatted down. "Some twelve-steppers keep a God box that they put their problems in. But the best way I know to turn over my problems to God is to turn over some dirt." She dug a shallow hole next to one of the tomato plants.

That's what she was doing out here the night I arrived.

"Write whatever comes to you, whatever you want to let go of," she said, looking up at me. "Rip up the paper and spread the pieces like mulch. When the paper breaks down, it makes the soil richer. Come spring, your problem will help the plants grow."

"I don't think so."

Sunny erupted into a coughing fit. Nona looked over at her. She was off her trike and was feeding rose petals to a large orange cat.

Nona called Sunny to her, and the cat ran under the lilac bushes into the neighbor's yard.

"Sunny has asthma," she said. "Let me hear you breathe," she said to Sunny.

Sunny coughed while Nona put her head down next to Sunny's body.

"We better do a nebulizer."

"I don't want it," Sunny whined.

"I know, baby, but your chest is rattley."

Sunny started to stomp her feet and jump up and down, gearing up for a world-class tantrum.

"Sunshine Rose, don't start with me," Nona said. "You gonna get more than a knuckle sandwich this time."

Sunny stopped.

"Just try it," Nona said to me. "Take some breaths and sit quietly for a while and see how you feel, what you might want to say about your life." She and Sunny went into the house.

I didn't want to take any breaths, and I didn't want to sit quietly next to a bunch of vegetables, but I was glad she was gone. If contributing to her little fairy tale that she was helping me got her to leave me alone for the rest of the night, it was worth it. I plopped down on a piece of wood that bordered the flower-and-vegetable bed so my butt wouldn't be in the dirt, and stretched my legs out straight and put the notebook and pen in my lap.

What happened to me? How did I end up here? Women my age were starting their careers, running their own businesses, winning Pulitzers, getting married. When I was ten, I decided that when I was twenty-five my life would be so much better. Twenty-five was a sophisticated and powerful age. At twenty-five I'd have an exciting career and own my own house and paint every room a different color because I wouldn't have to worry about landlords, and I'd never have to move unless I wanted to. And I'd be popular too, with a cool best friend and a fine boyfriend. I never envisioned that I'd still be in school, that I'd be unable to afford new clothes, let alone a house, because I'd owe tens of thousands of dollars in student loans. It never crossed my mind that I'd still feel the same: like a dorky, stupid child and a bone-weary old woman at the same time.

I looked at the house, but I couldn't tell if Nona was spying on me through a window. I turned a little so that if she was looking, she wouldn't be able to tell what I was doing. I slipped a couple of strands of hair from under my bandanna, checked nonchalantly over my shoulder to make sure she hadn't come back outside, and then closed my eyes and pulled one strand, then the other, really fast.

I thought about what Nona said about letting go of things. But I couldn't think of anything to write. Instead, I put the two strands of hair in the hole she had dug, and in case she was watching, I ripped a piece of paper out of the book and wrote some lines from a Nina Simone song: "Yes, I'm tired of paying dues. Having the blues. Hitting bad news. Ain't no use, baby."

Record Store Boy

MAYBE THE GOD BOX WORKED BECAUSE THE NEXT morning, I felt like I was ready to get out of the house. When most people leave home, they go away to a bigger city, looking for glamour, action, adventure. But by the time I moved out, I had had enough action to last a lifetime. I was looking for less excitement, fewer surprises. That's why I went to the University of Iowa. It sounded so regular and so real. Just over sixty thousand people lived in Iowa City and half of them were students. My dream town.

I felt coddled in Iowa City, with its old farmhouses, tree-lined streets, and the Iowa River rolling through the center of campus like a green ribbon. I especially liked that the town was filled with people trying to learn things. Of course, that was truer in grad school than undergrad. But still, in a city set up around the purpose of learning, I could ignore the frat parties and football games. For a long time in

Iowa City, I felt safe. I understood the rules, the expectations.

For now, though, I was in Denver and all my expectations were out the window. I got in my car and headed out of Park Hill, Nona's neighborhood in northeast Denver, not far from where we'd lived when we stayed with Bill. I always liked this neighborhood. Park Hill boasted that it was the first community in the country designed from inception to be integrated. It probably is more integrated than most neighborhoods. Though most of the whites live in the south part in cutesy bungalows or imposing mansions, and most of the blacks and Latinos live in the north part in small ranch houses, many of which have bars on the windows or rottweilers or pit bulls in the yard. Nona's house was in the middle, walking distance to a co-op bookstore, two coffee shops, a gourmet grocery, an Italian restaurant, and a library to the south, and a rec center, a post office, a public health clinic, another library, and a half dozen liquor stores to the north.

I shifted into second, then third gear. I turned west on 28th and met a view I hadn't seen in so long I had forgotten it. Most cities have a defining characteristic, but what do you say about a city whose defining characteristic is not even a part of it? What Denver is most known for, being in the Rockies, is actually wrong. On clear days, you can *see* the Rockies, but Denver is not *in* them. The city sprawls flat and friendly on the plains east of the mountains. Today, between the trees and houses on either side of the street, in front of me was a purple peak that already had a little snow on top, even though it was in the eighties down here. When

I got to Colorado Boulevard, the vista opened up and the mountains stretched in front of me to the left and right in a jaw-dropping view.

I drove past City Park, the natural history museum, and the zoo. Once, in third grade, our class was going on a field trip to the zoo. All the kids were so excited, though even at that age we were supposed to act cool. The boys puffed out their chests and pimp-walked around the playground, daring the lions and tigers to try to eat them. The girls chattered in squeaky voices about the baby animals. I wanted to see all the animals. I was fascinated by the idea that zebras, penguins, baboons, and giraffes lived right in Denver, just like me.

I had taken home the permission slip and left it on the table so Nona would be sure to see it. For two weeks, I waited for her to sign it and give it back to me. All she had to do was scratch her name across the bottom, but every morning she had some reason she couldn't get to it. The day of the field trip came and she still hadn't signed. I made a cup of instant coffee with lots of milk and sugar and took it and the permission slip to the pullout couch in the living room. She had the blankets pulled over her head and a pillow on top of the blankets. I talked to her through the bedding, reminding her that it was field trip day and she had to sign my permission slip right then or I wasn't going to be able to go. Without whining, whining gave her a headache, I filled my voice with hope and longing so she would know how important this trip was to me. She didn't even lift her head from under the pillow. She just mumbled, waved me away, and rolled over.

I left the coffee on the floor next to the couch and took the permission slip to the kitchen table. Willing my hand to stop shaking, I signed her name in the best cursive I could manage. When I handed it to Mrs. Douglas, my heart was thumping hard. I'm sure my signature looked like that of an eight-year-old, but a bunch of us turned in our slips of paper that morning and Mrs. Douglas, assuming we all had mothers who cared that we went to the zoo, collected them without even looking at them. I knew I had done a bad thing, but I was thrilled. I felt like I had developed a super-power. I had taken care of myself. I knew I would have to do it again, and I knew then that I could. Looking at the Bengal tiger that had come all the way from India I vowed that I wouldn't wait for Nona again. I would be careful never to put myself in a position where she could let me down. I would keep my expectations low enough that even a drunk stumbling home in the dark could step over them without tripping.

Downtown had changed completely since I had last seen it. New buildings had sprouted like mushrooms after a rain, and all the old warehouses had been turned into shops, restaurants, bars, and lofts. After circling through down-town, I got on Colfax and drove past ethnic restaurants, fast-food places, gas stations, liquor stores, the Fillmore auditorium, African braiding salons, and shops selling comic books, water pipes, cigarette papers, used furniture, vintage clothes, candles for Wiccan ceremonies, and X-rated DVDs.

Near East High School I saw a store with a sign that read simply *Records and Tapes* and zipped into a parking space right in front. I had about a hundred dollars left in my checking account, and Nona didn't have Internet access so I couldn't download any music, so I decided to invest in a new CD.

The sign on the door said *Shake It Up*. The windows were covered with posters of Miles Davis, Johnny Cash, Tupac Shakur, Eminem, Bob Marley, the White Stripes, Beyoncé, Jennifer Lopez, and Al Pacino in *Scarface*. I walked in and was immediately hit with the smells of damp wood, dust, and incense, and the sound of loud punk rock music. Two young guys, one white and one black, worked behind the counter. The white guy had tangled, strawberry-blond ringlets passing for dreadlocks. His eyes were closed and he bobbed his head fast along with the music, swinging his matted dreads. The black guy was tall, skinny, and light-skinned, with a big, haphazard afro and glasses with thick black frames so ugly they were supposed to be cool. He nodded his head at me.

The only two other customers were Goth kids with Mohawks. There were racks of vinyl albums and CDs, and a section for mix tapes. I found the jazz CD section and started browsing.

"Help you find something?"

I looked up and saw the kid with the afro smiling at me from the other side of the row of CDs. I shook my head.

"You dig jazz!" he yelled at me above the crashes and screams of the music.

I shot my eyes at the sign that labeled this the jazz section and yelled back, "You figured that out on your own?"

"That's cool! Not many young sisters have an apprecia-tion! Mostly, even older black folks like the so-called 'smooth jazz'!"

Mattlocks turned the music down.

"I'm Oliver . . . Ollie . . . Ol," he said without yelling and stuck out his hand, which hung there like a dead fish until he figured out I was not going to shake it. I kept flip-ping through the CDs. I wouldn't let him see that he was bothering me. Some guys like that. Some of them seem to believe getting under your skin is only one step from get-ting in your panties.

He stroked the peach fuzz above his lip. "It's nice to see someone who likes it rough. Music I mean." He grinned, his teeth like the tiny, hard marshmallows that come in cocoa mix.

Mattlocks hooted.

What is it with guys that they think their interest is such a compliment, that when they hit on you, no matter how crudely, they think they're doing you such a big fat favor? No matter how young or how old or how ugly or broke down they are, they all seem to think they are the sun and truly expect any woman to bask in their glow.

"Listen, Record Store Boy, why don't you pick on somebody your own age? What are you? In middle school? You read that in your daddy's *Playboy*?"

The grin disappeared and he looked down at the floor.

Mattlocks doubled over the counter like he was punched in the stomach and laughed. "Duuude! Playa, that was cold!"

I steeled myself for what Record Store Boy would say,

but when he looked up at me, his face was so sad I could see his smile had been more hopeful than cocky.

"Sorry. I didn't mean . . . I . . . sorry," he mumbled and scurried behind the tie-dyed curtain into the back room.

The punk music started screeching again and Mattlocks glared at me. But I picked Nina Simone's *Compact Jazz* and took it up to the counter, daring him to say something to me, daring him to even look at me the wrong way. But he was young and chicken too. He took my money and gave me my CD.

I didn't mean to hurt the boy's feelings or embarrass him in front of his friend. But *he* chose to come on to me while his buddy was watching. And so very lamely too. Plus, I knew that as soon as Oliver Ollie Ol heard the little bell above the door tinkle when I left, he'd be back out to watch for some other girl. And by that time, I would be back at Nona's listening to the High Priestess of Soul.

I HAD NONA'S STEREO in the living room cranked up loud. "The Gal from Joe's" blared hot, jazzy horns. In real life, I dance worse than small-town Iowa white girls, but in my imagination, I can really move. I was shimmying and shaking for all I was worth. I was in a smoky nightclub wearing a crimson flower in my hair and a silver dress that slipped and slid around my brown skin like water. Unlike most of the time, right now I was in my body, connected to it, instead of lost inside my head. I could feel my heart beating, sending oxygenated blood running through my veins. My arms and legs were not bony sticks. They were lovely and willowy. My small breasts sat high on my chest, my stomach was flat, my hips flared, and I felt womanly. I could feel wetness on my brow, on my scalp, under my arms, and between my legs, and it was okay. I was okay. And I could dance my ass off. I was facing the stereo, which was the big band on the stage. Someone was holding out a hand for me and I was just about to take it when I heard a throat being cleared behind me.

I dropped my arm and froze. Mor-ti-fied! I vowed I would never, ever again pull a single hair out of my head if Nona wasn't standing behind me. I turned around. She and Sunny were just inside the front door, looking at me in my track pants, t-shirt, and head wrap, looking nothing at all like the woman in my mind. Nona was holding two plastic grocery sacks, and had her lips pressed together to keep herself from laughing. "Nina Simone, right?"

I turned off the CD.

"Don't let us stop you." Nona carried her bags into the kitchen, chuckling. Sunny ran past her.

I felt ridiculous, outed as a silly, dreamy girl with too much time on her hands and no access to the beat.

Sunny returned wearing the pink tutu over her jeans. "Let's dance! Turn the music back on!" It was the first time she spoke directly to me, and it was to order me around.

"I don't think so."

She went over to the stereo and turned it on herself, then came and stood in front of me. "You dance good," she told me.

It was a safe bet I was never going to hear that from anyone else, and I was just pitiful enough that I was grateful for praise from a preschooler. "Thank you."

"Wanna see how I can dance?"

Before I could answer, she was skipping and twirling on her tiptoes and shaking her hips in an offbeat, and a strangely risqué, bump and grind that made me understand how she could believe I was a good dancer. Poor thing, we shared the same lack of rhythm. But she was so happy and her happiness was so pure that a smile broke through before I knew it. She understood. This three-year-old got me. Then I noticed Nona in the doorway watching me watch Sunny, and the smile went back to where it came from.

"Nobody in my family can keep a beat," she said. "Me and you used to dance together when you were little. I used to play Prince and The Time, you remember? You really used to like Morris Day, with his crazy self. 'Jungle Love' and that one about doing the bird." She flapped her arms.

"Fine, make fun of me because I can't dance." I got up and turned the stereo back off. "Ha, ha, ha. Hilarious."

"I wasn't making fun of you!"

Sunny stopped dancing. "Why'd you stop it?"

"Don't be that way, Shay."

Sunny was just a kid. It wasn't her fault. But I didn't have to stick around and be insulted and I sure didn't have to stroll down memory lane with Nona. I turned Nina Simone back on and went into my room. The music played on. Nona started making dinner and I guess Sunny was still dancing her little brains out.

I did remember Nona playing Prince. She listened to

this song "Still Waiting" over and over for hours while she wept. It was a song about being lonely and unloved. Her behavior scared me so much, I threw the cassette away. I had expected her to know I had done something to the tape and confront me. After all, we lived alone and she didn't have a boyfriend at the moment, and I do mean "moment" since she never went more than a couple of weeks before she was hooked up again. Who else would have thrown it out? But I didn't know yet how the alcoholic mind becomes accustomed to strange disappearances. She didn't even seem to notice it was gone.

When dinner was ready, Nona came to the door and knocked, but I had lost my appetite. The memory of her being so desperate and weak-willed with men put me back where I started before my trip downtown. I didn't know why the way she had behaved so many years ago should still affect me today, but it was depressing. And feeling anything about her made me feel like a fool, which made me feel even more depressed. I snatched off my scarf and pulled thirteen hairs before I made myself stop. When I was done, I felt better and worse at the same time.

CHAPTER 5

The High Priestess of Nada

THE NEXT DAY WAS A SATURDAY. I WOKE UP AT 7:07
to the sounds of cartoons, the scents of bacon and coffee,
and, as usual, Sunny's questions, most of which seemed to
boil down to *Why?* Why was a big thing for her. This kid
had a burning desire to get to the bottom of things, which I
was starting to admire. She'd make a great scientist.

I was about to start my period and bacon was just what
the doctor ordered. If only I could have it covered in chocolate and served with French fries. Along with being starved,
especially for greasy, salty food, I was feeling evil. Every
month I got visits from the three PMS dwarves: Sleepy,
Grumpy, and Piggy.

I walked into the kitchen and Nona turned around from
the stove. "Good morning," she said like she really meant it,
like this was the best beginning of the best day ever. It was
disgusting. "Got some pancakes and bacon going on over

here. Want some? Re-al ma-ple sy-rup," she sang out, trying to tempt me. But it wasn't necessary this morning.

"Yeah, thanks. But first I gotta go. . . ."

I jogged to the bathroom. When I was done, I noticed a new note on the mirror.

Stop worrying. Start praying.

She didn't act like she had a care in the world anymore. I wondered what she had to be worried about.

I went back into the prairie room and sat at the table.

"Didn't realize breakfast was a formal affair, did you?" Nona asked nodding toward Sunny, who was wearing yellow footie pajamas, a pink boa, and a tin tiara.

Nona was wearing hot-pink satin pajamas and fuzzy leopard-print slippers.

Well, my cotton nightshirt and bandanna were going to have to do. I was planning to stay in my pajamas all day long. All I wanted to do was eat and go back to bed and turn my face to the wall.

"I'm the Princess of Dancing," Sunny said. "What are you the princess of?" Now that she had decided to speak to me, she had just as many questions for me as she did for Nona.

"Nothing." That was me: the High Priestess of Nada.

"Shay's the Princess of School," Nona said. "She's really, really smart."

I choked on my coffee and started coughing. Nona didn't go to my high-school graduation. She didn't fill out the financial-aid forms or help me with my college applications. She had never once even checked my homework or praised me for getting good grades. Now she wanted to talk about how smart I was?

"You okay?" she asked, rushing over to bang on my back.

I jerked away from her and croaked, "I'm fine."

"Wanna dance with me?" Sunny asked.

"Maybe later."

"See ya later, crocodile."

"It's 'See you later, alligator.' It rhymes," I said.

"What's 'rhymes'?"

"Words that sound alike," I explained.

"What's 'sound alike'?"

"Words that make the same sound, like cat, hat, bat, rat, mat. Those all rhyme."

Nona brought the bacon, pancakes, and heated syrup to the table, and sat down.

"I know my numbers," Sunny volunteered. "Onetwo threefourfivesixseveneightnineten!"

"Very good," Nona said.

"And my letters. ABCD—"

"You can do your letters later. It's time to eat now."

She didn't have to tell me twice. It was the best meal I had eaten in forever, and I'm a pancake snob. These were fluffy but substantial at the same time. They tasted *real*. Real flour, real eggs, real butter. Nothing out of a box. And the bacon was overcooked almost to the point of being burned, just the way I like it, which made me wonder if my taste had been set as a little girl in Nona's kitchen, just like Sunny's.

I scraped syrup off my plate with my last bite of bacon while Nona refilled my cup of coffee. I took three ibuprofen and between that and the food and caffeine I started to feel like I might just live after all.

"I'm going to be taking Sunny down to Belinda's shop in a little while to hang out with her granddaughters while I go to a meeting. Want to go with and see if Belinda can fit you in today, so you can get your hair done?" She put the coffeepot back and sat down.

There went my good meal and my good mood right down the drain. "Uh-uh."

"If you need money—"

"I said no!"

She took off her glasses, cleaned them with the hem of her pajama top, and put them back on. "I'm sorry. I didn't mean to upset you. I only meant there's no need for you to be wearing rags on your head if you need to get your hair done."

"It's not a rag! I like head wraps." When the effects of pulling first started to show, I had bought half a dozen scarves to wear to class and work. I was prepared to tell people it was my new look, but nobody asked. At a university, it was probably politically correct to assume it was an African American–culture thing; and other black folks knew there are no circumstances under which it is ever okay to question a sister about her hair when she's covering it up.

Nona wasn't buying it, but she would never guess I was part bald under my scarf. She didn't know about my trichotillomania, but she knew enough to shut up about my hair and change the subject. "After my meeting, some of my friends are going to be coming over for lunch."

That's why she was so concerned about my hair. "I'll be out." Doing what, I didn't know, but I wasn't about to participate in this little drama, being the prodigal daughter swept into the bosom of her loving family.

She looked down. "I see. I wanted them to meet you, but maybe another time."

"Whatever." My new not-so-favorite word, but I couldn't stop saying it.

AFTER NONA AND SUNNY LEFT, I decided to call Stephanie, my best friend from high school, to see if we could hang out. I picked up the phone twice to call her father to ask for her number, but I hung up both times. There was nobody else to call, so I walked down to the Park Hill library. Entering the double doors, I relaxed instantly. Surrounded by books, I was on familiar ground. I browsed the fiction section fighting the guilt that crept up my spine. I hadn't read a novel for pleasure since high school. I didn't know what to look for, didn't know what I even liked, but I couldn't take another day of Nona's ladies' magazines.

"Ansa," said a tall, tea-colored woman with short hair that was just beginning to gray.

"What?"

She reached by me and picked a battered hardback and handed it to me. "Can't go wrong with Ms. Ansa. You ever read this?"

The book was called *Ugly Ways*.

I shook my head. "What's it about?"

"Three daughters after their mother dies."

"Who has the ugly ways, the mother or the daughters?" I asked suspiciously. I had no desire to read any stories about Perfect Black Mothers and Their Adoring Daughters.

"See, your just asking that question tells me you should read the book."

I liked that she didn't tell me the whole plot. I decided to give it a shot. "Any other suggestions?"

She carefully scanned the *A*s and *B*s, and jumped with recognition when she got to the *C*s. "You've probably already read this. It's been out forever. But it's excellent."

It was *Your Blues Ain't Like Mine*, by Bebe Moore Campbell. I loved the title, but was embarrassed to admit I hadn't even heard of it, let alone read it. "This is my first break from school in a long time. I haven't read anything but textbooks in years."

"Then, you have to read this! Oh my God, it's so good!"

I smiled at how animated she got. This was a woman who loved books.

"What else?" she said to herself, scanning the rows. "You want just African American authors?"

"Not necessarily."

"*The Red Tent* is amazing. And *A Yellow Raft in Blue Water*."

"Thank you."

"You're so welcome. It's a joy to turn people on to a good book." She stared at me. "You look familiar. How do I know you?"

"I don't think you do."

"Yes I do. I've seen you here before with a little girl, right?"

"No, that was my mother."

"You tell her I said go 'head on with her bad self! Sisters age well, but I wish somebody would mistake me for my daughter one day."

I took the book and thanked her again, but the last thing I was going to be telling Nona was that someone had thought I was her.

She snapped her fingers. "Oh! *This Side of the Sky*. Local author. Elyse Singleton. Really, really, really good. That's the last one."

ON THE WALK HOME, I tried to imagine what kind of a woman would be Nona's sponsor. I pictured a woman like the one who helped me pick out the books, but I liked her too much to think of her as an alcoholic, even a recovering one. I realized I didn't know Nona well enough to be able to guess what type of person she might pick as a mentor.

Whoever it was seemed to be helping. I had checked the house many times for liquor bottles, but didn't so much as find a hidden empty Coke can, which would hint at some Hennessy in the house. It seemed like Nona really had stopped drinking.

By the time I got back, Nona was home. In the prairie room, Sunny was showing a book to the white woman who was in the picture with Nona on the bookshelf. She was tall and stout with a firm jaw and a glossy platinum braid sitting on each shoulder. She was wearing denim overalls, a blue T-shirt, and lots of rings and gold bangle bracelets. I imagined her with one of those horned helmets that cartoon opera singers always wear. Nona's very own Warrior Princess.

"Hi! You came!" Nona said.

I held up my stack of books. "I got something to read. I was just going to—"

"Now that you're here, let me introduce you."

Lois smiled, deepening the lines around her blue eyes and mouth, and shook my hand, her bracelets clinking. Like Nona, she radiated vitality. Where were the signs of the wrong choices they had made? Years of drinking should have ravaged these women. I wanted scars.

Lois looked around the room. "Every time I come over, I can't believe this place. You should have seen it when your mother bought it. Half the windows were broken. There were holes in the walls and green outdoor carpeting on all the floors. There must have been ten *Beware of Dog* signs. And the people who lived here probably had about that many dogs. The whole place reeked of piss. I gagged the first time I came in here."

"This house was on the market over a year before I came along," Nona said, putting Sunny to work emptying a bag of baby carrots onto a ceramic platter. "I got it for a pretty good price. And I had a lot of help. Soon as I put the bottle down for good, it was like the path ahead of me opened up and whoever and whatever I needed just came to me. All the guys at our Saturday group worked on this house like they were volunteering for Habitat for Humanity, and a woman I met in another meeting hooked me up with a Realtor and helped me get my mortgage. She even helped me fill out the papers for a first-time homebuyer's program, so I barely had to put any money down."

"Fellowship," Lois said, and she and Nona shared a warm smile.

Sounded beyond fellowship to me. Making friends was something I never really learned how to do. It's hard when you move all the time, and damn near impossible when you're too embarrassed to invite kids over to your house for fear of what your mother might say or do.

I could turn to Carl and a couple of other professors for guidance and maybe an occasional pep talk, but I didn't have anybody in my life who would help me as much as these people were willing to help Nona. When I left Iowa, I didn't even have anyone who could help me move my furniture into storage; I had to pay a couple of undergrads.

Nona set the platter of vegetables and a bowl of black bean dip on the table.

"How you coming on your list?" Lois asked Nona and then scooped some dip on a pepper and popped it into her mouth.

"I'm working on it," Nona said quickly.

"Give me a 'for instance.'"

Nona glanced at me. "I'm not sure we should be talking about that now."

I turned toward my room. "You're the one who wanted me to meet her. I'll go in my room."

"No!" Nona said. "It's no big deal. I'm supposed to make a list of things to do to be good to myself, that's all."

"Just tell me, have you started it yet?" Lois asked.

"Where the party at?" a girlish voice called from the living room.

"In here," Nona answered quickly.

"Saved by the bell," Lois muttered.

"Miss Ivy! Miss Ivy!" Sunny dropped her carrot on the table and ran into the other room.

A stringy girl wearing a tank top, jeans cut so low you could see the top of her yellow thong, and pointy high heels walked in the room carrying Sunny. She was the one in the photo with Nona and Lois.

"Look what Miss Ivy gave me," Sunny said. She was holding a doll that looked exactly like a newborn baby, with a puckered mouth and wrinkled brown skin in a pink little onesy and knit cap. It was so real-looking it was creepy. I never liked baby dolls. I played with Barbie. I especially loved her stuff: the Dream House, the furniture, the Corvette.

"What a nice baby!" Nona said in her teacher voice. "What are you going to name her?"

Sunny shrugged.

"None of her dolls have names," Nona said. "She can never think of one she likes." She turned to Ivy and said, "What'd I tell you about presents?"

Ivy had a white woman's nose and a black woman's lips. Pimples glowed across her sand-colored skin like tiny red stars and her cheeks were pockmarked from previous galaxies that had died there. Her hair looked naturally straight, and was pulled into a high ponytail. When your head is covered with bald patches, you pay attention to other women's hair. Long, short, nappy, straight, dreads, Mohawks, weaves, braids, it doesn't matter. You notice it.

Ivy put Sunny down, and Sunny wrapped her arms around Ivy's legs. "I know, I know. But I feel bad if I don't bring something," she said, blinking her eyes anxiously.

"All you have to bring is you. Look at Lois. She don't bring nothing."

"Hey!" Lois protested, her mouth full of bean dip.

"Can I still get a hug?" Ivy asked.

Nona held open her arms. Ivy fell into them, with Sunny still attached to her legs, and wrapped herself around Nona. The three of them turned, and still entwined, Nona introduced us.

"Nona's my girl! Your mom has been really good to me," Ivy gushed, pulling Nona closer to her, exposing the leafy vine tattooed around her right biceps. "Better than my own mother. That's fo' sho. Like, these last two months in A.A. have been the best of my life."

"I'm Ivy's sponsor," Nona explained.

Ivy must be the one Nona was always talking to on the phone.

"I thought you weren't supposed to tell that kind of stuff," I said.

"I wouldn't have brought it up if Ivy hadn't."

"I'm not ashamed to be in A.A.," Ivy said, her eyes moving up my body, from my Goodwill Levi's to my black-and-white-flowered head scarf, where they lingered. "I like your wrap. Very Erykah Badu," she said with a condescending smile.

I touched my head and glared at Nona.

"I didn't say anything," she said.

"I like it too," Sunny repeated.

"I do hair sometimes, braids and weaves," Ivy said. "I'll hook you up if you want."

"What's for lunch?" Did I care? No. I just wanted everybody to stop staring at my head!

"Curried chicken salad with couscous," Nona answered.

"With whose whose?" Ivy asked.

Sunny cracked up and kept repeating, "Whose whose? Whose whose?" It was perfect preschool humor, or maybe Sunny thought anything Ivy said was worth repeating.

"You'll see."

Sunny grabbed her booster chair. Nona handed us all plates and dishes of food to carry to the patio and we trooped outside. A couple of crows yelled at our intrusion and flew off. Nona had the orange umbrella open over the table, though it was overcast. It was hot and the sky threatened rain, but by now I knew that was a hollow warning. Every afternoon dark clouds rolled in from the west, but they would only spill a few drops, then the sun would come back out. I missed Iowa, the river and humidity. The damp air turned everything green and made my skin soft (and my hair, but I was trying not to think about hair at the moment).

Tall, fat flowers were climbing out of their pots and spreading across their beds. The sunflowers were tipping over from the weight of their blossoms. A plant by the patio was bearing deep red tomatoes the size of grapefruits. But fall was coming. The light was changing and there was a coolness in the breeze. Tiny white petals were all over the patio and the air was thick with the scent of dying roses.

The bush that climbed over the doorway was more thorns than blooms.

We arranged our dishes on the table. I sat down.

"Move, Shay!" Sunny demanded.

"She always sits next to me," Ivy explained.

I moved over, and Ivy got Sunny settled in her booster seat.

Nona said, "Let's bless the whose whose." She made us hold hands, Ivy on one side of me and Lois on the other. Everyone but me bowed her head.

Sunny said her usual, "God is good. God is great. Letusthankhimforthisfood. A'mam!"

Soon as she was done, Ivy dropped my hand and reached over to tickle Sunny. Sunny seemed to adore Ivy, and it looked like the feeling was mutual.

Nona looked at the gray sky. "I'm hoping if we sit outside, it'll make it rain. I washed my car today too to see if I could get some water out of these clouds. I'm scared another month like this will dry everything up for good."

"This garden isn't the only thing that's going to dry up for good," Lois said.

"Lois!"

"Ummmmm," Ivy said with her eyebrows raised.

Lois chuckled. "Forty ain't dead."

"I'm forty and raising a preschooler. It's the next closest thing." Nona shook her head like she couldn't believe the direction the conversation was going in. Neither could I. Unless I was missing something, Nona seemed to be *rejecting* the idea of getting a man.

She changed the subject. "Lois, you want to state your intentions first?"

Lois kicked off her Birkenstocks, and folded one foot under her behind, waiting for a car blasting tejano music to go by. She took a deep breath, letting it out in a whoosh and rubbing her right hand over her breastbone as if to warm herself, even though it was plenty warm enough. Then she laid both hands on the table with her long fingers spread and sat up straight. "I intend to stay healthy and well in mind, body, and spirit. I intend to do more than just survive. I intend to *live*. Every day of my life."

Nona reached over and clasped Lois's hand. "Amen!" Then she explained to me, "Lois just officially became a cancer survivor."

"Five years cancer free," Lois interjected. "But it could always come back. At any time."

One thing I knew is that diseases don't arise out of thin air. They start because of genetic abnormalities and our interactions with our environment, our exposure to pollutants and chemicals, and the choices we make. Like drinking. Alcohol consumption raises a woman's risk of getting breast cancer.

You might not be able to keep bad things from happening, but you could minimize the damage. That's why alcoholics pissed me off. Some shit didn't have to happen. Life was already out to get you in some form or fashion, so why add to your troubles? Why make things worse? If you're a poor, black, single mother with a high-school education, why in the hell would you add liquor and drugs into the mix?

"LaShay?" Nona nodded at me.

"Jesus, Nona. How many times do I have to tell you? My name is just Shay! You know I hate *La*Shay."

"You could just tell me in a normal voice—"

"I've told you a million times! You don't listen."

"Shoot!" Ivy frowned and started working her neck. "You call *her* by her first name like you some kinda stranger off the street or something, not her daughter!"

"Ivy, it's okay," Nona said. She closed her eyes, took a deep breath, and opened them again. She said to me, "I'm sorry. I think LaShay is a beautiful name. It's why I gave it to you." Then she said to Ivy, "But *Shay* is right. I should remember and respect what she wants to be called."

"That's what I'm saying!" Ivy responded. "She wanna *get* respect. She gotta *give* some respect."

"Really, Ivy, this is between me and Shay."

Ivy looked around like *Is it just me?*

"Shay, you want to state your intentions?" Nona asked.

I just stared at her.

"Fine. Ivy?"

Ivy neatened her ponytail for a few seconds before she started so she wouldn't say what she wanted to say to me. "I intend to be on time to my job, like, every day," she muttered, counting her intentions on her fingers. "I intend to show up to my parole officer every week."

Parole! I wondered what she could have done. Using drugs? Dealing drugs?

Then she got more in the groove. "I intend to get my GED. I intend to keep going to meetings and keep working the steps so one day"—she turned and looked directly at me—"I can be just like Nona." She all but stuck her tongue out at me.

Ivy held up her hand with all five fingers accounted for. Nona gave her a high five, even though she sounded like she was only repeating what her lawyer told her to say.

"You're up," Lois said to Nona.

Nona spoke without looking at anyone. "I intend to make up for my mistakes. I intend to right my wrongs if it takes me the rest of my life."

Sparks of blame started shooting off Ivy again. But this wasn't my fault. Nona couldn't make it up to me. Ever. It was too late. No matter how many healthy meals she cooked or how often she dragged me out into her yard, it was never going to change things.

After the intentions, we began the meal. The alkies talked about "higher powers," "willingness," "surrender," and "keeping it simple." Ivy clung to Nona's every word, as mesmerized as if a prophet was speaking. You would have thought Nona hung the moon. You would have thought she was the sun.

When we finished eating, Sunny picked up her new doll and hopped onto Nona's lap.

"You think of a name?" Nona asked her.

Sunny looked up at the sky like a name was floating in the clouds. Finally, she said "Laaaaa . . . Shay!" like a sneeze.

For a heartbeat nobody said anything, then Ivy burst out laughing, throwing her head back so you could see the fat silver stud in the center of her tongue. She laughed so hard and for so long I knew for sure I had an enemy.

Two Kinds of Jif

GAINING AN ENEMY REINFORCED HOW MUCH I NEEDED a friend. It took me a couple of weeks to gather up the courage to call Mr. Berry, but he remembered me right away and even scolded me for not keeping in touch. He gave me Stephanie's phone number and made me promise to come visit him. High on his attention, I called Stephanie right after I hung up with him. She squealed and cooed at me like the long-lost friend that she was, which was another relief, and invited me over.

Stephanie and I used to be able to really communicate. Before we met, we had taught ourselves the alphabet in sign language, using the same book we found in separate elementary school libraries. In high school, we would sign to each other in class. Because neither of us had learned many signs for words, we would talk to each other letter by letter, flattening our palms to signal the end of one word and the beginning of the next, like cavewomen. It was painfully slow, but fun to talk in plain view of the other kids (but not the teachers). There were no deaf kids in our classes, so we could tell each other whatever we wanted.

After the warm responses from her and her dad, I was suddenly hopeful we could pick up where we'd left off. I started to let myself imagine what it would be like to have someone to talk to again. When I got to her apartment, though, it was obvious right away that she wasn't the same girl. In high school, we used to say we were two kinds of Jif: She was chunky and I was smooth. Which only meant that we were both the color of peanut butter and she was thick and I was thin, because, as our little saying demonstrates, neither of us was smooth.

But the girl who opened the door was skinny. Her hair was up in a ponytail showing off what had become a long, graceful neck. Early September was giving us the last hot breaths of summer, and Stephanie was taking full advantage in impossibly short turquoise shorts and a hot-pink tank top showing obvious definition in the muscles of her arms and legs. She looked slim and powerful at the same time. She grinned and held out her Venus Williams arms for a hug. I leaned into her now-sleek body, and was engulfed in her body spray, which smelled like waffle cones. A girl goes away for a few years and everybody changes.

"Hey, girl," she said.

"You look like you should be in a magazine!"

She grinned, showing the little gap between her top front teeth. At least that was still there.

"You look good too."

That was kind. Stephanie looked like she was on a vacation in the tropics. My outfit screamed grad student. I had on a white button-down shirt, tan pants, and clunky but comfortable black Teva sandals. I'd been working and going to college for seven straight years. My wardrobe was made up of black, white, beige, and gray basics so that everything went with everything else and everything could be worn to work or school. Nona had noticed. She had bought me three scoop-necked t-shirts in lemon, tangerine, and the same periwinkle as the house.

"Yeah right," I replied. "What did you do to yourself?"

"Love, girl. Love! Love! Love! We go to the gym together. He works me out," she said, fanning her face and raising her eyebrows up and down. She sounded like the popular girls back in high school, who spoke crazy-sexy-cool instead of English.

"Um-hum." I tried to laugh like I was crazy-sexy-cool too, but ended up sounding more like a mad scientist in an old movie.

She waved her left hand in my face until I noticed the big rock on her finger.

"Is this . . . ?"

"*I'm getting married!*" She jumped up and down like she had won the lottery.

"Wow." I tried to smile. I knew I should be happy for her, and I was. I *was* happy. But I was also feeling the familiar sensation of being incompetent at life. It always seemed like everyone else knew what was going on and how to be in the world, and I didn't. I was twenty-five and didn't know how to do the things that every other girl seemed to be born knowing. Like how to slow dance and have a sexy telephone voice. Like how to fall in love and get married. Stephanie had clearly grown out of her awkward phase, whereas mine seemed to be permanent.

She stopped jumping. "And you're invited. We're so thankful for each other we decided to make it a Thanksgiving wedding. Actually, it's the day after. A Friday night. We're doing a whole fall theme. We're going to decorate the church with garlands of orange and red roses and maple leaves on the ends of the pews. My flower girl is going to scatter rose petals and maple leaves as she walks down the aisle. The guys will wear black tuxes with red vests and orange boutonnieres. My bridesmaids are going to be in deep cranberry red, off-the-shoulder dresses, and they'll carry single long-stemmed orange roses."

"Sounds amazing."

She smiled, pleased with the vision in her mind. "Elegant. Girl, I saw an article that suggested bobbing for apples at a fall wedding! Like I would want my wedding to be like a kids' Halloween party!"

"What else were they going to come up with, turkeys wandering around the ballroom?"

"Actually, I'm going to have peacocks on the grounds."

I started to laugh, then realized she was serious.

She picked up a thick cream-colored envelope off the coffee table and handed it to me. My invitation.

We sat down on a wicker couch. The cushions were covered in pink and red tropical flowers and green vines. In front of us was a wicker-and-glass coffee table, on which was arranged a green glass vase with red silk roses, some magazines, and a couple of remotes. A tall plastic palm tree sat in front of the sliding glass doors across the room. A framed print of a travel poster for Jamaica with a black couple walking on a white-sand beach was on the wall over the couch.

Stephanie and I used to talk about getting out of Denver. She always said she was going to live on an island—Jamaica, Hawaii, Barbados. Her father's family tree goes back to the Seychelles. She used to say she had salt water and island breezes in her blood. But she stayed put after graduation and got her degree in journalism from CU-Denver. She had told me on the phone that unlike most of her classmates she was able to land a job in her field upon graduation. She'd been a features writer at the *Denver Post* for a couple of years. Even though she had been a nerd, she was never as bad off as I was. Stephanie had it like that. Things came easily to her. Except getting out of Denver. Now it seemed she was never going to live on an island. She had nothing but Greg Sandoval, that was Mr. Wonderful's name, in her blood.

She filled me in on Greg, a lawyer, and handed me a picture of a handsome brown-skinned man in a suit.

After an hour of gushing about the Finest, Yummiest, Sweetest Man on the Face of the Planet Ever! she got around to asking about me. "So what made you come home? I thought you'd"—she made air quotes with her hands—" 'stick needles in your eyes' before you came back here again?"

My hope that I could talk to Stephanie about what was going on with me dwindled. She was so different, and so happy, I couldn't see how she could possibly relate. "I'm taking a little break." It wasn't the whole truth, but it wasn't a lie either.

"Well, he ain't little, but I've got just the break for you. His name is Desi Gordon. I thought about him as soon as you called."

What happened to the chubby girl whose idea of a good time was staying up all night playing Monopoly and eating popcorn mixed with M&M's? And when did taking a break start to mean taking a guy? Especially a guy named *Desi*? "As in Ricky Ricardo?"

"As in desi-rable. As in Desmond, as in Tutu," Stephanie answered. "He's a good man just like the Desmond who dedicated his life to freeing his brothers and sisters from apartheid. And he happens to be single, *o-kay*? Don't tell me you're still bashful?"

Bashful was a nice word for what I was. Socially retarded was more like it. I didn't go through the normal developmental stages like you're supposed to. I didn't have boyfriends in middle school because boys are no fun when your mother is also chasing them. When I got to high school I was painfully behind the curve, and I was determined not to end up with a baby daddy and a diaper bag full of lost dreams, so I stuck my head in my books and dodged boys like bullets. By college, I was an out-and-out loser as far as relationships go. I was so standoffish, guys thought I was stuck-up. It was easier to let them believe I was a snob than for them to know I was petrified.

"I would have thought with all that college partying you'd be over it by now."

What college partying? I frowned. "I'm tired of partying. I'm kind of done with men for a while. That's why I came back. I'm taking a sabbatical." It wasn't a lie exactly; I was taking time off . . . just not because of men.

She shook her head. "I'm so glad I'm done with wannabe players. But you know the best way to get over one man is to get another one quick. Trade his ass in for a better model."

In a last-ditch appeal to the Stephanie I used to know, I signed n-o, flat palm, w-a-y.

"God, I forgot all about signing. I can't believe you still do that. What'd you just say?"

"No way."

"Just one date. It won't even be a date. It'll just be a . . . friendly meeting. You can meet my man and our friend and we'll have some food and that's it."

I grimaced. "I don't want to meet people. I hate people. People suck."

"You know I'm gonna keep on you, so you might as well just say yes now and get it over with."

Was it possible Stephanie was always this pushy and I just forgot it?

"Well? Well? Well?"

I supposed even a blind date would beat sitting around Nona's. Ever since they did the intentions thing and I snapped at her, she had been acting like a wounded bird. I made my thumb and pinky into the bull's horns that stand for a *y,* bent my thumb and placed the other four fingers on top for an *e,* then made a fist with my thumb in the front of my fingers for the *s.* Stephanie smiled. I wondered if she knew what I signed or if she was going to take whatever I said as a yes.

One Great Secret

THE FIRST TIME I PULLED MY HAIR I WAS TEN. IT WAS
at night and Nona was gone, as usual. Two men banged on
the front door. They were loud, slurring their words and
laughing at everything. Obviously drunk, obviously at the
wrong place. There was loud music and people-noise coming from next door. "Come on!" they shouted. "Let us in.
We wanna party."

I was scared, but something told me to get out of bed
and go to the door. As I was walking up to it, I saw that it
was unlocked. My heart started to pound violently and my
hands shook. "You have the wrong house!" I yelled, trying
to sound mean with my little ten-year-old self. "Go next
door!"

The sound of my high-pitched voice only made it
worse. "We wanna party with *you*!" they said. "Come on,
baby!"

My stomach dropped to the floor. I was immobilized,

but I knew I had to lock the door. I forced myself to walk toward it, terrified that if they could hear me coming nearer it would set them off more.

"Open up! Open up!" they chanted.

I got to the door and slowly turned the small handle on the knob that would lock it. They started to quiet down. I went to sit down, when I heard something. I turned back toward the door and the doorknob was moving. They were trying to get in. I started trembling like I was having a seizure, my muscles locked and shook at the same time. I don't know how long I stared at the doorknob turning, but finally they stopped and went away. I shook-walked to a chair and collapsed. I stayed there for hours thinking about what would have happened if I hadn't been awake, if I hadn't gotten out of bed. Thinking about how Nona had left me without even being bothered to lock the door behind her.

I could have been hurt. But I didn't feel lucky that it didn't happen. The idea that something that bad could happen to me wasn't in my head until that moment, and when it came it opened the door to a whole world of un-thought-of fears.

It was too much. I couldn't stand my own mind. Somehow I knew that pulling my hair would relieve the stress, get me out of my head. And I was right. With the first pluck, pressure was released, like popping a balloon or taking a pin out of a hand grenade, and I sucked air way down into my lungs. I twirled the hair around my fingers and kept breathing deeply. By the third pluck, I stopped shaking. I tugged and twirled my hair until I could go back to bed, just before it got light. When Nona got home, I was in bed pretending to sleep as usual. I never said anything to her about it.

STEPHANIE DIDN'T WASTE any time setting up the "friendly meeting." The next day she called me and a week later I was looking down at a pile of drab blouses and pants on my bed, trying to figure out what to wear and talking to myself. "Calm down. Relax. It's just dinner with a friend. So what, a guy is invited? It's no big deal. You don't have to do anything you don't want to do."

It didn't work. I had to pull three hairs before I could force myself to throw on black jeans, black shoes, and a white t-shirt and tie my black head wrap in a ball at the nape of my neck. I looked at myself in the little mirror over the dresser. "Even if you don't feel like it right now, you are young, gifted, and black. You almost have a master's degree and you are nobody's baby mama."

Ivy was in the kitchen putting dishes in the dishwasher. It seemed like she was always around now. When I closed the door, she looked up at me and snickered. "I thought you was lying about going out with a girlfriend. I just knew you was gonna come out looking all good for some nigga. My bad."

She had a way with backhanded compliments. I looked around for my backpack. Sunny was always taking off with it, looking for pens and pencils to "write" with.

Ivy scraped leftover food into the trash can and rinsed the plate. "Twenty-five and you don't have no man, no kids, and no job? Man, I wish I could take a few months off and just, like, hang."

Yeah, moving in with Nona was like being on vacation. I moved the kitchen chairs out of the way and looked under the table.

"But it's good you're here. Your mom has really been wishing for that." Ivy slammed the dishwasher door, and I stopped what I was doing. She was looking at me with her faux good-girl smile.

I couldn't figure out why she hated me so much.

"She's like really happy now," she said.

Then it dawned on me: She was jealous. If Ivy were a dog, she would have been pissing a circle around Nona to mark her territory. She had done everything she could think of to say *Back off. Nona is mine.* I wanted to tell her *You can have her. She's all yours.* But I was so surprised I laughed.

Big mistake. She took a step toward me and I stepped back. Ivy was like one of those ghetto-tough girls in high school. Always ready to fight. The last fight I had was in second grade. I won, but that wasn't exactly a good enough record to take on anybody now.

Sunny ran into the kitchen, interrupting us. She grabbed my legs. "Can I go with you?"

"No, I'm going with some friends." I pried her arms loose. "Where's my backpack?"

Ivy shook her head to let me know I wasn't worth the trouble. "You don't even know you got it like that."

"I wanna go with you," Sunny whined.

"Where'd you put my backpack?"

Sunny sulked and shrugged.

Ivy held out her hand to Sunny. "Come on, Itty Bitty. Let's go outside and get your mama so we can watch a movie."

"I'm not itty bitty! I'm three and a half!" Sunny said, but she obeyed.

I kept looking around and finally found my backpack on the floor in Nona's room, with all the contents scattered all over. This time the little monster had even opened my wallet. I was going to have to start locking it up in my car or something to keep this kid out of it. After I checked to make sure everything was present and accounted for, I left. When I got outside, I hurried past them all on the patio, yelling a rushed good-bye over my shoulder as I dashed down the path.

STEPHANIE WAS WEARING a short fuchsia sundress and strappy high heels showing off miles of gym-toned flesh. The ponytail I had seen last time turned out to be a hairpiece, which she wasn't wearing today. Her real hair was short, and slicked back with gel. It looked like water was dancing across her scalp.

"I didn't know you'd be this dressed up. You said it was just dinner."

"Yeah, dinner at a restaurant. Indoors. With grown-ups. O-kay?"

In a college town, what I had on were going-out-to-dinner clothes.

She looked at her watch. "They're going to be here in a few minutes. You'll have to do as you are. Come on. We'll just put some makeup on you."

I quit wearing makeup in eighth grade. "No thanks."

"Just a little blush." Stephanie dragged me into her bathroom and closed the toilet seat.

I sat down.

"You could have worn something a little more . . . colorful."

The t-shirts Nona gave me were still in the bag with the price tags on.

"Can we at least take off this scarf and do something with your hair?"

"No!" I put both hands on my head. "I need a touch-up."

"Okay, okay. Fine. Just the makeup." She perused the containers on the vanity, then picked up a black plastic square. "Close your eyes."

I obeyed.

"You should pluck your eyebrows."

Yep, definitely bossier than I remember. Her new muscles seemed to have gone to her head. She started dabbing liquid foundation on my cheeks. So much for only a little blush.

"Hmmm," Stephanie said. "Mascara."

I opened my eyes so she could brush my lashes.

When she was done with the mascara, I closed them again. I felt the tickle of a brush against my eyelids. Being made up was relaxing, like getting a good shampoo at a beauty salon. Something I hadn't done in a long time. I wanted to just stay there and go to sleep. Stay there and not go to dinner with some guys I never met.

In seventh grade I started wearing makeup. Every day for a week, I woke up two hours before school so I could do my face. I wore foundation, powder, blush, lipstick, lip liner, mascara, the whole works. I thought I was pretty. I had my hair in a Salt 'N Pepa asymmetrical bob. For the first time, I liked looking at myself in the mirror. The next week, Mrs. Martin took me aside after Social Studies and said, "You know your mother doesn't let you go out of the house looking like that. You have such a pretty face. Don't ruin it when you get here. Now go wash that mess off before I call your mother."

She didn't know Nona was passed out when I left for school. She didn't know that if Nona had been awake, she wouldn't have cared. Afterward, I ran into the girls' bathroom and looked in the mirror. I saw raccoon eyes and too-red cheeks and lips. I saw what everyone else had been seeing for days: a clown. After that, I went to the store and got a magazine and learned how to apply makeup. I practiced and practiced until I got good at covering up my face. By the next year when I was thirteen, high-school boys and men Nona's age and older started looking at me, saying things they shouldn't have been saying. I stopped wearing makeup.

Stephanie rubbed a cream blush onto my cheeks with her fingertips. Then topped it all off with powder. I wanted to keep my eyes shut, but I was afraid it would seem weird now that she was done with anything that would get in my eyes, so I opened them. Her head was tilted to the side and she was studying my face like a painting. Her lips were red and shiny, and her long gold earrings gleamed next to her face. Her newly thin neck was that of a swan's.

"Not too glossy, I think." She took the lids off three lipsticks before she found the reddish brown she wanted—plainer than the bright red she was wearing.

"Open your mouth a little."

I did and she dabbed the lipstick against my lips.

She handed me a Kleenex, and I kissed it to get the extra color off.

She snapped her fingers. "Earrings!"

She left, and I stood to check out her work. Since our complexions were similar, her makeup was right for my skin tone, but I wiped off some of the shadow and blush before she got back.

"Try these." She handed me a pair of large silver hoops. "But don't lose them. Greg gave them to me."

I put the earrings on, and was pleased to see that I didn't look too terribly ridiculous.

Stephanie gave her work the thumbs-up. Then she checked herself out in the mirror, smiling to make sure food wasn't caught in the gap between her teeth. She had always been self-conscious about her front teeth. "I need a cigarette. You smoke?"

"No." I was surprised she did, but it helped explain the weight loss.

She went out on the balcony and I sat on the couch feeling the makeup settle into my pores.

"Don't tell Greg. I'm supposed to be quitting." She

came back and sprayed herself with body spray, which explained the strong waffle-cone scent, and popped in an Altoid.

"Want a spritz?"

I skipped the spray, but did take a mint. No reason for a bad night to be even worse.

STEPHANIE WAS RIGHT. Greg showed up dressed in slacks and a leather blazer, and Ricky Ricardo had on a raw silk shirt. At least he was in jeans. Each couple was going to ride in separate cars. We went to the parking lot and Ricky walked up to a pristine red vintage car.

"This is yours?"

He smiled sheepishly. "I know. Everybody out here drives an SUV. I'm gonna have to get something that does better in snow, but it was my grandfather's. He left it to me last year. I brought it out here on a trailer."

He opened my door and held it for me while I got in, then walked around and got in the driver's side. The interior was white leather, and at a glance I didn't see one crack.

"What is this?"

"A '63 Ford Falcon." He backed up. "Don't tell me you like it? I think it's kinda ugly, but it was Papa's."

"It's beautiful. That '72 Bug over there is mine. Thankfully the last owner added a cassette player and seat belts in the back. But it gets really hot with no air-conditioning in the summer."

He smiled wide and said, "Ah, so you know."

I felt like I had passed a test, but I was still anxious so I didn't say anything else on the way over, and neither did Ricky. Maybe he was anxious too, or maybe he didn't want to ruin the good start we seemed to have made.

When we walked into La Naranja, the hostess ran up and hugged Greg and Stephanie. Ricky and I exchanged a surprised glance. "They must eat here a lot," he said.

"This is my cousin," Greg explained. "I worked here every summer from the time I was fourteen until I was twenty-three."

"We're having our rehearsal dinner here," Stephanie added.

The cousin led us to our table. We sat boy-girl, so that Ricky was next to me and Stephanie was across from me. They ordered a pitcher of margaritas and I asked for a Coke with lime.

"Still?" Stephanie raised her eyebrows.

"Still." People get all up in arms about crack and meth and every other illegal drug, and totally ignore the damage alcohol does just because it's legal. But I knew. Alcohol makes people stupid, selfish, destructive, and crazy. And I was crazy enough on my own, thank you very much.

After everyone else had finished their first drink and everyone but Stephanie had killed a basket of tortilla chips, Ricky poured another round. He lifted the pitcher and looked at me. "Want some?"

I shook my head.

"Oh, come on, Miss Goodie Goodie. Have a little fun." Stephanie wagged her glass of frothy green liquid in my face. Having drunk her first one on an empty stomach, she was already tipsy.

"I'm surprised you drink. Alcohol slows down metabolism. It's also a depressant. And do you know what it does to your brain? Your liver? Not to mention ulcers, pancreatitis, heart disease?" I thought of Lois and was about to add breast cancer to the list when Stephanie started laughing at me.

"Damn, just when I was getting ready for some class A binge-drinking," she said.

"*O-kay?*" Greg said, sounding just like Stephanie. They matched like a pair of salt and pepper shakers.

"*Lighten* up, girl. You sound like you need a drink now more than ever."

Suddenly, I was embarrassed. As usual, I had gone too far. As usual, I was the odd one out. I hadn't meant to keep going, but liquor strikes a nerve in me. I knew I should have driven myself, met them at the restaurant. Then when it turned bad, like I knew it would, I could have driven myself home. I could have been heading out the door right now.

Ricky Ricardo put the pitcher down. He wasn't laughing. "I like a woman with strong convictions."

I looked at him, really seeing him for the first time all evening. Stephanie was right: Desi was handsome. Muscular, but not in an icky bodybuilder way. His body was more like a dancer's or a runner's. His face and head were shaved so smooth he looked like polished onyx, and he had long eyelashes that women would kill for.

He smiled at me. He liked me.

Now I was really nervous.

During dinner, Desi told us about his move here from Chicago, where he had lived his whole life except for the years he attended Howard University. He talked about wanting to learn to ski, downhill and cross-country. He and Greg discussed mountains and gear for a while, until Stephanie caught Greg's attention, and the two of them started their own conversation, leaving Desi and me to talk.

I kept my mouth shut, which seemed all right with Desi. He had a nice voice—deep and smooth, but not obnoxiously so. He talked about his job—he had an MBA and worked for a consulting firm—very passionately, using his hands a lot. They were like coffee-colored birds flying around the room.

I was trying to figure out what to say, when suddenly he was silent and just staring at me. He must have asked a question.

"Oh! Sorry?"

Stephanie sneaked a glance at us.

"I said, Do you want some of my fajitas?"

"No thanks."

He speared a piece of steak and red pepper and lifted his fork in front of me. "It's really good."

I took the bite, aware that my lips were where his had been just seconds before.

Across the table, Stephanie was raising her eyebrows and pointing at her mouth.

"Um . . ." Desi said. "You've got a piece of cheese on your chin."

I hurriedly wiped my face.

"Didn't get it."

I wiped lower on my chin.

Stephanie grimaced and shook her head.

"Can I taste yours?" Desi asked.

The hair on my arms rose up and my blood rose to the surface. I was warm, but I had chill bumps at the same time. I cut a bite of chile relleno and lifted it—it fell with a plop on the tablecloth. I grabbed a napkin and started wiping it up. "Sorry."

I tried again. This time, he touched his lips to my fork.

After dinner, he drove me back to Stephanie's to get my car. When we parked, he asked me out. He was a nice guy. Smart. Ambitious. Considerate. Smelled good. He even drove a car with character. There was absolutely nothing wrong with him, but I said no.

He replied, "You have a secret."

The floor dropped out of the Falcon. "What do you mean?"

"You have a secret. Come on, tell me."

"I don't know what you're talking about." My head itched. I touched my earlobe, and discovered I was still wearing Stephanie's earrings, so I couldn't rub my ears. My neck started itching like crazy. Suddenly, nothing was more important than scratching my neck. Then my arms started.

"See. All that itching is 'cause you know I'm right."

I stopped scratching. "It's the dry air."

"All great women have at least one great secret," he said.

"I guess I'm not a great woman."

He stared at me for what felt like a very long time. "Too late. I already think you are."

In bed that night, with the sounds of water trickling through the wall next door, I touched myself to relieve some pressure, but I don't mean my head. And I became aware of a sensation so pervasive I managed to forget it for long stretches of time (weeks, months, maybe even years). I'd been feeling this way so long that it was as familiar to me as my face in the mirror, but I had never stopped to name it. But after feeling close to someone for the first time in a very long time, the awareness of what was in my heart rushed to my brain: loneliness.

The Right to Be Pissed

"THE PEACE CORPS?!" NONA SQUEAKED.

"The Peace Corps," Lois repeated gently.

It was Sunday afternoon. Nona, Lois, Ivy, Sunny, and I were in the prairie room and Lois had dropped a bomb. She was joining the Peace Corps and Nona was going to be without a sponsor. Nona was flipping out. Her eyes had gone dark and she was chewing her bottom lip. The strange thing was that I felt the same. Though I knew better than to believe Nona wouldn't ever drink again, my own heart started racing at the idea of her without her Warrior Princess here to keep her straight.

They had just gotten home from church. I had spent the morning reading the *Denver Post*. The national news was all about the wars in Iraq and Afghanistan. Stephanie had a story on the front page of the Sunday Styles section about a couple that paid for their wedding by selling advertising— the invitations had a little blurb about the printer on the back, the cake was brought to you by Mile High Auto Body, etc. Well, reading the paper wasn't all I did. I also ruminated about last night, about Desi, but all that flew out of my head now.

"Why didn't you tell me?" Nona asked, her voice a little less high-pitched.

"I didn't want to say anything until I was sure," Lois answered. "I know this is going to mean a change for you, but—"

"It's fine," Nona said briskly, shaking her head. "Fine. I'll be fine."

"You mean 'fucking insecure, neurotic, and emotional'?" Lois asked.

Sunny gasped.

"Will you please give me a real feeling?" Lois continued.

"I don't know, okay? I just heard about this. I feel . . . I feel . . ."

Abandoned. I would have thought I would enjoy Nona getting a taste of what it feels like to be left behind, but I didn't. And I didn't understand that at all.

"What?" Lois pressed.

". . . Shocked as shit, okay? How's that?" Nona said.

"Mama, that's a bad word!"

"Thank you," Lois said.

Sunny pulled on Nona's arm. "You not supposed to say bad words!"

"How could you not have told me?" Nona asked.

"That's messed up," Ivy reached over and picked up Sunny.

Lois sat back in her chair and played with her bracelets.

She was wearing a long navy skirt and a sky-blue blouse. "I wanted something that was just for me. Something that was all mine. It was a secret, and it felt good to have a secret that wasn't shameful. I've always wanted to join the Peace Corps, but a drunk can't very well spend two years in a jungle or a remote village where there might not be a liquor store or a bar, now can she? But that's not an issue now. And since they let old broads like me go as long as you're healthy, and now I know that I am, I'm going."

Nona kept shaking her head.

"I'm sorry," Lois said. "I didn't mean to hurt you. You know that."

"Hey, I'm not your man. I'm not your mama," Nona said dismissively. "You don't have to tell me all your business."

Ivy laughed sarcastically, as usual quick to take Nona's side, not getting that Nona was only pretending not to care.

"Where are you going?" Nona asked.

"Bulgaria. To teach English."

"For how long?"

Lois took a deep breath. "Two years, actually almost three. Twenty-seven months."

Nona was so stunned she spit her bottom lip out like it was sour. Her mouth hung open and she stared at Lois.

Lois smiled sadly. "You *will* be okay, Nona. Not fine, but okay."

"I'll make sure she is," Ivy said, beside herself with joy at the opportunity to have Nona even more to herself. "Don't worry, Nona. You and me will hang. We'll help each other."

Great, I thought.

Lois agreed with me. She frowned and said, "That's not your role."

"How you gonna tell me my role? You don't know what it's like for us."

"Ivy," Nona warned.

"How many days have you been clean?" Lois demanded.

"Sixty-five," Ivy said, her eyes blinking rapidly.

"Good for you. But here's a little tip, if you want to stay that way, keep your mouth shut and your ears open when anybody with more time than you is speaking, no matter what color they are."

"Y'all always quick to tell a sister to keep her mouth shut, ain't you?" Ivy spat. "That's why I don't like nothing to do with white folks."

"You're half white yourself."

"Yep, but it ain't the good half."

"Whoa!" Nona put her hand on Ivy's arm. "In the movies, it's always some magical black person who comes to help the white characters heal. Don't you think it's about time to let white folks carry some of the spiritual burden for a change?"

Ivy stayed tense, but Lois smiled.

"Ivy, all I'm trying to say is that Nona is going to need a sponsor," Lois said.

"I never said she wouldn't!"

"And it can't be you."

"Before we start on my new sponsor," Nona interrupted, "can I finish finding out what's going on with the sponsor I got right now? When do you leave?"

"Next month."

"Next month!"

"I know it's fast. But we'll stay in touch. We'll write. I'll have access to e-mail when I go to Sofia. It's the capital." Lois leaned in and held both of Nona's hands. "Don't be sad."

"I'm not sad," Nona said sadly.

After dinner, long after the water sounds started and ended, long after I heard Nona come back in from the garden, we were both still awake. At 4:07, I could hear her in the kitchen. She wasn't going to sleep the whole night. Not good. This is how it would go when I was a kid. She'd stay up prowling around the house all night for a few nights in a row, then she'd go out again. Since I'd been back, she had been able to go to sleep after she came in from the yard, but not tonight. Just like that time at Bill's house, something compelled me to get up and check on her.

She was sitting at the table with half a loaf of bread, butter, and grape jelly spread out in front of her.

"I thought you were such a health nut."

"When the going gets tough, the tough eat carbs," she joked, tears forming in her eyes. "Most alkies go for candy or cookies. I go for squishy white bread. Instant carb rush."

This was new. In the past, Nona didn't cry until *after* she had been drinking. I didn't like it. And I didn't like her talking about rushes either. She made it sound like white bread was the beginning of the slippery slope.

She wiped her eyes. "Want some toast?"

"I'm going back to bed. Aren't you? You have to go to work in a few hours."

"I think I'll read awhile. Maybe it'll make me sleepy enough that I can doze for an hour or two. I'll go in the living room so I don't disturb you."

She cleared the table and I went back to my room. I was still awake when her alarm went off at 6:15, and I knew she was too.

NONA MOPED FOR DAYS and went through two more loaves of white bread. Not even working in the yard seemed to make things better. True to form, Ivy leeched onto her even more. I told myself that I'd be long gone back to school before Nona spun out of control, but still I found myself listening carefully to her A.A. hotline calls, waiting to see if she mentioned a new sponsor. She did not.

On the sixth night she came in from the garden, covered with dirt and with leaves in her hair. She looked like she was turning into a plant. "We're having a going-away party," she announced.

All the next week, after dinner and after Sunny was in bed, she cleaned like a maniac, scrubbing floors and walls and windows until everything sparkled and the entire place smelled like lemon furniture polish. Then she came home with bags of food, cooked a giant meal, cut bouquets of flowers, put on a gospel CD, and opened the house to the twelve-step folks.

I stuck around to see if Nona's new sponsor presented herself. I sat on the patio and watched a parade of unusually jolly people arrive. Most of them were white, but there were a few black people and some Latinos. Seemingly every recovering person in Denver had been invited to the party. Though Ivy didn't come. They had all lied to people, scarred them, failed them. Yet here they were, alive, smiling, moving on, all the lies and failures and hurts seemingly left safely in the past. But were they? Or did they have spouses and children at home waiting for them to slide off the wagon too?

After about an hour, I was still sitting outside. I had moved to a lounge chair on the grass after groups of people spilled out of the house, smoking and talking. Lois came out and blew her nose. Her hair was loose, hanging past her shoulders. As usual, she was dressed in a shade of blue. Today, she wore a sleeveless, flowing teal dress. With all the rings and bracelets, she looked like a fortune-teller, a giant Viking fortune-teller.

She walked over to my single chair and sat in the grass. "It's a little overwhelming in there. That many people haven't bawled over me since I was diagnosed." She stuck her long legs out in front of her. "I wish I could have gotten to know you a little better before I left. I hope I get to see you when I get back."

"I'm not coming back to Denver after I graduate."

"Not even to visit?"

I shrugged.

"You know, you have every right to be pissed at your mom. She's not trying to take that away from you. She just wants you to address it with her."

"She thinks she can change things, but it's too late."

"That's true. Nobody can change the past. I can't go back and not drink. All I can do is my best from this point on. That's all any of us can do."

"How long do you think it's going to be before Nona starts drinking again?"

"What makes you think she's going to start drinking again?"

"She doesn't have a sponsor yet. You said yourself she needed one."

"I've never seen anybody in A.A. work harder than your mom. She'll find somebody. And until she does, she's got all those people in there." She nodded toward the house.

The sun was starting to set, the clouds had turned coral against the turquoise sky, and the evening air was cool.

Lois rubbed her bare arms. "You can't change the past, but you can stop living there. That's something you always have a choice about."

I shook my head. "I know you want to take up for her, but—"

"I'm not saying this for Nona's benefit. I'm talking about *you*. Don't you want to get on with things? Isn't it a drag going around being pissed all the time?"

"You just said I had every right to be pissed!"

"And you do. But is that really how you want to spend the rest of your life?"

I rolled my eyes. Yeah, pretty much. This is what every girl dreams for herself: to have an absentee father and a drunken mother, so she can spend her adult years all messed up.

"You have the right to be angry at what happened to you, but you also have the right to be happy." Her eyes softened. "I didn't mean to upset you. You seem like such a bright, accomplished young woman. It's amazing what you've done with your life. And that's clearly to your credit. Lots of adult children of alcoholics don't end up nearly as together as you are. I hope you feel proud of yourself."

That was the first time anyone had acknowledged what I had gone through, that I had been all on my own. I didn't know how much I longed to hear those words until she said them. Suddenly, I envied the village that would get to lean on her thick shoulders. I wanted to thank her, but I didn't trust my voice.

She seemed to understand. She reached over and patted my arm, then kindly changed the subject. "I'm going in. Come have some cake and coffee." She struggled to get up. "Shay, give me a hand, will you?"

I stood and pulled her up. She shivered. "Let's go before they eat all my cake."

It *was* getting chilly, and my sweatshirt wasn't cutting it anymore. But even if it was still warm, I would have followed Lois anywhere right then. I stopped at the front door, wanting to have just a little more time with her. I asked the first thing that came to mind. "Why do you always wear blue?"

She looked down at her dress. "When I got out of rehab, I needed a way to remind myself to stop lying about everything and I read somewhere that blue is the color of truth and sincerity. Now I wear it 'cause it brings out my eyes." She grinned, and we went inside.

Everybody was crowded into the prairie room.

"There you are!" Nona snagged Lois as soon as we walked in. "I want to make a toast."

They made their way to the center of the prairie room

and Nona began. "When I first came to A.A., I was terrified, like everybody is. I didn't know any of y'all, and on top of that, I was usually the only black person in the room. But as scared as I was, I was more afraid of what would happen if I wasn't there. So I kept showing up, trying different groups, but I don't know how long I would have made it without Lois. After my fourth meeting, she took me aside and said, 'Let me tell you: The truth will set you free. But first it will blow your f-ing head off.'"

The drunks laughed.

I looked around. Was Lois right? Could these people replace her and keep Nona from drinking?

Nona turned serious. "I wouldn't have made it these last four years without you," she continued, her voice thick with emotion. "'Specially after I got pregnant. You showed me I didn't have to live like I had been living. You gave me reason to hope. You saved my life."

"You saved your own life," Lois said.

Nona smiled, but her eyes filled. She shook herself and tried to make herself laugh. "Everybody, lift your nonalcoholic drinks in honor of my sponsor, my friend, my sister, and my baby's godmother. Here's to Lois. All the blessings you can stand."

Lois gave Nona the credit for getting sober, but I knew better. Nona was never able to stop drinking before. I watched them hugging, knowing that I was thinking the same thing Nona was: *Lois, don't go.*

Record Store Girl

"DID YOU KNOW A SUNFLOWER IS TECHNICALLY A WEED?"
Nona asked.

I stopped shoveling cedar mulch and looked up at the drying sunflower stalks. They were at least six feet tall and headless. Some of the flowers had been yanked off and eaten by squirrels. Nona had cut the rest to dry the seeds for us to eat and to plant next year. One flower was as big as a throw pillow.

"All these years I've been planting them, and they're weeds. I just read it in a magazine."

"Uh-oh, she's gonna get deep on us," Ivy said.

For once I agreed with Ivy: We were in for a "Nona-ture" (a lecture by Nona).

She had dragged me outside this morning to help spread mulch. Nona, Ivy, and Steve, one of her A.A. friends, had brought home a heap of mulch in the back of his pickup. It was hard work, but I didn't mind for the first few hours. It was a beautiful September day and the air was perfumed with cedar. But after about four hours of shoveling with only a short lunch break, it was getting old.

Nona was still trying to get me to be as garden-crazy as she was. I was never going to be into weeding and pruning and dirty hands, but I had come to enjoy sitting on the patio surrounded by flowers. Her garden was lush and wild, yet organized. After hours of study, I noticed patterns—colors, shapes, and textures that repeated in a way that was soothing to the eye. I noticed that shorter things were planted in front of taller things so that the blooms on the taller plants seemed to float like candy-colored clouds above a green sea. That stalks leaning toward the sun seemed to be reaching out to shake your hand or give you a high five. That brushing against certain plants made them release lemon, ginger, cinnamon, or chocolate scents. There was even one that smelled like root-beer candy.

I never would have admitted it to Nona, but the yard was starting to make sense to me. And I was feeling a little less overwhelmed, a little calmer, and more energetic. But that didn't mean I was in the mood for one of her self-improvement lectures.

She laughed. "It does seem profound to me. Something about perspective, you know? It's all how we choose to see something."

Steve said, "One person's weeds are another person's flowers."

"Exactly!" Nona smiled. I watched them carefully. I could tell they liked each other. I just couldn't tell how much. There was no touching or secret looks, but they were definitely friendly. Steve was handsome in a manly-man way. He wasn't gym-buff like Greg. He had more than a little tummy, but he was strong and square-jawed, with a blond, shaggy charm. Plus he shared Nona's weird A.A. humor.

I wondered if Steve was the remedy she had decided on, now that Lois was leaving. If it was, it was bad. Men were always what got Nona in trouble.

"You want mulch by the angel?" I asked.

Nona turned away from Steve and said sure, then went right back to talking with him. I wondered what Ivy thought of Steve getting so much attention. Somehow, she didn't seem to mind. Maybe because he was a guy. Maybe Ivy was smitten too or maybe she thought he and Nona would get married and they'd be a happy little family. I could have told her not to hold her breath waiting on that one.

Actually, I was surprised by Nona, and surprised at my surprise. There was a time when I would have expected her to be focusing on some man, but I had already grown accustomed to this new Nona who didn't play around.

One day the fence got tagged with graffiti. Nona saw it when she came home from work, and without even changing her clothes, she went in the shed and got the paint out and painted over it. "You let this mess stay up even for a day, and they'll be back," she said. "Let them know you won't stand for it and they leave you alone."

Ivy wiped her brow. "How much longer do we have to do this? We been out here like forever."

The pile of mulch was getting low, maybe another hour to go. But even one more hour sounded too long to me too.

Nona looked at her watch. "Go on in," she said. "There's some leftover chicken and potato salad in the fridge, and plenty of tea. You know where it is."

Ivy and I both put down our shovels gladly.

"Aren't you coming?" Ivy asked.

Nona shook her head. "No, take Sunny inside. I'm going to keep going until this is done."

Steve bent over and stretched his sides. Even strapping young Steve wanted a break. "Do you mind if I go get a drink? Then I'll be back out to help you finish up."

"Of course," Nona said. "I'm sorry. I didn't mean to be a slave-driver."

"You're tough."

"I just want to get it done."

The rest of us trooped into the house. Steve had a quick glass of water and went back out. Nona stayed outside until every piece of mulch was swept out of Steve's truck and into the yard.

THE PHONE RANG and for once it wasn't for Nona.

"I can't believe you called me!" I blurted to Desi, my heart beating crazily. I didn't mean for that to come out. Almost three weeks had passed since our date, and I thought I was out of the woods. Incongruously, I had been relieved and disappointed that he hadn't called. But now, here he was.

"I don't scare off that easy, now," he said. "Let's go out again. This time without an audience."

Sunny was asleep and Nona was cleaning the kitchen. I could tell she was eavesdropping. She had grilled chicken breasts and peaches for dinner. A row of peaches from the Western Slope, the other side of the Rockies, sat ripening on the windowsill above the kitchen sink. The kitchen smelled like an orchard.

I turned my back to her. "It's just not a good time right now. I'm kind of going through some stuff."

"What kind of stuff?"

"I'd rather not say. It's a long story."

"You had a good time with me, right?" he pressed.

"Yes."

"Well, then? Why not?"

Because I knew how this would end up. We would go out a few times and he'd start looking at me like a pork chop and I wouldn't be able to go through with it and he'd start wondering what was wrong with me and I'd just end up feeling more like a freak of nature.

"I'm sorry."

"You have a secret lover?"

"No."

"You're gay?"

"No."

"Did my breath stink?"

I smiled. "No." *And you're never going to guess. Not in a million years. So. Just. Stop.* I was good at keeping secrets. That's what happens when you're raised by an alcoholic. You learn to keep things to yourself.

"Look. I don't hardly know anybody here. You just moved back. We can just hang out. Go to a movie. I'm not asking you to marry me. I never propose to a girl before the third date. I promise, unless you tie me up and beat me, we don't even have to be romantic. We can be friends. I know I'm always interested in having a friend. What about you?"

I walked into the living room and said faintly, "Why me?"

He whispered back, "I like you. Why are we whispering?"

I thought to ask myself WWNSD, but Nina Simone had long since given up on me when it came to men. And she was right. I was hopeless. Desi liked me now, but it was easy to like someone before you got to know them, before you found out how weird they were. Even though I was lonely and longed to say yes, I couldn't. I *did* have a secret, and it was too messed up and bizarre to ever give away, especially to someone as confident and cool as Desi.

This time I didn't whisper. "I'm sorry. I just can't."

In the seconds it took him to respond, I pictured his eyes closed, long lashes on his smooth dark cheeks.

"That's too bad," he said. And it was.

When I went back in the prairie room, Nona was grinning. "So Ivy was right. You gonna see him again?"

"No." I picked up *This Side of the Sky* and sat in the rocking chair. I was getting a kick out of the feisty character, Myraleen. She had just exacted her revenge on her evil mother by putting a pair of her panties on her mother's head after she was dead. Though, now in my dreams everyone spoke with a Southern, dirt-road accent.

"Didn't you like him?"

I shrugged.

"Do you want to talk about what's going on with you? I wouldn't say anything stupid like 'Get over it.' I know it's hard."

I turned the page.

She sighed and rubbed her fingers together. Her rough hands made a scratching sound. "Did . . . something happen to you? Did somebody . . . do something to hurt you?"

I thought about the time the drunk men came to the door. "No."

Nona was visibly relieved. "Really? That's the truth?"

I nodded reluctantly. She shouldn't get to be relieved. It's not like I wasn't terrified all those nights she was gone. It's not like I wasn't in real danger. Something bad could have happened to me and it would have been all her fault.

"Well, something's bothering you. If you don't want to talk about it, I already told you working in the yard is one of the things that helps me. I also take St. John's Wort. You could try that."

I turned the page, still pretending like I was reading.

"Or you could come to church with me sometime."

I snorted. "I am *not* going to church. Besides, I saw what works for you."

"What are you talking about?"

"Your blond friend."

"Steve?"

I nodded.

"He's Lois's boyfriend," she scoffed.

I was shocked. Steve had to be almost twenty years

younger than Lois. I had to admit as low as Nona might go, I didn't think she'd start something with Lois's boyfriend.

While I was digesting Steve and Lois, Nona had been planning to continue whatever point it was she was trying to make. "I know you have lots of . . . issues—" she said.

"*I* have issues?"

"With *me*. Because of your upbringing, my substance abuse. Have you ever thought about seeing a thera—"

"I'm not having this conversation with you!"

"You said you prefer reality over make-believe, right? Well, the reality is you've got to do something, Shay. You can't just sit around here sleeping and feeling miserable. Don't you want something better for yourself?"

Of course I wanted something better for myself! I wanted to be normal. I wanted to be finishing up my last semester, writing my thesis, looking for a new job. I wanted to be able to go out with friends instead of hanging around this place. I wanted Desi to be my boyfriend. But I was frozen, stunted, a little girl trapped in a twenty-five-year-old's body. "What about quote therapy, why don't I try that?"

She looked puzzled. "What's quote therapy?"

"I'll just tape up little notes everywhere, little happy phrases everywhere, and one day I'll be happy. Isn't that how it works?"

She walked over and closed the door to her bedroom so we wouldn't wake up Sunny. "You can make fun of me if you want to, but at least I'm doing something to get better. *Something*? I'm doing every goddamn thing I can think of! And if I think of anything else, I'll do that too. Whatever it takes. If I have to paper these rooms with quotes from floor to ceiling, if I have to go to meetings and church every day for the rest of my life, that's what I'm going to do! You of all people should know how hard this was, *is,* for me. How much it took for me to stop drinking. Shit, I am a middle-aged single mother of a preschooler. I barely make my bills every month. It's a miracle I'm not running around talking to aliens and wearing tinfoil on my head! It's only by the grace of God and these quotes and my meetings and my garden that I'm alive and sober today. Have you even read the book I left for you?"

About a week after I arrived, a book about adult children of alcoholics had appeared on my bedside table. I tossed it into a drawer and didn't think anything more about it.

"People in depressed houses shouldn't throw stones," she said. "You haven't had your hair done in God knows how long. You hardly ever leave the house. You really think you can afford to be criticizing other people? You have it so together?"

"Why might that be, Nona?" I threw the paperback on the floor. "Why might my life be so shitty, do ya think? Do you have any idea why I don't want to go out on a date again?"

"Fine, let's get down to it. Why?"

Now that she asked me straight out, I didn't want to answer.

She started pacing. "This ends with you and me. I fought my mother. She fought her mother. I don't want this to go on for another generation. This needs to end with you and me."

"I don't even want kids." And this was precisely why. I didn't want to mess them up. She was right. It should end here.

"Just say what you came to say! Please. Let's end this. Let me have it."

She wanted the big scene. She had been poking me and prodding me since I arrived, trying to make me split open so she could put me back together. I was supposed to list the crimes against me so she could plead guilty to every one of them and get credit for time already served. I was supposed to scream till I cried so she could hold me and make it all better. Well, she could apologize to me for the rest of her life and it would never make it up to me. And I wasn't about to pretend that it would.

"Come on. Why is your life so terrible? Tell me. I can take it. Let's get it out so we can move past this. I'm just as tired of carrying this baggage as you are."

On top of everything else, the apology that was just dying to leap from her lips wasn't even to make me feel better. It was to make *her* feel better. She was making even *my* pain about her!

"Okay, tell me this: Why did you come back? If there's absolutely nothing I can do for you, why are you here?"

But I was done acting in her dramas, playing whatever role she directed me to. Very Mature for Her Age. Accomplished Young Woman. Now I was supposed to be the Wounded and Vulnerable Prodigal Daughter. Well, I would die before I gave her the satisfaction. She called this the everything-but-the-shouting room. So be it. I stood and walked oh so slowly and deliberately past her into my room, closing the door gently behind me. I would not even give her the pleasure of a slammed door.

My whole body was shaking from the effort to hide my feelings. I paced quietly back and forth on the yellow rug. She wanted to give me advice, to fix *me*? There was so much she didn't know about me. She didn't know I pulled out my own hair. She didn't know why I was scared to go out with a perfectly nice guy. I wanted to scream at her so badly. To yell at the top of my lungs, *This is not about you! This is about me!* I wanted to ask her if she ever once thought about me during those times when she was gone all night long. I wanted to tell her the gruesome stories of cleaning up her vomit, and sometimes urine or blood, the mornings after. I wanted to tell her how petrified I was at night and how I made up whole worlds in my head to pretend that I wasn't home alone, and how all that pretending had messed me up so much that now sometimes I felt like I couldn't tell what was real and what was pretend. That the reason I came home in the first place was because a dead singer told me to!

But uh-uh, not even in the privacy of my own room would I let her make me cry. I didn't care what Lois said. I blinked back my tears. "Fuck you, Nona," I whispered, the words sharp and sweet on my tongue, like fresh-cut onions. I wanted to say them loud and smack my lips after. I wanted to shout them like a Baptist. It was all I could do not to run back into the kitchen and let her have it, but she wanted it too much. Silence was how I could make her pay.

The next morning Nona knocked on my door.

"Come in," I said as calm as you please, even though I

had been arguing with her in my head all night, even though I had pulled so many hairs my scalp was tingling.

She was already dressed for work. "Here's the deal: You can babysit Sunny while I'm at work or you can get a job."

"You must be drinking again."

She glowered at me. In her mind, she was slapping me up one side and down the other. "In A.A. we say 'Fake it till you make it.' It's one of our 'happy little phrases,' as you call them. Maybe if you stop acting depressed, you'll stop feeling depressed. You don't want my help? You don't want to spend time with me and your sister? You don't want to go out with your friends? Fine. But you need something to do with yourself and I sure could stand to save what I spend on day care."

"I didn't go to college to be a babysitter."

"Then get a job. Oh, and you can start helping out around here too. From now on, the laundry is on you." She shut the door.

"Fine!" I couldn't help myself, I yelled through the closed door. I had always been responsible for myself. Why should now, when I was exhausted and overwhelmed and falling apart, be any different?

WWNSD? I asked, though I didn't know why. Nina Simone was the one who got me into this mess in the first place. Then I remembered that record store I went to had a *Help Wanted* sign in the window. What Nina Simone would do is get off her ass and go get a gig. I hauled my butt out of bed, dressed, sped over to the record store, and asked for the manager.

A fiftyish guy with a gray pompadour dressed in a bowl-ing shirt with "Pussycat Lounge" and the silhouette of a naked woman in a martini glass handed me an application. After I filled it out, he reviewed it and asked in a baritone voice, "You like ramen?"

"Excuse me?"

"The noodles. You like 'em?"

I shrugged. "Yeah, they're all right."

"You're hired. Twenty-six hours a week. Come back Monday morning at ten."

Alrighty then. That was one strange interview.

"You know why he asked you about the ramen, right?"

I turned around. The question came from the guy who had hit on me. "He's got a noodle fixation?"

He pushed his big black glasses up the bridge of his nose. "It's 'cause that's all you'll be able to afford to eat with the money you make here, *Record Store Girl*." Then he grinned, showing his little marshmallow teeth.

The Oliver Branch

DIE, CLOCK, DIE! SOMEONE HAD TAPED TO THE CLOCK behind the counter. I was ten minutes early for my new job. Just over a month ago I couldn't get out of bed and now I had reverted back to my old habit of being early. A rapper who spoke so fast I couldn't understand a word he was saying blared from the speakers.

I was surprised to discover it wasn't the Pussycat Lounge guy who was going to train me. It was Oliver who was there to show me the ropes, even though, with his bouncy fro, high-water jeans, and Converse All Stars, he looked like somebody I should be babysitting.

"Greetings, Record Store Girl," he said, this time with less bite.

"You don't have to keep calling me that. I get it."

"Oh, but I like it. Tell you what? For short, I'll call you RG."

"Why don't we just start over and you call me Shay and I'll call you Oliver?"

"Extending an Oliver branch, huh?"

I had to smile. "Something like that."

"Okay. Deal." He offered his hand for me to shake, and this time I did. He waved me behind the counter, and we went behind the tie-dyed curtain into the back, which served as office and stockroom. It wasn't much. Stacks of boxes on the floor, a couple of desks buried under invoices, mail, *Vibe, Spin, XXL, Billboard,* books, CDs, and file folders, tall metal shelves filled with more boxes, and a life-size cardboard cutout of Britney Spears. Somebody had taped a cartoon bubble over her head that said *Oops, I did Oliver again.* I pointed to it. "Your girlfriend?"

He looked sheepish. "Yeah, we go way back. There's probably a lot of stuff around here that . . . well, it can get a little raunchy here sometimes."

He cleared his throat and got back to business. "If you have a purse or backpack, you can leave it back here, or under the front counter. We haven't had any trouble with anybody's stuff getting 'disappeared,' but I still wouldn't bring anything too valuable."

"I locked my backpack in my trunk." I knew the drill. I'd flipped burgers, scooped ice cream, shelved books, filed letters, made copies, operated the teacup ride at Elitch Gardens, and tried to sell life insurance over the phone. This was just one more, hopefully the last, less-than-interesting job I'd have before I entered my profession. At least, that's what I hoped as we went back behind the counter, which wasn't in much better order than the

stockroom. It was awful. How could anybody find anything? How could they keep track of anything?

There was one good thing, though. The disarray and
general funkiness made me feel like I didn't have to worry
about my hair. Everyone would simply think my head
wraps were a religious requirement or a hip-hop fashion
statement (though my boring khakis and t-shirts would
keep them guessing). My hair was getting so nappy that
I wasn't sure anybody would ever be able to get it
straight again. At least I washed, conditioned, and braided
it up once a week now. That was progress. I was feeling like pretty soon I might be able to stop balding
myself.

"Always count your money when you start your shift
and before you go home. Write it down and get somebody
else to initial it and leave it in the drawer. Put big bills—
anything over twenty—under the money box, but don't
forget to count them before you leave."

The music was loud and distracting. I felt like an old
lady for even thinking it, but still it was worth a try. "Think
we could turn it down a notch?"

He frowned like I had asked if we could have Big Foot
over for tea, then kept going. "We don't take checks. Except: A dozen cats—regulars—are gonna come in here and
write checks, and we'll take 'em."

"Who are they?"

"They'll tell you."

"So I just believe anybody who says 'I'm a regular'?"

He looked at me like *Duh, isn't that what I just said?* "You
smoke?"

I shook my head, and wondered just how old Oliver was. Maybe about twenty.

He leaned in. "Let's say you do. You can take smoke breaks. I don't smoke, but when it's nice outside, it's a good excuse to get some weather. Half hour for lunch. If you bring your lunch, keep it in your purse. Put it in the refrigerator and it's gone. Do *not* eat the Chinese down the street no matter how starvin' like Marvin you are, no matter how desperate. Do not, do not, do not. Stick with the Greek Pete's. I'm a vegetarian so I stick to stuff like grilled cheese and pancakes, but the gyros and hamburgers are supposed to be good."

The way he spoke about food made me lower my estimate of his age to sixteen or seventeen. We left the counter and walked through the store. The CD player shifted to the next CD, also rap, and I knew a headache couldn't be far behind. This guy rhymed about "working it hard" while a woman moaned and groaned in the background.

"Last thing: the music. Organization is mostly, how shall we say, eclectic. And we have a loose relationship with the alphabet, so for example, say you're looking for Nina Simone."

He knew *and remembered* the CD I had bought. I didn't know whether to be impressed or creeped out.

"Could be in *N* or *S* or, sad to say, under the name of the album, or, hell, under *H* for High Priestess of Soul. You just gotta be creative. Mostly, if you can't find it, get the customer's name and number, and if it shows up we'll call 'em. They'll be back anyway. We're pretty much down to regulars now. That's everything you need to know to run the register. When it's slow, you straighten up. Any questions?"

"No, this is only temporary. I'm only here a semester. I go back to grad school in January." I didn't know what made me volunteer all that information.

"Where?"

"University of Iowa."

"You from here?"

I realized I had opened the door to a conversation I didn't intend to have. "I grew up here. But I just want to keep this about work."

He tensed up. "Just trying to be friendly."

What was it with guys wanting to be my "friend" all of a sudden? Was I putting out some kind of desperate vibe? Was *No Boyfriend* written on my forehead? I didn't want him to think that the Oliver branch was going to lead to anything else. "Nothing personal, but I'm not really—"

He held up his hand. "No, heard you loud and clear. Trust me. I won't be getting in your business again. You, my sister, will be left alone."

Shake It Up

THE NEXT DAY WHEN I GOT TO WORK OLIVER AND Mattlocks were there sitting behind the counter. They stopped talking when I walked in. I dropped my backpack in the back room and introduced myself to my new coworker.

Mattlocks tilted his head at me and said, "Matt."

"Excuse me?"

"My . . . name . . . is . . . Matt. What . . . is . . . your . . . name?" he said very slowly, like he was talking to a mentally challenged person.

"Your name is Matt?" Mattlocks was named Matt! That was too good.

He rolled his eyes theatrically. "Yeah, okay, you're going to fit in just fine around here."

I went behind the counter. "What should I be doing?"

"Let's see. Well, Dudestress, you're new. You'll probably be looking at a lot of Internet porn in the back room, am I right?" He held up his hand to high-five me.

Oliver snickered and shook his head.

When I didn't slap Matt's palm, he said, "It's okay. They *don't* mind."

Oliver grabbed paper towels and a bottle of glass cleaner and handed them to me. "You can clean," he said. "Both of you."

"Can't never let a brother have any fun, can you?" Matt griped playfully. He got the vacuum cleaner from the back room and started on the floors while I polished the glass display cases.

Oliver was true to his word and left me alone. Business was slow to nonexistent until after school when the kids from East High strolled through. It would have been really easy to do nothing but surf the Net and listen to music most of the day, but Oliver worked hard. He was busy the whole shift, stocking and rearranging products, and breaking down boxes and taking them to the Dumpster. I had misjudged him that first day I came into the store.

Shake It Up was a small independent record store trying to make it when most kids downloaded music from the Internet and adults bought CDs at Best Buy, Borders, Target, Wal-Mart, and Starbucks. I could see they had to hustle for their income, and I was impressed that Oliver didn't slack.

Right before it was time for me to leave, a middle-aged white guy came up to the counter with a stack of vinyl big band albums. I rang them up and told him the price. Just like Oliver had told me, the guy pulled out his checkbook and told me it was okay to take his check, so I did.

——

LEAVING ME ALONE lasted two whole days. I was helping Oliver take inventory to order new CDs. We were in the country section. We hadn't been working more than ten minutes when he cracked. "What's your theme song?"

I looked at him, puzzled.

"I'm a communications major and a Gemini," he said. "I have to talk. I can't help it. Not that I really believe in astrology. My moms is into it. It's one of those things that gets in your head whether you want it to or not. So . . . ?"

"I'm not sure I have a theme song."

"Yeah you do. Everybody does. What's the one song you have to listen to to get yourself going?"

I could give him this one. " 'House of the Rising Sun.' Nina Simone's version."

"Why?"

"The feelings. The intensity. The energy."

"Who do you listen to besides Nina Simone?"

"Billie Holiday, Ella Fitzgerald, Sarah Vaughan."

"Um. Okay, that's all good. All cool. But, you listen to any music cut in this century?"

"Like what?"

"Like anything. I know you like female vocalists. What about Cassandra Wilson and Rachelle Ferrell?"

"I haven't heard them."

"What about Diana Krall? Jane Monheit? Norah Jones?" I shrugged.

"Wow. Okay, but you've heard of Mary J. Blige and Erykah Badu?"

"I'm not really familiar with their music."

He peered at me over the top of his glasses. "Not really familiar with their music?"

"I've heard of them. I just . . . I work and go to school. I don't have time to worry about what other people are listening to. I like what I like."

Oliver rolled his eyes. "What about Lauryn Hill, Jill Scott, Angie Stone, Floetry, India.Arie?"

Matt called out from across the room, "Dude, how could you leave out Dianne Reeves? She lives like ten minutes from here." He was checking stock from local bands. The store sold almost anything on consignment, and Matt was intensely loyal to local artists. It didn't matter what kind of music: hip-hop, emo, metal, salsa, jazz, punk, bluegrass, rap, blues, or country. As long as they were from Colorado, he played them and did his best to sell them.

"Yeah. Dianne Reeves?"

I shook my head.

"Me'shell Ndegéocello?" Matt asked.

Obviously, I should have known who these women were, what their music was like, but some of them I hadn't even heard of. I had been making $13,000 a year writing grants part-time while I went to school full-time. I couldn't afford cable, didn't belong to a gym, didn't go to bars, and didn't have time to read magazines. Where would I have heard about anything new?

"Where have you been hiding for the last decade?" Oliver asked. "Come on, every university has a student radio station where you can hear this stuff."

"Where'd you go to school?" Matt asked.

"Iowa," Oliver answered for me.

"Faith Hill!" Matt shouted like he was a contestant on a game show.

Oliver laughed. "Maybe we need to go back closer to Nina Simone's time," he mused. "Start with the sixties and move forward. Let's see . . . you have to like Aretha Franklin, right?"

"Yes," I said. Whew! I did know and love Aretha.

"Okay! We have liftoff. Who else?"

I sighed. "I told you already."

"How 'bout Roberta Flack?"

"Gladys Knight? Mavis Staples? Ann Peebles? Dionne Warwick?" Matt added.

It didn't even matter that I wasn't answering. They were playing a private game of Name that Girl Singer.

"Good ones. Chaka Khan? Minnie Ripperton? Phoebe Snow?" Oliver threw out.

"Um . . . Whitney Houston?" Matt said, which Oliver thought was hysterical. Now they were having fun with me.

"Okay, okay, very funny. Are you done tormenting me now?"

Matt shook his head. "How can you work in a record store and not know any recent music? Dude, that's like a vegetarian working in a McDonald's!"

"You might be missing the next Nina Simone," Oliver said.

I smiled, on firm and familiar territory. "Which of those singers you just named sings jazz, blues, pop, classical, show tunes, gospel, *and* protest songs? Which of them writes her own music, does covers, *and* is a civil rights activist?"

They just looked at each other.

Uh-huh, so I thought. "I'm sure all these women are very talented. But there was only one Nina Simone."

Ivy's First Time

"CAN YOU PLEASE, FOR THE LOVE OF ALL THAT IS GOOD and holy on God's green earth, shut up?" I pleaded.

Matt had been telling stupid, vaguely sexist, racist "jokes" all day, and I thought my head was going to explode if I heard another story about Chinese dry cleaners, priests and altar boys, Michael Jackson, tiny pianists, or the number sixty-nine.

"You don't laugh much, do you?" he asked.

"When there's something funny, I'll laugh."

"No, I don't think so. I don't think you have a sense of humor."

On top of everything else, I was about to start my period. I was in a foul mood. I sighed heavily.

"Come on, Dudette, I'm just playing with you."

"No you're not! You're getting on my case. First, my taste in music didn't meet your approval. Now it's my sense of humor. Who died and made you the culture police? You should arrest yourself for those things on your head."

He touched his matted dreads. "What things?"

"It's almost time for me to go. There're no customers. Can we just listen to the music?"

Oliver and Matt had taken to dramatically announcing each CD they played. They were "educating" me about music. Right now, Dianne Reeves was singing "Loads of Love," and I was enjoying it.

"There're *never* any customers. We're dinosaurs," Matt said. "Working in a record store. A *record* store. Do you know how many people there are in this world who've never even seen a record? Let alone owned one. Pretty soon it's going to be the same for CDs. I'll chop off my left ball if this store is open this time next year."

"If we're in such sad shape, how come they hired me?"

" 'Cause the owners are ostriches." He stopped to consider his own words. "Extinct dinosaur ostriches. They're just going to keep doing what they do until they retire, which *will* be before this time next year."

It turned out that Pussycat Lounge guy was one of the owners, and I'd only seen him again once. He came in once a week or so to sign checks or drop off vinyl he found at some estate sale or garage sale. Not exactly the action of someone who planned to stay in business for a long time. Maybe Matt was right.

"They could be having local bands in to play and sell their music. They could be selling vinyl on eBay. Well, they could be doing a lot of stuff. My point was going to be that a sense of humor will come in handy around here. But now I've just depressed myself." He slumped against the counter. "You're right. Why bother?"

It was fifteen minutes before the end of my shift. "In that case, I think I'll go ahead and go home."

"Might as well," Matt said. "Might as well."

WHEN I GOT HOME, Ivy's car was parked behind Nona's. A bad day made worse. If Ivy had acted like Nona's personal protector before, she was going to be an outright pit bull now.

Since Nona and I had our little chat, which I'd come to think of as the Jack Nicholson incident ("You want the truth? You can't handle the truth!"), I had ticked the lock, zipped my lips, and given myself every other lockdown I could think of. She didn't have much to say to me either. When we did speak to each other, we were exceedingly polite. It was our way of fighting without fighting.

I sequestered myself more than usual, and she and Sunny stayed out in the yard as late as the fall light would allow. She was still harvesting zucchini, tomatoes, jalapeños, and bell peppers, cutting flowers for bouquets, and even planting things. She had replaced one addiction with another. Almost every day new potted plants with bright sale tags appeared on the patio to acclimate to the yard for a few days before they went into the ground.

"My first time scared the hell out of me," Nona was saying as I walked into the kitchen. She and Ivy were sitting at the table holding hands. I stopped dead in my tracks, as if someone had yelled "Freeze!" Could they be talking about what I thought they were talking about? Why would Nona be talking about losing her virginity? It wasn't possible that Ivy hadn't had sex yet, was it?

I started to back out of the room and tripped over nothing but my own clumsy feet, falling noisily on my ass. They turned in unison to look at me.

"I . . . I . . . didn't mean to hear . . . You . . ." I sputtered, getting up. "You keep . . . I'll go."

"What in the world is wrong with you?" Nona asked, dropping the distant tone she had been using with me since our fight.

"Obviously, this is a very personal conversation. . . ."

She stared at me, trying to figure out what I was talking about. Then her wide eyes grew even wider behind her little glasses, and she started laughing. "Girl, I was talking about my first time *speaking at a meeting*. Ivy shared her story for the first time. She got her ninety-day chip tonight."

"You thought . . . ?!" Ivy whooped and bent forward, her long auburn hair falling into her eyes. She sat up and brushed the hair out of her face, still laughing. She had filled out a little. The sleeve of her t-shirt rode up revealing a strange new tattoo, four purple spots around the vine on her arm, as if it were blooming.

I felt the blood rush to my face. "I didn't know."

Nona went to the refrigerator and pulled out a bottle of sparkling apple cider.

"I'm twenty-three! Like, it is waaay too late to be havin' that conversation!"

"I didn't know."

Ivy grinned wickedly. "I guess you could say my A.A. cherry just got popped."

"Ivy!" Nona opened the cabinet to get glasses for the cider.

"My bad," Ivy said, but she was still chuckling. She got a rubber band out of her pocket and pulled her hair into a ponytail. Her shirtsleeve moved again. The circles on her arm weren't tattoos, weren't flowers. They were bruises, four fingerprints.

"It's a powerful accomplishment," Nona said. "Say it out loud: I'm Ivy and I'm proud."

"That's so corny!" Ivy said, but she was beaming. She stuck out her hand. "Wanna see?"

She handed me a bronze coin slightly bigger than a quarter. It had a triangle in the center with the words *To Thine Own Self Be True* around it. That's the alcoholic's motto all right. I wondered how in all these years nobody in A.A. had realized that being true to their own selfish selves was exactly their problem. I handed the chip back to her.

"Shay, would you care for some apple cider? We're having a toast." Nona was getting glasses out of the cupboard, her back to me and her I'm-taking-the-high-road tone restored.

"No thank you," I said equally cool. I went to the stove to dish up a plate.

"Snap! Almost forgot." Ivy ran out to her car and returned with a gift bag from Crabtree & Evelyn.

Nona looked at her sternly.

"I know, but I saw it and thought of you."

Nona reached inside and pulled out something wrapped

in tissue paper. It was a bar of gardener's soap. She smelled it. "Mmmm. That's wonderful." She reached in again and retrieved a bottle of lavender hand lotion and a tube of cuticle cream. "Thank you, Ivy. But this stuff is expensive. You shouldn't be spending your money on me."

"Like, I can afford it."

Nona cocked her head to the side. "How?"

"I'm just dancin', not trickin'," Ivy said quickly.

Tricking as in *prostitution*?! She was right. It was way too late for me to be thinking she was talking about losing her virginity! How naïve and stupid she must have thought me.

Nona threw her head back and groaned. "Ivy . . ."

"I don't want to talk about this in front of her," Ivy said, nodding her head at me.

She was the one who showed me her stupid chip and started telling all her business. I took my food and went into my room and closed the door, but I could still hear them.

"Ivy, you know being in a bar every night puts you at risk."

"They wanna buy me a drink, I say no. If they push it, I get the bartender to give me a Coke with nothing in it. They do it for lots of the girls."

"Is this because of Justin?"

Was Justin the one who left the fingerprints on her arm?

"It's because I can make a hell of a lot more than six dollars an hour! Like, I'm saving my money so we can get a better place and get my kids back from my mom."

Kids! She has kids? I hoped passionately they got to stay with her mother forever.

"I understand. I know you want your kids, but this is a mistake. This is your old pattern. If you want your life to change, *you* have to change. Everything has to change."

"Everything *is* changing! I'm clean! I'm straight! You heard me tonight. And Justin is so different now. He's ready to take care of his family. You'll see."

"I hope so."

"You said I made a powerful accomplishment." Ivy pouted.

"You have. It is," Nona said.

"Well, then, can we please go back to celebrating?"

They went into the living room, and I couldn't hear the rest of the conversation.

I was putting my dirty dishes in the sink when Ivy returned with their empty glasses.

One of the glasses slipped out of her hands and shattered. "Shit!" She turned toward me and spoke like we were in the middle of an argument. "Why don't you just leave? You ain't doin' nothin' but, like, trying to drive everybody crazy," she said in a low hiss so Nona wouldn't hear. "Just go on back to school and leave us alone."

Us? "What I do is none of your business," I whispered just as forcefully.

"It is if it has to do with Nona. I don't like the way you treat her."

Obviously, Ivy didn't believe in fighting without fighting. "Like I said, it's none of your business."

We stared at each other, neither of us backing down.

"Watch yourself," she said, bending to pick up the broken glass.

"You watch *your*self!" It was a lame comeback, but I was proud of myself for saying something back. At least she didn't have the last word, and now she knew she couldn't push me around.

She swept up the glass and went back into the living room, eyeing me over her shoulder as she left.

I wasn't scared. It wasn't like she was really going to do anything to me. She was just talking trash, like a girl who had watched one too many action movies starring rappers. What could she do? Slash my tires? Wait for me after work one night and jump me on the way to my car? Suddenly I remembered that Ivy was on parole, and it dawned on me that jumping me might be *exactly* what she could do.

While I waited for Ivy to leave, I did a load of laundry. To keep from waking Sunny, I sneaked in Nona's room and got her and Sunny's dirty clothes. Going through the pockets of a pair of Nona's jeans I found a handful of yellow dandelion heads. I wondered if they were from the seeds I scattered.

After Ivy left, Nona was surprised to find me in the prairie room instead of in my room. But I had something I needed to know. She put her purse on the table and went to the counter and picked up a small stack of bills and stamps.

"Why is Ivy on parole?"

"I can't tell you that." She sat at the table across from me. "Why do you ask?"

"It's not really a good idea having a criminal hanging around, is it? I mean, what about Sunny?"

"She's not a criminal."

"*Hel-lo!* She's a prostitute!"

"Was," Nona said calmly. "And you shouldn't have been eavesdropping."

"Did she do anything violent?"

"Of course not!"

"How long is she on parole?"

She narrowed her eyes. "Why are you suddenly so interested in Ivy's background?"

"I told you already."

"You've seen Ivy with Sunny. She loves that girl, and she loves me. She'd never do anything to hurt either one of us."

Nona and Sunny might be safe, but I still had to worry about a girl who not too long ago made her living on the streets, learning very different lessons than I had in the classrooms of tiny, sheltered Iowa City.

A Very Pregnant Pause

BY THE TIME OCTOBER HAD ROLLED AROUND, THE WHOLE town including the trees and the sky above had turned orange and blue in honor of the Broncos. That's how most of the rest of the city saw it, anyway. Denver is Jockville, and the Broncos are their gods. During football season when I was a kid, male teachers used to wear orange-and-blue-striped ties and the women would wear horse earrings, orange scarves, or a Broncos pin on their lapels. By the time I got to high school and the Broncos were actually winning Super Bowls, even Nona was wearing a Broncos sweatshirt on Sundays. Of course, she'd be passed out for most of the game, but she'd have on her colors.

When Stephanie invited me over to her dad's house to watch the game on Sunday afternoon, I was so grateful for the Broncos I dressed in the tangerine top Nona bought me, a pair of blue jeans, and tied a blue scarf over my hair.

Sunny was waiting for me when I stepped out of the bathroom. "Whatcha doin'? Little pooin'?"

"Getting ready to go somewhere."

"Where you going?"

"A friend's house."

She followed me through the house back to my room. I was starting to think of her as my little shadow.

"Can I go with you?"

Nona looked up from the lasagnas she was preparing; she was making one for us to have this week and one to go in the freezer for later. For once, Ivy wasn't there on a Sunday.

"No."

Sunny stood in the doorway while I put on my shoes. "Who's your friend?"

"Nobody you know."

"Pleeeeze can I go with you?"

I picked up my keys and backpack. "I said—"

"Sunny, come here, Sweet Potato." Nona wiped her hands on her apron.

Sunny sulked over to her. "I need you to be here with me so I don't get lonely. Say 'See you later.'"

"See you later, crocodile," Sunny mumbled.

"It's 'alligator,'" I mumbled back, feeling almost guilty.

Nona picked Sunny up and gave her loud smooches on her cheeks and forehead, and blew raspberries on her neck while Sunny shrieked and giggled.

MR. BERRY GREETED ME at his front door. "If it ain't my bonus daughter." He was a tall, dark-skinned man with wavy white hair. He looked like a man out of an old jazz movie, one of the cool cats Nina or Billie would have hung out with. He didn't become a father until he was in his forties, but even though he was old enough to be Stephanie's grandfather, he was always energetic and still seemed to be so today. He was wearing pressed jeans, a Broncos sweatshirt, and a red apron that said *BBQ King* in black letters. The Q had a little gold crown on it.

"How come it took you this long to come and see me?" He mock-frowned at me.

I tried to think of a clever answer, but I hadn't heard "bonus daughter" in so long I got teary. "I didn't think you would remember me."

"I may have Alzheimer's Junior, but how could I forget you?" He pulled me into a hug.

I remembered his smell. Soapy, but not like that earth-mama, herbs-and-flowers body wash Nona bought. He smelled like Irish Spring and barbeque smoke. I could have stayed sniffling in his arms the rest of the day.

He let me go and crooked his fingers under my chin to lift my face. "Come on now. You hungry, sweetheart?"

I nodded, smiling, and wiped my eyes.

"Follow me."

The Berry house was a large split-level ranch in Aurora, a suburb east of Denver where a lot of middle-class black people moved in the seventies and eighties. Like all the suburbs around Denver, the houses were varying shades of beige and gray on streets that dead-ended into one another to discourage drive-through traffic. Nona used to say the layouts were "to keep the rats in their mazes." But where

Nona saw monotony, I saw stability and security. I saw homes where fathers mowed lawns and mothers helped children with their homework and, above all, stayed home at night with their kids.

We walked down a short hall past the living room, which was filled with the same powder-blue carpet and blue and white furniture that Stephanie's mom had bought twenty years ago. We entered the large kitchen, which overlooked the family room that was a half flight down.

"Cleo, look who finally came to see us," Mr. Berry called into the family room.

Cleo trotted up the stairs. "Shay! Shay! Shay!" she squealed and leapt up the final step, landing right in front of me. Stephanie's little sister was still round, not fat really, but strong-looking and thick. "Healthy," older black folks would say. Her hair was in baby dreads and she wore low-slung jeans, a pistachio-colored sweater, and in her only nod to the occasion, bright orange socks. She looked like she should be chasing fall leaves in a Gap ad.

"You know I'm mad at you, right?" she chided, but she was grinning, showing the same charming space between her two top front teeth that Stephanie had.

"I know, I know."

"All right, then. Give me some." She opened her arms. We hugged each other, and I wanted to smack myself for taking so long to get in touch with them all. I had wasted all that time wondering if they would even remember me, and they had missed me as much as I missed them.

Mr. Berry had been busy bringing in pans of meat and

vegetables from the grill. "Come on, y'all. Game's about to start."

Stephanie and Greg came upstairs. Even in gym clothes they looked stylish and pulled together. This time Stephanie had long extensions braided into her hair. She looked totally different every time I saw her, like she was still searching for the right look to go with her new body.

Greg nodded *What's up*.

Stephanie said, "I'd hug ya, but I'm funky. We came straight from working out."

"Health girl." Cleo rolled her eyes.

Stephanie ran her hands over her stomach and hips. "I'm going to look fat enough in my dress as it is."

"Wow, five whole minutes without mentioning the wedding. A record," Cleo said.

I wondered if Stephanie had an eating disorder, because there was no way she was going to look fat in her wedding dress.

Then Mr. Berry put a stack of paper plates on the table and told us to get in line, and I understood why Stephanie had gone to the gym first. The spread was ribs, chicken, hot links, grilled corn and red peppers, baked beans, sliced onions and tomatoes, greens, potato salad, and rolls.

Greg rubbed his hands together and nodded, his eyes glistening at the thought of the damage he was about to do. He went over to Mr. Berry and bear-hugged him. "I am *so* happy to be marrying your daughter, I can't even tell you."

"Hurry up and bless the food, boy," Mr. Berry said.

Stephanie, Cleo, Greg, Mr. Berry, and I stood holding hands around the table.

"Bless us, O Lord, and these your gifts which we are about to receive from your bounty through Christ our Lord. Amen." Greg made the sign of the cross when he was done and everyone else said amen.

We helped ourselves to the food and went into the family room. Greg and Mr. Berry sat on the sectional sofa in front of the TV and bent over their plates on the coffee table; and Stephanie, Cleo, and I sat at the card table.

I told them about my job at the record store, and about Ivy being on parole for what I assumed was prostitution. They were even more scandalized than I. They had grown up in one house with a devoted father, loving aunts, plenty of food, pretty clothes, and good schools. Other than their mother's death, their lives had been so nice and normal they couldn't fathom anything else.

After I finished telling them about Ivy, Cleo had some gossip. "Must be something in the water. Guess who's pregnant?"

"Not you!" I said immediately and Stephanie's eyes widened.

"Daphne," Cleo said.

"Shay doesn't even know her. We should be talking about something else," Stephanie said.

"I don't know Ivy, and we just talked about *her* like a dog. Besides, if you don't know the person, it's not gossip. She and Gerald are talking about getting married, but I'll believe it when I see it. Gerald ain't Greg."

"She was trying to trap him?" I asked.

"She *says* it was an accident."

I laughed, delighted to join in the girl talk. "Accident, my butt. I don't buy it. The only way a woman gets pregnant today is if she wants to be pregnant."

Stephanie put down her fork. "Accidents happen."

"How?" I scoffed. "Shots, patches, pills. It ain't rocket science. And genius Nona somehow did it twice."

Stephanie threw her napkin on the table and ran out of the room.

"What's wrong with her?" I asked Cleo.

"I think she thought you were coming down on her."

"But . . . why . . . ?" Oh no! I put my fork down. "*That* was why the talk about being fat in her dress . . ."

"She didn't tell you?"

I shook my head. I wouldn't want to start out a new marriage with a baby on the way, not that I was in any danger of getting married or pregnant. Stephanie must feel miserable. She and Greg weren't going to have a chance to be a couple before they had to worry about a kid. Sunny was fairly low-maintenance, and she was still a lot of work. Changing poopy diapers isn't the most romantic way to begin a marriage. And here I was going on about how there's no such thing as an accident. "I feel terrible."

Cleo cleaned the last bit of pork off a rib and set it daintily atop the small mountain of bones on her plate. "I wouldn't worry about it. Between being pregnant and planning the wedding, she cries at the drop of a hat anyway."

I went upstairs and found Stephanie sitting on the white canopy bed in her old room, mournfully clutching a pack of cigarettes. Her bedroom still had the lilac shag carpet and old-fashioned, white nubby bedspread she had in high school. Posters of Boyz II Men, Brandy, TLC, Denzel Washington, and the Jamaican beach plastered the walls. The mirror on the matching vanity was almost invisible under pictures, postcards, and concert ticket stubs. I wished that I had a room filled with my old things, but I never wanted time to stop when I was growing up. I had desperately needed it to go forward.

I sat next to her.

"I want one so bad," she said, looking at her cigarettes.

I knew what she meant. That's how I felt about pulling my hair. I handed her the silver hoops she had loaned me when I went out with Desi. "I'm sorry."

"I'm pregnant."

"Cleo told me. I know it's not the best way to start your marriage. Are you going to be okay?"

She looked perplexed. "What do you mean? This is the very best way to start. Other than how fat I'm gonna get. It totally screwed up my dress. I had to exchange it for another one with a wrap that I can wear to try to hide the bulge."

I didn't believe her, but I wasn't going to push it. If that was how she wanted to play it, I'd go along. "You're not even showing."

Still holding the cigarettes, she lifted her sweatshirt, and sure enough there was the tiniest little pooch. "I'm ten weeks along. I was hoping to be able to wait until after the wedding to tell people, but I'll *definitely* be showing when I walk down the aisle. Aunt Baby Mae says the women in my family get big early."

I was still trying to wrap my mind around this idea. "But you were drinking margaritas. . . ."

"I didn't know yet. The doctor said it should be okay. I only had a couple."

I struggled to think of the questions one was supposed to ask an expectant mother. "Do you know what it is?"

She shook her head. "Typical man, Greg wants a boy. I want a girl. We're going to wait till the delivery to see who wins." She sighed. "I miss my mom. She was supposed to help me plan everything. She's supposed be here to see my big ass in my dress on my wedding day. She wasn't there when I graduated from high school or college. She's not going to be there when I have this baby. It's like there's a huge empty spot where she's supposed to be, and there always will be."

I knew all about that empty spot. I had one of my own, for different reasons.

She stood up and shook her arms and legs, as if she could shake off emotions like lactic acid pooled in sore muscles. "We need to get off this. Let's watch a movie." She put the cigarettes in a drawer, and went out into the hallway to yell down to Cleo.

A few minutes later Cleo trotted into the room.

Stephanie held up the choices: *Father of the Bride, The Best Man, My Best Friend's Wedding, The Princess Bride, American Wedding,* and *The Wedding Planner.*

Cleo groaned.

"I'm sensing a theme," I said.

Stephanie smiled. "It's less than seven weeks away."

"It's going to be seven long-ass weeks if we have to keep watching wedding movies," Cleo grumbled.

Cleo and I both voted for *The Princess Bride*. Cleo probably did because it's not really so much about getting married, and I did because there are no mothers in it at all.

The Great Divide

"I NEED YOU." NONA WAS SHAKING ME AWAKE.

I had been dreaming of driving through mountains filled with golden aspen trees, forests, waterfalls, and lakes. "Wha—" I cracked one eye open and muttered groggily. The aspen leaves shimmering in the sun in my dream turned out to be caused by the yellow-curtained sunshine hitting my eyelids. I took my earphones off.

"I need a favor. You have to watch your sister today. She's sick, and I can't stay home." Nona was already dressed for work.

Today was my day off. I was planning to do nothing, even though nothing was starting to get a little old, but I wasn't going to admit that to Nona. The only way I could get out of babysitting would be if I was going somewhere.

"I'm going to the mountains," I said, dancing aspen leaves still fresh in my mind's eye.

Sunny coughed in the next room.

"You've barely left the house in weeks, but now you just have to go to the mountains?"

"You're always on my case to get out of the house and now today I have to stay in?"

"I'm sorry," she said. "I didn't know you had plans." She looked at her watch. "Please do this for me. I might be able to leave early this afternoon and you can go out then," she said, turning and heading out the door before I could answer.

She called from the kitchen, "Her temperature is just a little high, if it goes down and she feels better, you can take her to school later if you want. My work number and the Children's Tylenol are on the table. Try to keep fluids in her. Let her drink whatever she wants. See if you can get her to eat some soup."

She was acting like I had agreed to stay home. Apparently, a response from me wasn't needed. But spending my day off with a moany-groany preschooler wasn't what I had in mind. I got up and went into the kitchen. Sunny was sitting at the table in her pajamas. She looked a little tired, but not too worse for wear. Nona was packing her lunch for work.

"They don't have a way to take care of sick kids at the preschool? What if a kid got sick while she was there, they wouldn't always be able to send her home, right? What would you do if I weren't here?" But along with Sunny's cough, I could hear the unmistakable swish of the rug being yanked out from beneath me. The next sound I would hear would be me landing right on my butt.

Nona stopped what she was doing and stared at me. "I

don't know what I would do if you weren't here. The point is you *are* here. I'm out of sick time, so I can't stay home unless I take it unpaid, and you know I can't afford that. I'm asking you for one favor."

Before I could answer, she said, "We did a nebulizer a few minutes ago. I'll try to be home early, but call me at work if she seems even a little worse."

She walked over and kissed Sunny on the forehead. " 'Bye, Sweet Potato. I'll see you later. I'll bring you a present."

Sunny nodded.

"I'll call and check in," Nona said to me, and bent down and kissed and hugged Sunny one more time. "Be good," she said to her, and my mind raced through all the times she had said the same thing to me when she skipped out on me in the middle of the night.

After Nona left, Sunny took a bowl of dry Cheerios and went into the living room to watch cartoons. I sat in the kitchen, fuming. When I was eight I had the kind of evil virus only kids get that's half stomach flu and half plague. Everything hurt: my stomach, my skull, my teeth. And my fever was off the charts. Nona must have been worried, because she had stayed home sleeping next to me two nights in a row. I started to think being sick was a good thing and wished I had some kind of illness that would make her stay home all the time. We had a girl in our class who had sickle cell anemia, and I started plotting to sit next to her and to hold her hand so I would catch it.

In the middle of the third night I sat up in bed and I could tell I was going to be sick. I looked next to me and

Nona wasn't there. I knew better, but I told myself she was in the living room or in the bathroom getting a cold cloth for my forehead. I tried to call for her, but I couldn't open my mouth. My lips were so dry, they had sealed shut. I could feel the bile rising and was scared to death that I would vomit into my mouth with no chance for release. I forced my lips apart and threw up green liquid all over myself. My lips were bleeding and smelly green liquid was everywhere. I started crying for Nona, but she didn't come. She had left, and with her went one more idea about how to keep her home at night. I was so sick, but I quickly realized my choices were to sleep in vomit or to get up and clean myself off. I washed up, changed my pajamas and sheets, and went back to bed.

I woke out of my reverie, if that word also applies to bad memories, and found myself twirling a strand of plucked hair. Damn. I really didn't want to let Nona drive me to pull my hair anymore. I tried to distract myself by eating a bowl of cereal. Then I took a long shower in tepid water. Because of the dry air, my skin couldn't take hot water anymore. It was dry and ashy, even with lots of lotion, and what was left of my hair felt like straw. When I got out of the shower, I slathered myself with Vaseline, patted dry, wrapped a towel around myself, and opened the door to let the steam out. Sunny was there waiting, as was getting to be her habit.

"What are you doing?" she asked thickly, her nose still stopped up.

"Nothing." . . . *thanks to you,* I restrained myself from adding as I dressed.

"Want to dance with me?" she asked.

"Not right now." I took my pajamas back to my room. She followed me in, and watched while I made the bed.

When I was done, she repeated herself. "Now do you want to dance with me?"

She wasn't coughing anymore. I looked at her closely. Her nose was disgusting, so I got a tissue and wiped the crust and snot off. I felt her forehead. Barely warm. "You really feel like dancing, huh?"

"I want to be a ballerina."

"Let me take your temperature."

We went back into the prairie room. She sat at the kitchen table while I stuck the thermometer in her mouth. 99.9. Practically normal. She sneezed, and a river of snot came out. I grabbed a paper towel and cleaned her face.

"Let's dance," she pleaded.

I thought for a minute: It wasn't like I'd be making her exert herself. We wouldn't be hiking, or even walking. We didn't even have to get out of the car. She'd probably sleep for most of the trip anyway. "Want to go for a ride with me?"

"Okay!" She forgot about dancing immediately.

"Go get dressed."

She took off into Nona's room, and came out five minutes later in purple jeans, a red sweater, and yellow socks. I must have been getting used to her style because it didn't look that bad to me. I helped her tie her sneakers. We went into the bathroom and I washed the sleep out of her eyes and wiped up her snotty nose again. I picked up the brush and sat down on the toilet. "Let me fix your hair."

She stood in front of me while I unbraided her messy

braids and brushed her hair. It was unbelievably soft, and smelled like almonds and bubble gum. I swept it up into a ponytail, and we were good to go.

Or so I thought. When we got to my car, she said, "Where's my car seat?"

Damn, fuck, shit, hell. "I don't have one. You can ride in the back with the seat belt like a big girl." We wouldn't be gone very long.

She eyed me suspiciously.

In the fall Denver could be sixty degrees one day, and in the thirties the next. Unfortunately, today was one of the thirty-degree days. Even though the sun was bright, as it almost always was, it was too chilly to be standing out here arguing with a three-year-old. I unlocked the door and pushed the seat up so she could get in the back. "Come on. Get in. It's cold."

"I'm supposed to have a car seat." The child was a rock.

"Just get in the car. Now. Hurry!"

She didn't budge. I was just about to pick her up and stick her in the seat when I remembered: I squatted down and held my fist in front of her face. "You want a knuckle sandwich?"

The tiniest smile broke through and she nipped my hand.

"Okay, now get in the car."

She climbed in the back and I strapped the seat belt across her.

Going down 28th, "the brown cloud" blocked the view of the mountains. That's what Denverites call the dust and pollution that gets trapped over the city in fall and winter. I

got on I-70 and headed west. It was after the morning rush
hour so traffic wasn't too bad. I zipped along feeling better
the farther west I got. Just as I guessed, Sunny was asleep by
the time we got to the foothills. As the elevation started to
increase, my car slowed down and I had to get in the far
right lane. I didn't have the horsepower to go much faster
than fifty-five. Outbacks, 4Runners, Escalades, Explorers,
Avalanches, and Wranglers with ski racks on top (though it
was still too early to ski) whizzed by me, but I wasn't in any
hurry. There was no place I was trying to get to. That's the
good thing about a drive: It's the process of going, not the
arriving, that matters. I turned on Nina Simone and kept it
down low, so Sunny would stay asleep.

Soon as I passed Evergreen, just above Denver, the
brown cloud lifted, and it didn't seem like we were in danger of running into snow. I don't ski, so I'd never been in
the mountains in the winter. Another Colorado myth to
bust: Black folks *do* ski. I just didn't happen to be one of
them. A lot of people who grow up poor in Denver hardly
ever go to the mountains, so they become easy to take for
granted as merely jagged backdrops to the city. I'd only
been to the mountains during the summer with Stephanie's
family. Mr. Berry took us to Breckenridge a few times. I decided to go there. It would take less than a couple of hours
and I could stay on I-70. I'd get to go through the Eisen-
hower Tunnel, across the Continental Divide. It makes me
marvel at native people who had to go over these mountains
on foot and horseback without any brightly lit tunnels or
paved highways. I imagined the prospectors who came out
here looking for gold and silver, and the so-called settlers

who wanted to go farther west. What must it have been like the first time they looked at these mountains and realized they were going to have to climb over them to reach their dreams?

From the highway, I didn't see golden aspens. I saw pines and brown hills. But up and up I went. Not too far up I-70 I cleared a hill and the mountains opened up in front of me as if a curtain had been lifted. Nina Simone was singing "Here Comes the Sun" and I was glad I had come up with this bogus trip to the mountains.

When I hit Georgetown, about an hour into the drive, Sunny started coughing so hard she woke herself up.

I had almost forgotten she was in the backseat.

"I want my mama."

I looked at her in the rearview mirror. Her nose was nasty again. "We're going for a ride, remember? We'll see her later. Want to get a hamburger?"

The bribe worked. I handed her a Kleenex and kept going. There was snow on the tops of the highest peaks, and even though the aspens were mostly leafless, it was still beautiful. But Sunny kept coughing. When we were only twenty miles from Breckenridge, I got concerned. I stopped on the shoulder and felt her forehead. It was burning up, and I knew I wouldn't cross the Divide today. I got back on the highway and took the first exit that would allow me to turn around and go back east. At Georgetown, I decided to stop and buy some Children's Tylenol rather than trying to make it all the way home. I pulled over at a gas station.

"We have to go in and get you something to drink."

She shook her head.

"I can't leave you in the car. I have to go in to get you something so you'll feel better."

She started to cry. It wasn't the manipulative kind of crying either. We went in and I bought cherry cough drops, orange juice, and regular Tylenol because they didn't have the children's version. I broke one of the white pills in small pieces and tried to get Sunny to take one. But she wasn't having it. So I smashed it up with my car key and put the powder in her bottle of juice. "Drink this."

She took a sip.

"Keep drinking."

After she had a quarter of the bottle in her, I gave her a cough drop and got back on the road.

By the time Denver was in our sights, she was barking like an emphysemic trucker. Fear prickled up from the base of my spine. What if this was an asthma attack? We were God knows how many miles from a hospital. People die of asthma attacks. I didn't have a cell phone (one of the bills I hadn't paid in Iowa) and I didn't have Nona's work number with me. I didn't even know what kind of medication Sunny was on. I looked at her in the rearview mirror. "Sunny, can you breathe?"

She just looked at me.

"Say something, okay? Can you say your numbers?"

"One . . . two . . ." She took a deep, labored breath between each one, but she was able to keep going all the way to ten. I hoped that was a good sign.

"We're almost home. We'll get your medicine then, okay?"

She nodded.

I drove as fast as I could, glancing at her in the rearview mirror every thirty seconds, asking her questions so I could see if she had enough air to speak, all the while scared shit-less that I was going to get stuck in traffic. By the time I got home, even though I knew I was going to catch hell, I was relieved to see Nona's car in front of the house.

Soon as I walked in, she leapt at me. "I called and called. What happened? Where did you go? You didn't even leave a note. You scared me half to death!"

She ran over and scooped Sunny up.

"The mountains."

"You took a sick kid with asthma into a higher altitude in the cold?" She felt Sunny's forehead. "She's burning up!"

"I didn't know the altitude could make her have an asthma attack. She wasn't feverish when we left. You told me I could take her back to school if her fever went down, so why not just a little ride," I mumbled.

"Just a little ride? She's wheezing! And if I can't get it under control, we're going to have to go to the emergency room." She turned to Sunny and said in a calmer tone, "Come on, Sweet Potato, let's get you a neb going."

Sunny hated nebulizers, but she didn't even protest.

Nona turned to me. "Be mad at me all you want, but don't you dare drag Sunny into it."

My mouth fell open, but Nona had rushed off to the bathroom so Sunny could inhale her medicine before I could say anything. She thought I had made Sunny have an asthma attack on purpose?! She thought I was so crazy I'd take out my feelings about her on her precious darling? I had really freaked out, which was why I rushed back home.

It's not like I kept going west when I knew the child was getting worse. Nona had told me I could take her to school and *leave* her there if she was feeling better. I didn't abandon her or ignore her, I took care of her and brought her straight home.

The nebulizer calmed Sunny's wheezing and the Tylenol brought her fever back down. Nona fixed her some soup for dinner, and left me to fend for myself.

A couple of hours later, Sunny wasn't in dancing mode, but she wasn't coughing anymore. Nona didn't say a word to me. Even though it was no big deal, and everything had turned out fine, I hung out in the living room watching cartoons with Sunny until she went to bed. Nona sat on the couch, hovering over Sunny like she expected her to start wheezing again at any second, and I sat across from them in the chair. Nona and I were only a few feet apart, but our own version of the Continental Divide stretched wide between us.

The Smallest Beginning

ON SATURDAYS WHITE HIGH-SCHOOL KIDS DROVE IN
from the burbs. I was waiting on a boy who wanted to
prove to me how down with the brothers he was. The only
problem was I didn't know what the hell he was talking
about.

"Dude, you don't know Pharrell? N.E.R.D.? The Nep-
tunes, one of the biggest hip-hop producers, like, *ever*?"

He probably drove a brand-new SUV and lived in
wealthy Littleton. Probably went to Columbine High School
and had parents who could pay for him to go to college for
five, six, seven years before he was even forced to declare a
major, let alone be expected to graduate. And he was doing
his damnedest to act like a boy from the hood. He stood in
front of me in his baggy jeans and XXXL sweatshirt with
the hood up like he was a badass.

The CD of a local rock band, the Trip Heavy Badgers,
was blaring and I was getting a headache. But I had set a

limit of five hairs a day, and always saved them for at night before I went to sleep.

"I'm afraid I don't!" I shouted over the music, and rang up his CDs, some of which, apparently had songs produced by somebody named Pharrell. 50 Cent, Ludacris, Ghostface Killah, Kanye West, Chamillionaire, Ne-Yo, Young Jeezy, Three 6 Mafia, Mike Jones, Jim Jones, T.I., Nas, Snoop Dogg, Trick Daddy, Jay-Z, LL Cool J, Diddy, most of whom I'd never heard of. His haul came to $257 and he threw a Visa on the counter without skipping a beat.

I used to wonder why these kids even bothered coming into the store, why they didn't just download songs like everybody else their age, or go to a store in their own neighborhoods. Then I realized: They wanted the "urban" experience. They liked driving down Colfax, past the homeless people pushing shopping carts, the panhandlers on every corner, and the trash in the gutters. You can't get that feeling of being dangerously hip in the suburbs or on the Internet.

"What about Timbaland?"

I shook my head.

"Yo, yo, yo," the customer said to Matt, signing the credit card slip. "Dude, somebody put on some Fiddy up in here so girlfriend can learn about the music of her people!"

The Trip Heavy Badgers were in the middle of the world's longest drum solo, my head was throbbing, I had caught Sunny's cold so my nose was running, and I was tired of feeling judged by everybody, even strangers! I slammed the cash register drawer. "I know who my people are, and they don't run around rapping about smacking hos and getting high, pimping themselves out to ignorant sub-urbanites who would piss in their own pants if they actually met a real gangster, or a real ho for that matter!"

I held up his bag of CDs and smiled. "You have a nice day!"

He snatched the bag out of my hand, but waited till he got to the door before he said anything. "Bee-*yach*!" he yelled and ran out, slamming the door so the bell jangled loudly.

I turned off the Badgers and put on some Billie Holiday. Two young guys with their arms covered in tattoos moaned their disapproval, but a thirtyish guy in khakis smiled in relief.

Oliver walked up to the counter.

"Like I went to college to put up with that bullshit," I huffed.

"You think any of us did? More power to a sister getting her degree, but check this: I'm working on a double major: Spanish and communications. John's got an MFA. Asia's working on a Ph.D. Matt, well, Matt doesn't exactly know yet what he wants to be when he grows up, but the boy's got a hella high IQ and his crazy ass is in school," Oliver fumed.

"Almost everybody up in this joint has either got a de-gree or is working on one. When's the last time you was at the mall or a Starbucks? Everybody everywhere not in the straight-up ghetto got a degree these days."

He threw up his hands. "And *this* is where it gets you. No need to front."

"You're standing up for that asshole?"

"No. But damn, you act like your shit don't stink, reminding us eleventy million times that you're getting a master's like the rest of us are still walking on all fours. You dis everybody in here . . . Matt . . . me."

I pushed past him into the backroom and got my backpack.

"Shay, wait . . ." Oliver called as I ran out the door.

As I sped home, I thought about what he said, and felt ashamed because he was right. I wanted everybody to know that I could do more than work a dumb retail job. But I felt like an idiot for not putting it together that everyone there was in the same boat I was. Whether they were playing in bands or going to school, they were all doing more than working at Shake It Up.

By the time I got home I realized what the boys were looking for when they came from the burbs to Shake It Up. They wanted connection. They wanted community. They wanted someone else to know them.

I pulled up in front of the house. It was dark so early now. Just 7:41 and the only light was a pale blue glow around the houses and trees. The black sky above seemed to be sinking down over everything.

"Hey, Shay, May, Day," a female voice sang from the darkened patio.

I stopped on the path. Ivy. I hadn't noticed her car. Great. I kept walking, put my key in the lock, and opened the door.

"You gonna let me in, Shay-away?" she chortled and passed me into the living room.

"Does Nona know you're here?" What I meant was: *What are you doing here by yourself?*

"I tell her everything, because she's my friend. My very good friend. When she gets home, we are going to talk. Be . . . cause. . . we . . . are . . . friends," she said, carefully enunciating every syllable.

Something wasn't right. I walked to the kitchen.

Ivy followed me. "It's me again! I'ma keep showing up!"

"So Nona knows you're here?" I repeated.

"Now you're all worried about her? What about Sunny? Like, you want to know where she's at?" Her pale eyes were cold, and the nostrils of her button nose flared.

Something was definitely wrong. My heart started to thump faster. Ivy had hated me from the minute she met me. Actually, not even me. She hated the idea of me, the idea that Nona had a daughter and a life that didn't involve her. And now Nona had obviously told her about Sunny's asthma attack, probably told her it was all my fault. I moved to the other side of the kitchen table. "Where—" My voice broke. I coughed, cleared my throat, and tried again. "Where's Nona?"

She lurched in front of me—standing between me and my bedroom. "Her and Sunny went to go get something for dinner."

She was drunk. Or high. I could see it now: her too-bright eyes and hyperarticulated speech. High, jealous, and a jailbird. Not a good combination. "Does Nona know you've been drinking?"

"Does Nona know you've been drinking?" she mocked. "She's going to help me. She's . . . my . . . friend."

I tried to move past her, but she stood in the way. I stepped to the left. She stumbled to the left.

"You *still* haven't gotten your retouch?" she asked with a twisted little smile. "Like, I told you I would braid up your hair for you."

I rolled my eyes, trying to act nonchalant enough to gain the upper hand, but I held my backpack in front of me like a shield. "What do you want? A magic word?"

"No. You ain't gotta say, like, shit to me."

I moved to the right and so did Ivy. "Well, then will you please get out of my way?"

"Sure, *La*Shay." She took a step to my left.

As I brushed past her, she snatched my bandanna off in one quick motion.

"Oops." She giggled.

I gasped and dropped my backpack. My hair was in short thick braids all over my head except the empty spots where there was nothing to braid. My hands flew to my head. Ivy dropped my bandanna and grabbed my wrists. I tried to pull away from her, but she was strong.

"Let go of me!"

She forced my arms down and got a good look at the circles of bare scalp, much paler than the rest of my skin, one over each of my ears and one dead in the center near my forehead. She hooted and cackled. "Girl, what the hell did you do?"

I jerked my arms away, too mad to be scared anymore. "You low-life piece of shit!"

She stopped laughing and stepped toward me.

"What's going on here?" Nona demanded, she and Sunny standing in the doorway to the kitchen, each holding a plastic grocery bag. She stared at the two of us breathing hard and standing close enough to hug, but our faces clearly saying hugging was the last thing on our minds.

"Nothing," Ivy said quickly, moving away from me.

"Shay? Tell me the truth."

Ivy started talking fast. "I told her I didn't like how she treats you. I told her she needed to show you respect."

"Sunny, go watch a video, okay?"

Sunny stayed rooted to her spot. Nona took her sack, which probably had one thing in it, and pointed out of the room. "Now."

Sunny turned around and crept back to the living room.

"Ivy, what are you doing here? I told you to call me tomorrow, when you were sober."

"But I need you," Ivy whined. "I wanna stay here! You let *her* stay here."

"I'm not playing this game with you. This is not the way to get my attention. You want my attention? Work your program. Go to meetings." Nona sighed. "Come on, I'll take you home."

"I can't go home!"

"Why not? Is something going on with Justin?"

"Go ahead. Say it. I'm no good. You don't love me. Nobody loves me. You hate me." She fell into a kitchen chair.

Nona went to her and touched her shoulder. "You know that's not true."

Ivy clung to her and wept.

"We'll talk tomorrow. We'll go to a meeting. But I can't do anything for you in this shape. Come on."

Ivy struggled out of the chair.

"Shay, you okay?" Nona asked.

I couldn't let Ivy know she had gotten under my skin. The best way to face a bully is to stand your ground. If I crumbled now, Ivy would have all the power. "I'm fine." My voice was steady.

Ivy let go of Nona and whipped around, stunned. Good for me. She had either expected me to tattle or to be cowed and run in my room.

Nona put one of the bags of groceries in the refrigerator. "Shay, will you follow us in Ivy's car?"

"That bitch ain't driving my car!"

"Ivy, I won't have this. I mean it," Nona said evenly.

"*I'm* the one standing up for you! She's the one that, like, don't give a damn about you!"

"You cannot come between me and my daughter. I told you that. And I don't want you coming over here loaded. You shouldn't even be driving."

Ivy stomped out of the room. Seconds later the front door slammed so hard the windows rattled.

"I don't know how you could let that little drunk hoochie—" I started, but Nona butted in.

"Stop it! Stop it right now. 'Cause you don't know what you're talking about. I'm one of the only people in this world who's ever shown that girl an ounce of kindness. And she's scared she's gonna lose me to you. You're getting a master's degree and she didn't even finish high school. You already have everything, and now she feels like you're going to get me too. That doesn't give her the right to drink, and it doesn't give her the right to get up in your face. But you sure don't have the right to talk about her either. Got it?"

I tried to imagine someone who was so bad off that she thought *I* had everything.

"Now come on. We can't let her drive." Nona left to get Ivy.

That's when I realized my head was still uncovered. Had Nona noticed? Now she'd get all freaked out and start nagging me to see a therapist again or start spouting A.A. mumbo jumbo at me. I tied my bandanna on my head and followed them.

Nona and Sunny took Ivy home. I followed in Ivy's cigarette-smelling Chevy. We arrived at a run-down apartment complex on the eastern outskirts of town. I handed Ivy her keys and she went inside without a fight. I wondered what Nona said to her in the car.

On the way back home, Nona and I were quiet, without even the sound of the radio to distract us. Sunny had fallen asleep in the backseat. The only sound was the wheels on the road and the heated air blowing from the vents.

We were halfway home when Nona said, "I'm sorry about tonight. And while I'm at it, I'm sorry about the way I acted about Sunny. I should have told you what to look out for, that asthma wasn't anything to mess with. You did the right thing bringing her home when you did."

"I really didn't know how sick she was when we left. She was asking me to dance with her. She seemed fine."

"I know."

"Did you tell Ivy that I wanted to hurt Sunny?"

She looked at me. "Of course not!" She turned back to the street. "I did tell her that I got mad at you and that you and I didn't seem to be getting any closer. I shouldn't have let it go this long without talking to you. That's not exactly walking my talk. I'm sorry."

"What are you going to do about Ivy?"

"I'll call her tomorrow and take her to a meeting."

"You're still going to be her sponsor?"

She checked the traffic, changed lanes, then answered, "As long as she wants me to, I will." Then she said, "You put your scarf back on."

I had forgotten. Oh God, here we go. "When I get anxious, I pull it," I said, trying to sound defiant and composed at the same time.

"Thank you for sharing that with me. I'm glad you told me."

Moving back to Denver had brought many surprises, but nothing surprised me more than this. I didn't exactly expect her to point at me and laugh, but I had definitely expected her to think I was crazy. That's what I thought myself.

Nona got off I-70 at the Colorado Boulevard exit near her house. We stopped at a light and the car was illuminated by streetlights. She smiled gently. "You don't have to cover up with me."

I always felt such a tangled knot of emotions around Nona. I didn't know where to begin unraveling them. And now things were even more confusing. Nona was different, sober, the way I always wanted her to be, but instead of making me happy, it somehow made me angrier. And now with her shining all this . . . this *acceptance* on me, it was almost too much to bear. I didn't know what to say.

The light changed and she stepped on the gas.

Sunny piped up. "Mama, I'm hungry."

"I don't feel much like cooking," Nona said.

"I'll cook." I had been doing laundry, but that was the whole of my chores. It wouldn't kill me to fix a meal.

"I want pizza!" Sunny yelled.

Nona smiled condescendingly at me like I was Sunny asking to help in the kitchen. "Really?"

I wanted to say I've been feeding myself since I was eight years old, but I didn't. "Yes, really."

"Well, thank you. That would be wonderful."

I fried the catfish fillets Nona had brought home and fixed a salad.

"Mmmm," Nona said, tucking into her fish like a starved person. "I'm scared of you!"

"I don't like it," Sunny said. Of course.

"Girl, you better eat some of this. You don't know what you're missing."

Sunny folded her arms and shook her head.

I decided to handle the situation. "If you eat your fish, you'll get a wish."

Sunny giggled. "Big silly."

"Little silly."

Nona laughed.

Sunny held up her index finger. "One bite." The negotiations had begun.

"Five," I said.

"Three."

I smiled. "Deal."

After dinner, we watched *The Wiz*. Nona and Sunny were asleep on the couch by the end when Diana Ross,

Michael Jackson, and Nipsey Russell sing about feeling a brand-new day.

I didn't listen to my iPod when I went to bed, so I heard the song in my head all night. It must have slipped into Nona's dreams too, because the next morning there was a new sticky note on the bathroom mirror that said, *A beginning, even the smallest, is all that's needed.—Twelve Steps and Twelve Traditions.*

Glory

WHENEVER BLACK FOLKS SEE ONE ANOTHER WE MUST acknowledge one another. I didn't know that until I was in high school and had a reputation for being stuck-up, siddity. I didn't know that I was supposed to say hi or *What's up?* or just nod my head at any other black person, friend or stranger. Because, like millions of other things, Nona never taught me that.

I learned it by walking into Stephanie's house and passing her Aunt Baby Mae in the living room without saying hello. I didn't know her and I wasn't good at talking to people I didn't know, so I scurried through the room and into the kitchen.

She followed me. "Girl, don't you speak?"

I thought she was being sarcastic, like she meant didn't I have a tongue, and if I did why didn't I use it. But later, I noticed how Stephanie's father and aunts were always after her and Cleo about "speaking" to people. If a neighbor was outside when we walked into the house, Mr. Berry would ask us if we "spoke" to him. I started paying attention, and noticed Stephanie and Cleo saying hello or nodding at folks they didn't know. And I realized that "speaking" is a way of showing solidarity and respect, of making one another visible. Speaking is serious.

Which is why I still said hello to Oliver every day when I came into the store, even though it would set off a chain reaction of nonstop chatter. That, and because he was right when he told me off.

"History of Music Post-1975 is in session," he said. "Time to get off this continent and go to the Motherland. This is King Sunny Ade, 'Juju Music.' African funk. On vinyl. One of the most tremendous albums of all time, and one of the coolest, sickest things you'll ever hear."

He started the record. Spacey-sounding electric guitars and drums and a chorus of men singing blared from the speakers. It was a big band, lots of drums and singers. The song was dense and busy, and relaxing at the same time.

"I like it," I said.

Oliver was pleased. "There's hope for you yet. Hear how the drums and the singers are talking to each other? The call and response?"

I nodded. I didn't know what the people or the drums were saying and I didn't care. I was feeling too happy.

"It's what joy sounds like," Oliver said.

We listened more. The music washed over me and filled me. It was hard not to dance, but I didn't dare. Oliver was bobbing his head and playing air congas.

"You play any real instruments?"

"Bass. I was in a band in high school. Rap, hip-hop, and rock, sorta like Limp Bizkit meets The Roots meets Living Colour meets four suburban white boys and me."

"What was the name of the band?"

"The Usual Suspects. We were pretty lame. We only lasted a few months."

"What happened?"

"A girl. Yoko Ono in a cheerleader uniform. We didn't stand a chance."

I laughed. "Whose girl?"

He stroked the peach fuzz on his chin. "I better not say."

"Oliver the Ladies' Man," I joked.

"I'm always talking about me. Why don't we ever talk about you?"

"Because there's nothing to talk about."

"Like hell. What's your favorite color? What's your favorite food or book or movie or TV show? Do you have any brothers or sisters? What's your major?"

That one, I could answer. "I'm getting my master's in epidemiology."

"Now we're getting somewhere. Tell me about that."

"What do you want to know?"

"What interests you about it?"

"You really are a communications major, aren't you?" I teased. "Well, you sort of solve mysteries. Why diseases start and spread, and, hopefully, you come up with ways to fix things."

He nodded encouragingly so I kept going, and found myself energized about school and work for the first time in a very long time. I started talking about public health and getting to the root cause of a disease, and once I got warmed up I didn't want to stop. It was exciting to feel engaged in my own life again. I hadn't had a good meaty conversation about issues and goals with anybody in forever, and couldn't remember ever having such a conversation with a guy who wasn't in a study group with me. Oliver even used the word "cavalier" and didn't mean the Cleveland basketball team!

The music became spare—mostly the men and drums talking to one another—pure rhythm. It was beautiful and hypnotic. I realized I was enjoying myself.

When lunchtime rolled around, I offered to pick up a veggie burger for Oliver. When I handed him his sack of food, he said, "See? Now, that wasn't so hard, was it?"

After lunch I decided to e-mail Carl. I hadn't stayed in touch, as he'd asked. But all the talk about school made me think that I really could go back next semester and pick up where I'd left off. I didn't know until this minute how afraid I've been that maybe I'd never get it together.

I didn't know how to say all that to Carl though. So I typed,

HI CARL:

I JUST WANTED TO LET YOU KNOW THAT I'M FINE.

Then I remembered Lois telling Nona that "fine" meant "fucking insecure, neurotic, and emotional," which was pretty much exactly how I was before I came back. And now? I started over.

HI CARL:

I JUST WANTED TO LET YOU KNOW THAT I'M OKAY. REALLY.
I'M WORKING PART-TIME. I HAVE FRIENDS. I THINK I MIGHT
EVEN BE READY TO START WORKING ON MY THESIS.

Now I sounded like I was trying too hard.

WELL, MAYBE I'M READY TO START *THINKING* ABOUT
MY THESIS.

I ALSO WANT TO THANK YOU FOR

[buying my line that all I needed was a semester break.]

ALL YOUR HELP. IT MEANS A LOT.

SEE YOU IN JANUARY.

SHAY

I OPENED MY WALLET to give Oliver money for lunch.
We took turns going for lunch now. He had run over to
Pete's and picked up our Greek salads. He glanced at my
driver's license.

"LaShay, huh?"

I snapped my wallet shut. "Just Shay."

"The *La* too fancy for you?"

"Sounds like I should be sliding around a stripper's pole."

"You say that like it's a bad thing."

"Ha."

"Well, I like it," he said. "It's your name. It's who you
are."

"Easy for you to say. You have a perfectly fine name."

He put his pita bread down and wiped his hands on a napkin. "My last name is Toliver."

"You lie."

He pulled his wallet out of his back pocket and showed me his license.

"Your parents named you Oliver Toliver?"

"Actually, they let my grandmother do this to me. My paternal grandfather's name was Oliver and I'm my dad's only child. My dad is an only child. I was the only chance for a namesake."

"Why didn't they give her your middle name? Or, don't tell me: It's Boliver? No, Soliver?"

"She cried so they gave in. What's your middle name?"

"It's too country."

"Oh, come on. I'll tell you mine."

"I don't care about yours." I took a bite of salad.

"I'll tell you something else, then. Name it. What do you want to know?"

"I know enough, thanks."

"Damn, come on now. I ain't asking for money! Not your firstborn child. Just your middle name."

I rolled my eyes. "Glory."

"No shit? That's tight."

"Yeah right."

"Seriously. Glory rocks. Glory kicks ass. That's what I'm gonna call you from now on. Glory." His eyes were earnest behind his big glasses.

A kick-ass name. "You think?"

"I *know.*"

My name is Dixon, Glory Dixon. Why not? Nina Simone was born Eunice Waymon, and look what a name change did for her.

"So you wanna go get some food or something sometime when we're not at work? I wouldn't want to get sued for sexual harassment."

"You're asking me out?"

It was his turn to roll his eyes. "*Hello . . . !* It'll be fun."

Fun. There was that word again.

"My calendar gets booked up fast. You better jump on this."

I put my fork down and took in the big fro and the Muhammad Ali t-shirt. "How old are you anyway?"

"Nineteen."

I shook my head. "I'm twenty-five."

"That's about what I figured."

"And it doesn't bother you?"

"Why should it?"

I did feel comfortable with Oliver. He was young, but he was smart and thoughtful. And even though it might not look like it, it turned out we had a few things in common. "Okay, let's have some fun."

WE DECIDED TO meet the next day at the Museum of Nature and Science for a walk in City Park. I arrived about a quarter till two and waited near the museum, looking at the park's empty flower beds, tan grass, bare trees, and lake. Beyond the park was the downtown skyline, and, behind all that, the Rockies, looking purple and majestic just like the song says.

Unlike with my date with Desi, I wasn't nervous about meeting Oliver. Surprised at myself, but not nervous.

About ten minutes later he pedaled up to me, his cheeks flushed, wild hair blowing, and an orange Gerbera daisy sticking out of the pocket of his flannel shirt.

He circled around me once, then stopped. "I purposely came early so I could be here first. Are you ever just on time?"

"I just got here," I lied.

"No, you didn't. I was going to have my bike locked up and be standing here like Denzel with this flower in my hand waiting on you."

Denzel in nerdy-cool glasses and baggy cargo pants? I don't think so.

He climbed off his bike and handed me the daisy. "Give a brother a minute next time, all right? Operate on a little CP time, Glory."

Glory. I smiled. *So okay he wasn't Denzel, but I wasn't exactly Halle Berry myself.* "All right."

We walked his bike over to the railing near the parking garage and he locked it up. We headed into the park, taking a sloping path littered with goose poop. Oliver slowed to watch the kids at the playground, so I did too.

"You don't have any, do you?" he asked.

"God no! You?"

"No. Not till I'm out of school, working, and married. My father told me a long time ago: No glove, no love. Now I'm trying to set an example for my little brother."

I was impressed. "How many siblings do you have?"

"One. Michael. He's eight."

"I have a half sister named Sunny who's three and a half."

"Mike and I might have different fathers and different last names, but he's not my *half* anything."

I walked off quickly, and Oliver rushed to follow.

"I'm sorry. I didn't mean to upset you."

I slowed to a stroll. We reached the path that circles the lake.

"Are you all right?"

I stopped. "Nona was a drunk and my father left before I was born. I never knew Sunny's father. Nona met him in A.A. and he disappeared on her as soon as she was pregnant. I just met Sunny for the first time a couple of months ago. I guess the idea that I have a sister is still a little new."

Sunny *was* starting to grow on me, though. After all, the kid had taste. Sometimes I let her listen to my iPod, and she always requested Nina Simone.

A Labrador retriever ran by us and startled a large gaggle of geese, which flew complaining all the way into the middle of the lake. Oliver tugged my sleeve and we started walking again.

"My parents have been divorced since I was seven," he offered.

"Your mother is remarried?"

"She didn't marry Mike's father. And that's a good thing. Mike calls my father Dad. We don't see him much, though. He lives in Omaha now. Mike stays with me and my roommates sometimes on the weekends for a male vibe."

I could only imagine what a male vibe meant: smelly socks and fart jokes?

We walked past the boathouse and down a flight of steps. We got near the small pond that abuts the fence surrounding the zoo. Some animal on the other side of the fence was making an ethereal sound. *No-oo. No-oo.*

"Is that a monkey?" I asked.

"It's a peacock."

"It sounds like some kind of cat."

"It's a *peacock*," he repeated. "Can't you believe somebody else might know something you don't know?"

"I'm sorry. I'm sorry. Fine, it's a peacock," I agreed, even though I still wasn't sure I believed him.

Oliver talked about his classes. He was such a typical college student, bitching and moaning about midterms, but he grew more animated as he spoke. I noticed how big and expressive his eyes were. The peach-fuzz mustache and goatee needed to go, but he was kind of a cute guy really, with all those freckles and curly hair and big doe eyes. Sweet-looking, like he wouldn't hurt a fly. No wonder he was a vegetarian.

"What?"

I must have been staring. "I envy you," I said.

He looked at me like I was nuts.

"Seriously. I miss school."

"So, if you liked school so much and you're not close to your family, why'd you leave to come back here?"

"Just needed to get away from Iowa for a while."

He bumped his shoulder against mine. "Get away from *Iowa,* huh?"

"What?"

"What's his name?"

Just like Stephanie, he assumed I was having man problems. I opened my mouth to correct him, but what came out was, "Desi . . . as in Desmond."

"He cheated on you?"

Once the lie was out there, I went with it, trying to think of something that would have been big enough to make me leave school and move in with Nona. "Yes. With a man."

"No shit? Dude was on the down low?!"

I nodded, hating myself, but not hating the attention.

"How did you find out? Never mind, don't tell me. I don't even want to know. But . . ."

"What?"

"You got tested, right?"

I stared at him.

"For HIV."

"Oh! Yeah! Negative! Both times! Whew." I dramatically swept my brow as if I had been worried about getting a sexually transmitted disease from Desi, even though I had only seen the man once in my life.

We completed a circle around the park and went back up the hill to the museum parking lot. When we got to my car, Oliver said, "So, it's over with Down Low Desi, right?"

I laughed. He *did* make me laugh. "Definitely." It never really started with Down Low Desi, so it wasn't untrue to say that it was over.

"Good, 'cause I know a place for dinner I think you'll like."

I twirled the daisy Oliver gave me. It glowed in my hand like the sun of some really happy planet. "Okay." I opened the car door.

"Saturday?"

"Yeah. Sure." *Listen to me, Miss Agreeable!*

Oliver stood next to me. "All right. Well, I'll see ya later, Glory."

He leaned over to kiss me, and lo and behold I agreed to that too.

I closed my eyes and felt him peck my lips quickly, like he expected me to change my mind. When I didn't he kissed me again, a softer, slower, lip-on-lip smooch. It was nice. No, better than nice. *Way* better than nice. I felt warm and liquid, and . . . oh my!

He must have liked it too because when I drove away he was still standing there grinning idiotically, little marshmallow teeth everywhere.

BELINDA'S WAS LOCATED in Five Points and was renowned by black women from Cheyenne to Colorado Springs. It wasn't fancy, and nobody went there for anything too unusual—no microbraids or Nubian locks—but her staff knew how to put chemicals on just the new growth, not the scalp, to get their customers' hair stick-straight without burning them, a skill as valuable as the silver and gold that drew miners to Colorado more than one hundred years ago. But unlike silver and gold, Belinda's mine would never run dry: Black women would always pay for straight hair.

"Go off to school and don't come back for seven years," Belinda scolded when I sat in her chair. She was wearing a poofy burgundy wig and when she shook her head she looked like a wise, exotic bird. But she wasn't really mad.

She and Nona had been friends longer than Nona had been sober. One time, when I was in the seventh grade, so much time had passed before I had the money to get my hair relaxed, my nappy new growth was four inches long. It took her so long to get my hair untangled and straightened that she told me to come back in exactly six weeks, whether I had the money or not.

"Look at you, College Girl. Now what we gon' do?"

I took a great big breath and unwrapped my scarf. It was a long piece of blue cotton I had made from a sarong so it took a long time, or at least it seemed like a long time. I felt like Salome removing seven veils, except instead of John the Baptist's head, mine was the one that would end up on the plate for all to see.

After I was done, Belinda and I locked eyes in the mirror over her station. She sucked her teeth. "You should have come to see me when it started coming out. Don't you got a beautician in Iowa?"

After I started pulling, I had been too embarrassed to go. I shook my head.

Using her fingers, she parted my hair in several places, surveying the damage more closely. "This don't look like alopecia."

I wanted to fall through the floor.

She peered seriously at me in the mirror and, recognizing my chagrin, didn't go any further. "Well, let's see what we can do. What kind of style you like?"

I knew I might not have much of a choice, between the

bald spots and the damaged ends, but I didn't want my old, plain, curled-under bob. I didn't want to see nerdy little Shay when I looked in the mirror. I wanted to see kick-ass Glory. "Something different," I said, knowing that didn't help much. But Belinda had been doing heads for thirty years. She didn't ask for elucidation.

She washed and deep-conditioned my hair and cut off a few inches of dried-out split ends. She didn't straighten my hair, but added extensions to cover the blank spots. She put curling gel over old hair and new, and twisted it into many thick plaits, and sat me under the dryer. After four hours, my hair was about eight inches long and surrounded my face like a cottony black halo, like a lion's mane.

Belinda removed the shampoo cape and placed her plump hands on my shoulders.

I touched my hair. For the first time since I had been back home, it felt soft. I smiled at her, then at myself in the mirror. *So this is what Glory looks like.*

When I got home, Nona went crazy over my hair. "Look at you! I love it! Do you love it? I love it!"

"I love it!" Sunny said. "You look bee-yoo-ti-ful."

I couldn't stop smiling. It was fake hair, but it was mine in a way that felt important, and I was *claiming it.*

I waited for Ivy to say something sarcastic about my bald spots, but she didn't. She hadn't been able to meet my eyes since she came over drunk. She had called Nona, all remorseful, the next day and was going to meetings again. Nona was convinced she was sincere, but I wasn't. Nona hadn't heard the glee in Ivy's voice when she was pulling off my scarf. Alcohol didn't make her hate me that much. It only gave her license to show it. So I kept my distance.

"Let me get the camera." Nona dashed into her room. "Maybe sit in the rocker, in front of the books?"

I'd never liked getting my picture taken, but this time I wanted a way to commemorate the birth of Glory. I sat and smiled while she clicked a couple of shots.

Then Sunny ran and stood next to me. "Take my picture too!"

Nona waited.

"Sure," I answered, drawing Sunny into my lap and inhaling her almond and bubblegum scent. She touched my hair tentatively, then commanded, "Say cheese!"

And for once I was happy to obey her.

"Would you mind if we all took one together?" Nona asked shyly.

I shook my head.

"Ivy, will you?" Nona handed her the camera and stood next to the chair.

Ivy had a strained look on her face, but she snapped the picture.

"There, the brand-new you on record for the ages," Nona said taking the camera back.

Speaking of the brand-new me . . . "How did you come up with Glory for my middle name?"

Nona shook her head, trying to keep up with my change of subject. "You don't remember?"

"Remember what?"

"About morning glories . . . ?"

I stared blankly.

"Morning glories were my father's favorite flower. He used to say, 'Glories thrive in the worst possible soil and face the day with a smile every morning. What's not to love?' "

That was me. I didn't exactly face each day with a smile, but I was still here. I had survived.

"You don't remember that story?"

"You never told me that."

"Oh, I did too! Don't you have *any* good memories of me?"

The image of The Plaza in Kansas City at Christmastime popped into my head. Before we moved to Denver we went there every year. All the shops and restaurants would be covered in millions of lights. We'd walk all the blocks in the cold and the dark with hundreds of other people and Nona would buy me apple cider or hot chocolate with whipped cream and I would tell myself we were just like those other folks: happy.

"The Plaza," I said.

She gave a small smile and held up the camera. "Good. I hope we can make some new ones."

THE NEXT MORNING when I walked into the store the sound system blasted "Glory, glory hallelujah!"

Oliver turned around grinning, but froze when he saw me. "Wow! You have hair."

"Yes I do. You're a very observant young man."

"I know. I mean. It's . . . you . . . Glory, you look . . . wow."

That's how I *felt* too: Wow.

Mercury Rising

I WAS DOING SOMETHING UNPRECEDENTED: ACTUALLY looking forward to a date. No hair pulling. No agonizing over what to wear or worrying about what to say. The new me was going to make some new memories for myself. As promised, I arrived at the restaurant five minutes late. I saw Oliver standing on the corner. I parked my car and walked back to meet him. He was in jeans and a brown corduroy blazer over a black t-shirt, which was dressed up for him.

"You beat me."

"Been here half an hour just to make sure." He produced a long-stemmed red rose from behind his back and handed it to me.

I smiled. "Very suave."

"That's what I'm saying."

The door to the Mercury Café was open. Oliver went in first and parted red velvet curtains for me to enter, and I stepped into a large bloodred room. Directly in front of us up a couple of stairs was a long wooden bar with a large mirror behind it. To the right were booths and tables. On the far wall there was a neon red hoop with the front half of a stuffed tiger leaping through it. Jazz was playing and most of the tables were occupied by aging hippies, college students, and artsy-looking twentysomethings. I felt immediately at home and was impressed that Oliver had correctly guessed I would like it.

A white chick with pink hair, a tight pink dress, and a distinct underarm odor grabbed two menus and led us to a small table under the tiger, next to a stage that just barely fit a baby grand piano. Our table held a tall candle, a bud vase of red carnations, and dispensers of soy sauce and brown sugar. I stuck my rose in the vase with the carnations, and looked around. There were large colorful abstract paintings and photographs of nude women on the walls. There was another bar near us where cakes, pies, and cookies were displayed. The lamplight was bright enough to read by, and the red walls, fabric-draped ceiling, and heavy wood furniture made the room feel cozy and intimate.

A different waitress, this one wearing a silky white camisole, green fatigues, and combat boots, came to the table and brought glasses of water and silverware wrapped in white paper napkins. She set Oliver's water down first and reached across the table to give me mine. When she did, I noticed spiderweb tattoos on her elbows. But Oliver noticed something else: her breasts right at his eye level. Her right nipple just about poked him on the cheek. I watched Oliver watch her, and felt a stab of irritation.

He noticed me stiffen up. "What's wrong?"

I opened my menu. "Nothing. Everything's just fine," I said crisply.

"What can I get you to start?" the waitress asked.

"A bra," I muttered under my breath.

She didn't hear me. But Oliver looked at me curiously while he ordered coffee. Then he said to me, "You can get a glass of wine or something, if you want."

"I don't drink." I asked for coffee too.

After Nipple Girl left, Oliver said, "Because of your mom?"

I nodded.

The waitress took forever to come back with our coffee, but I didn't miss her. The menu was eclectic: steak sandwiches, breakfast burritos, hot and sour stir-fry, high tea, pasta dishes, soups. Oliver was going to get something called Dinah's Tofu, and recommended it to me, but I was suspicious. I had tried sesame tofu once and did not like it.

"Trust me," he said.

I wrinkled my nose. I was leaning toward the chicken-and-pasta dish. We closed our menus to signal to the waitress we were ready to order.

"I think it's really cool that you're working on a master's," he said.

"You told me I was frontin'."

"You kinda were, but still: A sister working on a degree, going places, doing something with her time . . . that's all right."

"I think it's cool you're a double major."

He pushed his thick glasses up. "Gracias. Sometimes,

though, I think I should be taking Arabic or Chinese. That's where the real money's going to be."

I looked closely at him in the candlelight. I could see the right girl going for him. Someone brainy and eccentric, a little shy, but cool enough to own a guitar and have a discreet, tasteful tattoo. A freshman English major who blogged and wrote prose poems in her journal, and kept her ta-tas covered in public.

Finally, the waitress came and brought our coffee and a basket of thick, brown bread and butter, and took our order. I went with the chicken.

I took a sip of coffee. "Whoa!"

Oliver grinned. "Strong, huh?"

I had to pour almost half the pitcher of cream in my cup before the coffee lightened to dark brown, which, of course, also made it cold. But I added some brown sugar and drank it anyway.

We continued to talk about school and work. Eventually our food came. Oliver insisted I try some of his tofu. It was breaded and fried in garlic and vegetables and served over pasta. I took a small bite and was extremely pleasantly surprised.

"Told you," he said. "One of these days you're going to learn to listen to me."

"What does that mean?"

"You didn't believe that what we heard in the park was a peacock. You didn't believe that this tofu would be good."

"Well, I barely know you."

"You're saying you begin from a position of distrust.

Why not believe me and see if I ever give you a reason not to?"

"Trust has to be earned."

"In my experience people who say that never trust anybody."

"So you just believe total strangers?"

"I'm not a stranger. We work together. My lips have been on your face. Doesn't that earn me the benefit of the doubt? Can you at least try to let me be innocent until proven guilty?"

Was this just one more way I was socially abnormal? Didn't everyone reserve their trust until they knew it was safe to give? Or did other people, normal people, simply take folks at their word and wait to see if they got fooled or hurt later? I didn't think I could have faith in someone I barely knew, whether his lips had been on my face or not, but I could try to give Oliver the benefit of the doubt about what to order. "I'll try."

After we had eaten and he paid the check, I thought we were leaving, but instead of going out through the red curtains, he said, "Come with me."

He led me through the back to another room—this one turquoise and green with a mural of palm trees and ferns, and filled with people listening to a poet on the mike at the front—and up a long flight of stairs. At the top was a dance hall. We entered and it was like stepping into the past. A big band with a female singer was onstage singing "Ain't Nobody's Business If I Do." Men and women on the dance floor—some in forties and fifties dress, some in jeans and sneakers—were jumping, kicking, twirling, and doing some very fancy footwork. Some of the couples were middle-aged and some looked like they were still in high school. Around the dance floor, small tables were covered in white or black tablecloths and topped with vases filled with red carnations. Red and white Christmas lights and garlands of white plastic flowers lined the rafters of the ceiling.

Oliver grinned at me and paid the cover charge for us to get in. "Would you like to dance?" he asked, holding out his hand. The music was loud so we had to practically yell to be heard.

"I don't know how to swing dance!"

"Neither do I!" He grabbed my hand and pulled me onto the dance floor.

"But—?!"

"We'll just do whatever!" He took my other hand and we kind of stepped back and forth and swayed to the music.

A girl in cat-eye glasses and a red-and-white polka-dot dress bumped into me and I stumbled. I yanked my hands away from Oliver. "This is stupid! I can't do this. I have no rhythm!"

He leaned in close and said, "Take a look around."

Some of the dancers were definitely better than others. A baby boomer in a black strapless dress with a handkerchief bottom was twirling around like a pro, her dress billowing around her legs. But a girl in a halter and jeans was being flung every which way by her partner. They were tripping all over each other and laughing heartily.

Oliver held out his hands again. "Trust me."

I placed my hands in his. This time I noticed his palms were a little damp and his smile was fragile. He was as nervous as I was, but he was willing to risk embarrassing himself. For me. When I first saw this room, I had felt like I was entering the past, but now I felt like I might be moving toward the future.

"Ready?" he asked.

"Ready."

We jitterbugged and Charlestoned (at least our version of them) and cracked up for two hours. Oliver even dipped me without dropping me. By the time I got home, I knew what I wanted to let go of. Before I went in the house, I pulled a piece of paper out of my backpack and wrote it down. My breath froze in the chilly night air. I scraped the mulch out of the way and dug a hole in the cold dirt. I'm not usually a praying person, but I looked up at the dark sky and implored Whoever might be out there to help me let go and move on, to help me take one giant leap for Shay-kind. Then I tore the paper into teeny tiny shreds, placed them in the hole, and covered them with dirt.

CHAPTER 18

Sisters

OCTOBER ENDED COLD AND WINDY. I WAS IN MY ROOM
reading, trying to stay warm under the covers, when I heard
screaming in the living room.

"Muthafucka!"

I jumped out of bed and ran into the living room. It was
Ivy. Blood had dried around her nose and mouth, and what
wasn't bloody was covered with snot and tears. She was crying, rambling. "Think he so bad . . . How could he? I'll kick
his muthafuckin' ass!"

"What happened?" I asked.

Ivy cried harder.

Nona rushed past me from the bathroom and handed a
wet washcloth to Ivy. "Maybe we should take you to the
hospital."

"What happened?" I repeated.

Ivy sobbed. "Get her out of here! I don't want her . . . I
don't want her . . ."

"Shay—"

Ivy sobbed louder and Nona held her, caressing her hair, swaying and shushing her like she was a baby. "Shay, take Sunny. Go get some dinner." Her voice was calm, as if having a bloody, screaming girl in her living room was no big deal.

I didn't want to stay, but I couldn't move. My heart was banging in my chest, furiously pumping blood to my feet but they wouldn't go.

"I don't want her to see me! Don't let her see me!" Ivy wailed.

"Go. Please," Nona whispered. "Sunny, it's okay, baby. It'll be okay. Go with Shay, okay?"

I noticed Sunny for the first time. She was sitting on the couch clutching a Barbie, and her eyes were as round as two full moons. I realized Nona wanted me to get Sunny away, and scooped her up. I recalled the night I came back to Denver and I had thought Nona was going out to drink. It hadn't even occurred to me that if Nona had gone out, Sunny would also have been left behind. I thought about my taking her to the mountains when she was sick and I felt small.

"We might not be here when you get home—"

"No!" Ivy shouted. "I don't want the hospital!"

"Okay, shush," Nona soothed, raising her eyebrows at me. "My keys are in my purse. Get the car seat out of my car and then leave the keys under the seat and don't lock it."

I grabbed Nona's keys and our jackets and rushed out of the house. We quickly put on our coats and dashed down the path to the cars. I got the car seat arranged and settled Sunny in the backseat of my car.

When I put the key in the ignition, my hands were shaking so bad I thought I'd better wait a minute to drive. I started the car to warm it up and took a couple of deep breaths.

"What's wrong with Miss Ivy?"

I turned around and felt like I was looking in a mirror, a mirror that reflected myself a long time ago. Worry was etched across Sunny's small face. I knew what it was like to realize that the grown-ups didn't know what they were doing and that you might not be in the best of hands. I didn't want Sunny to feel that way. "I don't know. But Nona . . . your mother . . . our mother will handle it. Everything's going to be okay."

She didn't look convinced.

"What do you want to eat?"

She looked at the floor.

I tried to think of what was around. "Hamburgers? Tacos? Chicken nuggets?"

She still didn't say anything. I was desperate, so I pulled out the big gun. "Ice cream?"

It worked. She looked up at me and nodded.

The child just witnessed a terrifying scene. She deserved an ice cream cone, even if it was only twenty-eight degrees outside.

I drove to Liks in Capitol Hill because the ice cream is homemade and because it would help ensure that we would be away from the house for a while, in case Nona couldn't

talk Ivy into going to the hospital. We both ordered cookie-
dough ice cream on sugar cones, and sat in our coats quietly
eating. Keeping her ice cream from melting all over her
hand and swinging her legs on the tall chair kept Sunny
busy for almost half an hour. She seemed to forget what
was going on back home, but the images of the bruises on
Ivy's arm that time and her battered face tonight stayed in
my mind.

Since I wasn't sure it was safe to go home, I took Sunny
to the Tattered Cover. It was just down the street from the
record store. We sat on the green carpet downstairs in the
children's section with a pile of books, some of which I read
to Sunny and some of which she "read" to me. *Click, Clack,
Moo: Cows That Type; Nappy Hair;* and *What a Truly Cool
World,* about Shaniqua, the angel in charge of everybody's
business, were my favorites. Sunny was a big Maisy fan, and
who could blame her? Maisy is one talented and resourceful
little mouse.

During the eleventh Maisy story, in which Maisy went
to bed, Sunny leaned against my chest and stroked my cheek
until she went to sleep, her hand still on my face. She was
wearing a little peasant blouse that Lois had sent from Bulgaria. Mixed with the sweet almond scent of her hair, I
could smell the ice cream she spilled on her shirt. I cradled
her in my arms, and we sat until our breaths and heartbeats
were in sync.

An older white woman carrying a stack of hardcover
books smiled at us. "Your daughter's precious."

I smiled back. "She's not my daughter. We're sisters."

———

THE NEXT MORNING, Ivy greeted me at the breakfast table with a bright "Good morning," awful damn perky for somebody who had slept on her sponsor's couch and whose face looked like a purple grapefruit. I looked at Nona, then looked back at her. "What's up?"

"I'm going to stay here until I get my own place," Ivy said. "I'll try not to get in your way."

I sat down. "What happened to you?"

"Shay—" Nona started.

"It's okay," Ivy said. "I owe the girl an explanation. Let's just say my boyfriend, my *ex*-punk-ass-boyfriend, decided I should be making more money."

Nona shook her head angrily.

It took me a few seconds to realize Ivy meant that Justin thought the line between stripping and screwing for money was as thin as a G-string.

Nona got up and came back to the table with a notebook and a stack of books.

Ivy's eyes widened. "All that's for me?"

"No drinking or drugging, work the steps, read the Big Book."

"I'll do it." Ivy pulled the stack closer to herself.

Nona patted her hands. "Good."

"So, what did my two girls do last night?" she asked me.

When Sunny and I got home, Nona and Ivy were in the bathroom talking. Sunny was still asleep, so I put her to bed, then went to bed myself.

"We had ice cream for dinner!" Sunny said, taking a big bite of turkey bacon.

"No wonder you're so hungry this morning," Nona said, smiling.

"What else did we do?" I asked.

"We read books."

Sunny and I recounted the Maisy-athon.

Nona reached across the table and took my hands in hers. "It's funny how God will give you what you want just when you aren't thinking about it."

I slowly pulled my hands away.

Ivy stood up, wincing.

"You okay?" Nona jumped up to help her. "You want some more ibuprofen? Some ice?"

Ivy picked up the little blue book, which was called *The Big Book* for some reason, and said, "I think another hot bath. Then I'll get started on my homework." She walked slowly to the bathroom.

I'm sure she was in pain—she looked like hell—but I wondered if she didn't decide to get up just then to get Nona's attention.

"How long is she going to be here?"

Nona sighed. "As long as it takes for her to find a place."

"That girl is trouble."

"I was trouble for Lois at first too. I'm going to tell you something you don't know." She ran the crust of her toast in circles on her plate. "I relapsed. When a certain someone left me"—she tilted her head toward Sunny so I would know she meant Sunny's father—"he stole some things: a gold chain, my stereo and TV, a little bit of money I had on my dresser. It broke my heart, and I sank into a bottle of Seagram's like it was a bubble bath. I was sick for days afterward and I thought it was the Seagram's, but it turned out I was pregnant."

"This is supposed to make me feel better how?"

"I'm not saying it was right. I hope to God I never do it again. But it happens. People make mistakes."

"That night she came here drunk. She wanted to do to me what Justin did to her. She hates me."

"I told you. She's just jealous."

Just jealous? I pushed back from the table. "Whatever. Don't listen to me. I don't care what you do, and I don't care what Ivy does. Be blind if you want to."

Nona stood and started clearing dishes off the table. "I have my weaknesses, but blindness isn't one of them."

The Princess Brides

"OH MY GOD! SHE'S ADORABLE!" STEPHANIE WENT GAGA over Sunny as soon as we walked into her apartment.

I beamed with pride, like I had something to do with it. But as usual, Sunny had dressed herself. She had on a red corduroy jumper, blue-and-green argyle socks, and red sequined *Wizard of Oz* slippers.

Every time I saw Stephanie, the conversation was always about her wedding or the baby. I could tell talking about Sunny was just going to make her launch into a conversation about the baby. But this time, I had something to contribute: I was going to tell her about Oliver.

"Maybe you were right about using one man to get over another. . . ." I prompted.

Stephanie looked at me. "Do tell."

"I'm kind of seeing someone."

"Duh. Who?"

"This is the part that's kind of funny. It's Oliver."

She stared blankly at me.

"From work," I said.

"Record Store Boy? Girl, tell me! Tell me how *this* happened!"

"He asked me out." My cheeks burned, and I put my hands over my face.

"Oooh . . . how old is he?"

"Nineteen." I peeped from behind my hands.

"You scandalous little cradle-robber!" Stephanie cracked up and slowly lowered herself onto the couch. Her stomach was only slightly more rounded, but she was really acting like a pregnant lady.

I took my hands off my face, trying not to grin.

" 'Bout time you listened to Mama Stephanie. I know what I'm talking about. What's he look like?"

"Cute. Young."

"Long as he ain't in diapers, go on and have your fun. You like him?"

"He makes me laugh."

She leered at me. "What else does he make you do?"

I sat on the floor and Sunny plopped in my lap. "Excuse me, my sister is here." I was embarrassed, but I was also enjoying myself. I finally had a real true guy to talk about.

"So how is he?"

"Nothing has happened. Yet," I said.

Stephanie started the movie: *Father of the Bride*.

Cleo was right. I groaned. "Another wedding movie?"

"I like weddings," Sunny said.

"Whose wedding have you been to?" I asked.

She shrugged, which I took to mean that at the ripe old

age of three she liked the idea of weddings—the idea of being a princess in a long white dress.

"Want to see my wedding dress?" Stephanie asked.

Sunny nodded.

Stephanie stopped the DVD and brought a garment bag out to the living room and carefully unzipped it. She slid the dress out and held it up in front of her. It was ivory with a floral pattern and seed pearls embroidered on the bodice, down the back of the four-foot train, and around the hem.

"Isn't it beautiful?" she said gazing down at the dress. "I am in love with this dress. I swear, I'd marry *it* if I could. I just wish I wasn't going to be as big as a house on my wedding day."

Sunny reached hesitantly to touch the dress, but Stephanie jerked it away. "Uh-uh. Let me see your hands."

Sunny held them out to show they were clean, so Stephanie let her touch it. Sunny looked like she was touching a dream.

"Try it on," Sunny ordered, and Stephanie didn't need any more encouragement than that. She all but ran into the bedroom to change.

She came out in the dress and a freshwater pearl–and–rhinestone tiara. The dress had a matching wrap that went around her arms.

Sunny gasped.

"Sunny, you okay? Can you breathe?"

She nodded.

I listened again and there were no more gasps, no coughing. I realized she was *that* moved by the site of this grown-up real-life Princess Barbie. She was about ready to faint from happiness. Stephanie had finally found someone as interested in her wedding as she was.

"It really is beautiful, Steph," I said.

"It better be. Daddy spent three grand on it." She turned and held down the silky wrap in front of her. "We'll pin this down to help hide my bump. Too bad they don't make one for big butts."

She put the tiara on Sunny's head, and picked her up. "Let's go see how you'll look when you're a bride. You want to come to my wedding?"

Sunny looked at me.

"Really?" I asked.

"Sure, the more the merrier. Bring your little friend too."

Stephanie took Sunny to the bathroom so they could look in the mirror. They made a perfect match. They both wanted to be princesses when they grew up.

CHAPTER 20

Losing It

TODAY WAS THE FIRST DAY OLIVER AND I HAD WORKED together since our date at the Mercury. When it was almost time to leave, he leaned on the counter, trying to be nonchalant. "Soooo . . . both my roommates are going to be gone tonight. Wanna come over? I'll get a pizza and something nonalcoholic for you?"

Even socially retarded geeky little me knew he was asking me over for more than pizza. But just in case I missed it, Oliver was playing Floetry's sexy "Say Yes." I did like the song said.

Oliver lived in Five Points, only a few blocks from Belinda's shop. Five Points had once been a happening part of town, sort of the West's very own Harlem. In the thirties, forties, and fifties you could have heard Duke Ellington, Billie Holiday, Count Basie, and the other big bands that toured the Midwest. When I was growing up, it was a forgotten, run-down ghetto. But now most of the Victorian houses looked freshly painted and sported new windows and landscaped yards. Row houses and lofts had sprung up everywhere. A new light-rail line ran through the neighborhood from downtown. It wasn't completely gentrified, though. The storefronts on Welton still looked pretty beat-up and the people waiting on the light-rail were mostly poor-looking blacks and Latinos.

Oliver's house was still part of the old Five Points, with cracking paint and a dilapidated porch. The inside was what you would expect from college boys: A couch and a chair covered in sheets, a beanbag chair, and a coffee table with a chunk of wood broken off one of the edges were placed in front of shelves made with planks and cinder blocks that held a giant TV, CD player, and record player. Next to the shelves, a CD tower and bookshelves held hundreds of CDs, and a dozen wood crates were filled with vinyl albums. On the wall behind the couch there was a large piece of fabric with a pattern of marijuana plants.

Oliver leaned his bike against the wall and slipped off his backpack. "Pepperoni?"

"I thought you were vegetarian?"

He shrugged. "It's the only kind of pizza I like. Besides, pepperoni isn't really meat. It's more like *meat product*." He ordered the pizza and a two-liter bottle of Coke for me, and went into the kitchen for a beer. When he came back, he sat next to me on the couch. "Does it bother you if I drink?"

You're underage, and by the way do you smoke dope? was what I wanted to say, but a lecture probably wasn't good for the libido. "I appreciate that you asked," I said primly, right when prim was the last thing I wanted to be.

Our knees touched, and he gulped his beer. "Sorry I don't have anything for you to drink before the pizza gets here."

"That's okay." I stared at the floor.

"You want some water?"

I looked back up at him. "I'm good."

He sat his beer on the coffee table and bumped his fists together to the beat of a song in his head. The drinking situation covered, we were out of things to talk about. He stood suddenly and loped to the stereo.

I listened for a few seconds. "Mary J. Blige, right?"

"Very good. You're learning."

Oliver bopped his head and bumped his fists. I closed my eyes and listened to Mary J. sing about wanting to steal away to spend a romantic day with her boyfriend. The pizza arrived and Oliver put my soda and the pizza box on the coffee table. He went in the kitchen and returned with a plastic tumbler of ice and a roll of paper towels. "We're out of plates," he said, handing me a paper towel.

"Out of plates?"

"Paper. We don't do no dishes here." He opened the box and handed me a large slice. "I asked for extra grease," he joked.

I took a bite. "You got your wish."

The pizza gave us something to do, which put us at ease and we were able to talk without the weight of the night's purpose on our shoulders. Oliver told me more about his family. He was really proud of his parents. His mother had finished her degree even though she got pregnant with him during her sophomore year. His dad worked at UPS and made a good living. A year after their divorce was final, his father married a woman who had two kids, a boy and a girl, so Oliver had a half brother and two step-siblings. He actually liked his family, even his stepmother! He spent time with them *voluntarily.*

"My mother used to leave me home alone at night while she went out," I said. "One time she was gone for a week. I didn't know where she was."

"Damn," Oliver said, setting down his fourth slice of pizza.

"I went to school every day like nothing was wrong. I lived on apples, peanut butter and jelly, and Hershey bar—and—saltine s'mores. And every night I stayed awake waiting for her to get home. In some ways it wasn't very different than any other week. But as each day went by it got harder to believe that she was coming back."

"What did she say when she got home?"

"Not a thing. One day I came home from school and there she was."

"You didn't ask her where she had been?"

"I was eleven. What was I supposed to say?" I took a sip of my Coke. "I've never told this to anyone before. I vomited every morning before school. After three nights went by and she didn't come back, I knew she was dead. I packed all our stuff—dishes, clothes, everything—in boxes and garbage bags. We didn't have suitcases. I thought I'd be going to a foster home, and I didn't want the landlord to just throw Nona's things away. I hated the idea of them being in a Dumpster. I figured if our stuff was folded and packed nicely he would at least give it to Goodwill. I kept her grandmother's ring and a few other things with me."

"And when she found all her shit in a box, she didn't say nothing?"

"By the time I got home from school, everything was unpacked. The boxes and bags were gone. We never talked about it."

"I don't mean to talk about your mom—"

"No, go ahead," I encouraged.

"That is seriously fucked up."

"Thank you! Yes, it is!" I was thrilled to hear someone else say it, but I still couldn't say what was really messed up, that my worst fear wasn't that Nona had died. My worst fear was that she was alive and had simply walked away, leaving me behind for good. That's what had made my stomach churn all night.

We finished our pizza silently, content to sit side by side and listen to the music. Oliver called the crusts pizza bones. Now Mary J. Blige was singing "No More Drama." It was a song about ending a relationship—something I'd never done before—but *no more* was a soulful mantra that spoke to me all the same. *I* wanted to free myself from pain. *I* was tired of playing games. As Mary J. grew stronger, I grew stronger too. Mary J. walked away from her man, but for me to end my drama I was going to have to go *toward* mine. When she got to the line about how good it feels to let go, I leaned over and kissed Oliver right on the lips. He was surprised only for a second, then he kissed me back.

The chorus swelled and the music was like a wave over

us. We lay back on the couch and he started running his hands over my t-shirt. Mary J. was still singing "no more," but now I was just thinking *more*. When he put his hands under my shirt, we both opened our eyes and he paused to see if I would stop him. When I didn't, he caressed my stomach and my breasts. Everything began to tingle and tickle. His mouth was warm and spicy-tasting. We kept kissing, clumsily, bumping noses, his glasses cold against my forehead. I started giggling, it was so crazy and silly: I couldn't believe I was kissing Oliver Ollie Ol.

He stopped again. His glasses were smudged and fogged. "What?"

I stopped laughing. "Your glasses are kind of in the way."

"Oh. You want to go in my room?"

The futon was on the floor covered with a sleeping bag instead of a bedspread. A bass guitar rested next to the dresser. There was a desk with a laptop and textbooks. We sat on the futon. Oliver put his glasses on the floor next to the bed and we leaned back. He rolled on top of me. Without his glasses, his eyes were shiny black marbles, and the freckles across his eyelids, cheeks, and nose stood out like jimmies on butter-brickle ice cream.

"I have something we can use," he whispered in my ear. It took me a second to realize he meant a condom. I debated asking him to go get the Mary J. Blige CD so we could play it in here. But he was moving fast. He raised my shirt up over my bra and kissed my breasts, then quickly unzipped my pants and pulled them and my underwear down to my ankles. He unzipped his pants while I tried to kick my jeans and panties off. I only got one leg free by the time he was out of his jeans and was opening the condom. The flip-flopping of my stomach and the heat I felt between my legs were uncharted waters. Suddenly, I was in so far over my head I felt like I was drowning. I jumped up.

'"What's wrong?" he murmured, squinting his eyes.

"I need a minute." I pulled my shirt down, put my panties and jeans back on, ran into the bathroom, and leaned against the closed door. My heart was racing and I was almost panting. The bathroom was like the rest of the place. No towels in sight and instead of toilet paper, they had a stack of fast-food napkins on the back of the toilet. I sat down and put my head between my knees, trying to get my breathing under control.

"Hard to lie to yourself in a bathroom, isn't it?" asked a voice as rich and smooth as caramel.

I almost fell off the toilet.

"A bathroom is a truth-telling room if ever there was one," Nina Simone said, standing next to the door. Nina Simone, hair braided and piled on her head like a crown, dressed in a long black-and-white dashiki gown, was in Oliver's bathroom! I couldn't remember the last time I had asked myself WWNSD, yet here she was.

"Just tell him the truth."

She knew. Of course she knew. "You don't think he'll think I'm weird?"

She waved her hand dismissively. The High Priestess of Soul didn't give a damn what people thought. "And if he does?"

"Then I won't go through with it and I'll lose my last chance to change."

She looked around the small, dirty room. "Honey, if this is your last chance, it's not much of a chance, is it?"

Again, she was pointing out that I had nothing to lose. Oliver had been a good guy so far. I put my fingers to my lips. There was only one other guy I had even kissed as much as I kissed him. In my junior year in high school this boy named Joseph and I had gotten close, we talked on the phone all the time and he was the first boy I had kissed since third grade. One night I went to his house and I really thought I was going to do it. We were making out on the couch in the family room in his basement, and he ended up just dry humping me and ejaculating on my jeans.

I stood and looked at myself in the mirror, remembering how Nona looked at me when she saw me without my scarf, how good it felt to have the secret done with. I marched back into Oliver's bedroom. He was sitting with his back against the wall, still in his t-shirt, his lower half stretched out under the covers.

"I'm a virgin," I blurted.

He cocked his head and stared at me like I spoke Swahili. He still had his glasses off.

"A *virgin* virgin. I mean I've done nothing, nada, zero, zip. I'm twenty-five years old and I'm a virgin." Now that I had spoken the truth, I couldn't stop. I was trembling and pacing, and the truth poured out of me like pure, clean water. "I didn't plan to be. I mean, I wasn't saving myself for marriage or anything. It's just one of those things that happened, or I guess I should say one of those things that *didn't* happen. I was always kind of shy, and I didn't have a chance to be a normal teenager and explore . . . things . . .

like other girls, I was too busy being this little grown-up. My mother was out partying and running the streets when I was in high school and junior high, and you don't want to be out there doing what your mother is doing, and I have to say, she didn't make it seem very fun. She was always getting her heart stomped on. Who would want that?

"Besides, I always thought that eventually it would just happen, like moving on to the next grade or something, but after a while it became like some immutable condition, like being black or female. Well, being female I suppose you can change, but you know what I mean. And the longer I went, the more freakish I felt. And by the time I was in college, I couldn't imagine telling someone that I hadn't done it yet. Then, pretty soon, I was twenty-one, an official adult. How do you tell someone I'm a grown African American woman and I've never had sex before? Then came twenty-two, twenty-three, and so on, and then twenty-five. A quarter of a century!"

I stopped pacing. I had started pulling my hair again right before my birthday, and my birthday was the first day I took to my bed listening to Nina Simone. I hadn't put it together before now that turning twenty-five had triggered all this.

I finally ran out of steam. "And now here I am. That's the real me." I stood there before him as Someone Who Had Never Done It Before shivering though the room wasn't cold, waiting to see how he would react.

He still looked stunned. He reached over and cleaned his glasses and put them on.

I knew he wasn't really, but it felt like he was moving in

slow motion. If he didn't say something soon, I was going to run out of there so fast. "I know that's not what you expected to hear."

"Uh, no, it's not. What about Desi?"

Huh? How did he know about—Oh God! "That wasn't exactly one hundred percent the truth."

He waited for me to finish.

"I met a guy named Desi after I got here, but nothing happened between us. I didn't come home because of a man. I came home because . . . because I was having some troubles at school. My advisor made me take the semester off. He wanted me to take a year, but I convinced him I'd be okay after a semester, which took some pretty fast-talking because I wasn't sure I'd be okay after a semester, or ever—"

He was eyeing me the way you look at a bag lady talking to a Dumpster or the way you look at a stray dog while you're trying to figure out if it's going to bite you or not.

"But that's not really what we were talking about. . . ."

"It's going to sound like I'm trying to get over on you, but I can't believe some brother hasn't . . . You look . . . well, damn! And you're smart and . . . and . . . I don't know how you could still be single, let alone . . ."

"I know, I'm a loser!" I held my fingers up in an *L* against my forehead.

"No, that's not what I meant. It was supposed to be a compliment."

"You're the first person I ever told." Not even Stephanie knew. Whenever the topic of sex came up I acted like I knew what I was talking about. It was easy. I knew how to make myself feel good, and I'd seen enough people rolling around in bed on TV and in the movies that I figured I knew the basics. Once, being a good little student, I had even tried online research, and somehow ended up at a website that featured dozens of pictures of the crotches of white guys, with red penises proudly curving up or pink ones tucked shyly into nests of hair. Circumcised, uncircumcised, big, little, they were all more like mushrooms or strange little mammals than hot dogs or baseball bats or any of the other crass metaphors I'd heard. I suddenly wondered what else about sex was different than people made it out to be. Did people really do all that moaning and rolling around? The irony dawned on me: Other women talk about faking orgasms. I faked talking about them.

Oliver finally spoke. "I haven't been with that many girls myself."

Calm flooded my body. He didn't think I was a loser! I was so relieved I didn't know what to say.

When I didn't answer, he said, "You could at least *act* surprised." He clasped his hands to his chest and mocked me in a falsetto voice, "Oh, Oliver, no, not you! I would have thought you'd have been with lots of women."

I smiled, even more grateful for his attempt to lighten the mood. "You're a lot younger than I am. It makes more sense for you to have less experience. Besides, being with even one person has me beat."

He patted the bed next to him. I walked over and sat down.

He spoke, looking straight ahead, not at me. "I'm not going to push you. We don't have to do anything."

Oh yes we did. I had viewed an online penis parade, been lectured by a dead woman, and told my biggest secret. There was no going back. I turned and kissed him so that he would know my intentions.

I had imagined it millions of times, imagined a man loving me awake like Sleeping Beauty. Though romance had nothing to do with it today. I wasn't in love. I only desired to end this part of my life and start the next phase, finally. But even with the help of movies, there are things you can't know enough to make guesses about: sounds, smells, tastes. And what it would really feel like at the moment when that thin membrane that stood between me and everyone else my age, between my past and my future, was finally punctured. I always pictured it like a finger stretching through an uninflated balloon, but the feeling, physically and emotionally, had to remain a question mark until today.

He did all the things I was sure a lover was supposed to do, caressing the right places and whispering the right words. I relaxed but stayed focused, waiting for the moment I was set free. Then it came. I felt it deep inside myself, and I stretched open like that balloon. Open and open and open.

Afterward, we lay there together for a minute, then he took the condom off and went into the bathroom. I heard him pee and flush the toilet and wash his hands. He crossed the room, holding the pizza box, grinning like a maniac, and squinting to see without his glasses. He was naked from the waist down, and his afro and his penis bounced as he jogged over to the bed.

I started laughing again and couldn't stop. It wasn't

pretty. I was snorting and tears were streaming down my face.

He shook his head at me, but after he put on his glasses, he kissed me three times quick on the lips, making loud smacking noises each time. Then he said "Yes!" like he was giving me a verbal high five.

"Yes," I said back, giggling so hard he probably didn't even know what I said. I just kept thinking, *I lost my virginity.* And it sounded so absurd, like it was my mind or a set of car keys or something I could recover and use again. I tried to say *Pardon me, Oliver, I seem to have misplaced my virginity. Have you seen it?* But I started howling again. I'd seen Nona on many a drunken crying jag. I didn't know there was such a thing as a laughing jag.

"I guess I should be glad that something finally got you laughing, but I don't know that this should be it," he said.

"I've been . . . I've been. . . ."

"What?"

"I've been *deflowered*!"

"You're trippin'."

"Buh-bye, flower. See ya!"

He picked a pizza bone out of the box on the floor, took a huge bite, and chewed happily.

THE NEXT MORNING, I knew it was asinine and cliché, but I couldn't help it: I had to look in the mirror to see if I looked different. Naturally I didn't, but I was a little disappointed. I had secretly expected that an act as momentous as losing my virginity would somehow show. I recovered from my disappointment quickly, though. I might be the same old Shay on the outside, but on the inside I knew I was a whole other woman. And that was good enough.

I had just stepped out of the shower when the bathroom door flew open, and there was Matt. I quickly grabbed a towel and covered myself. We stared at each other for a fraction of a second before I recovered. "What are you doing here?" I shouted.

"I live here. So the question, Dudalicious, is what are *you* doing here?" He grinned slowly. "And I think I have an answer." He started doing the white-boy cabbage-patch dance.

He looked so ridiculous, I laughed with him until I remembered I was dripping wet and wearing only a towel. I closed the door. Usually, I would quickly dry off and hop in my clothes, but today I went slowly. I patted myself dry, showing my thighs, stomach, arms, and breasts more attention than I'd ever shown them, as if I were seeing them for the first time.

When I came out, Matt was still in the hallway.

" 'Bout time! Almost made a dude hafta use the sink," he said as he slipped by me into the bathroom.

I went into Oliver's room. He was gone. I still couldn't believe what I had done in this sloppy room just a few hours ago. Did it really happen? I lifted the sleeping bag back and saw my proof: a small, dark stain on the sheets. In some cultures, it would be appropriate to hang the sheet out the window to show the world the man had claimed the woman. But surely, even in ancient times and primitive cultures, some of those women must have felt like I did: not so much claimed as the one who had done the claiming. I had claimed adulthood for myself. I had crossed over, at twenty-five, and left girlhood behind. Finally. I could hear Nina Simone saying *Brava*.

I put on my shoes and grabbed my backpack. In the living room, Oliver was sitting on the couch in sweatpants. Somehow he looked more substantial, as if his bony chest and chicken legs had filled out over night. Next to him was a cute, dark-skinned guy dressed in a Foot Locker uniform and eating a sandwich. He saw me first and said, "Hey."

Oliver smiled broadly, proud to have a girl over the next morning. "This is Will."

I said hi, then asked Oliver, "Matt is one of your roommates?"

"Didn't you know that?" He came over to me and stood close enough to whisper. "Want a cheese sandwich?"

The whoosh of air as he spoke and the energy pulsing from him like an electrical current that I was now plugged into made me shy again. I shook my head.

"I'll walk you to your car."

Outside, we stood next to my ladybug, blinking at each other in the morning sunlight. I put my hand on Oliver's suddenly stalwart chest. He had shepherded me over into my new life, and I would be forever grateful to him. "Thank you for being so understanding about . . . everything."

He rubbed his chin—his goatee also seemed to have filled out in just a few hours. "I'm the one who should be thanking you."

My face flushed, and he kissed me on my burning cheek. Brava indeed.

Four Women

ONE OF NINA SIMONE'S MOST FAMOUS SONGS IS "FOUR Women." When you first hear it, it sounds like a dirge about four African American women, struggling and abused, and how their different skin tones dictate their status in life. But as Nina Simone tells their stories and sings their names—Aunt Sarah, Saffronia, Sweet Thing, Peaches—she gives them each a voice, a place at the table, and by the end what seemed sad feels empowering.

Now that Ivy, Nona, Sunny, and I were living together, the bass line of the song went through my head often. I wondered what Nina Simone would think of the four of us. Was this what she planned? Me living with my sister, my mother, and my mother's A.A. protégée? I hadn't seen Nina Simone since she appeared in Oliver's bathroom. I wasn't listening to her songs anymore. I was too busy catching up on Mary J. Blige's work. But still "Four Women" was the sound track that ran through my mind.

At first, things with the four of us went along smoothly. Ivy and I didn't see each other that much. But our work schedules made it so that we were both home for dinner at the same time a couple of nights a week, and we all managed to sit and eat together like civilized people. No bickering. No snide remarks. Maybe it was because I wasn't carrying my big secret anymore, but Ivy didn't get to me as much. Also, it seemed like she had switched tactics. Instead of trying to get me to leave, she seemed to have decided "if you can't beat 'em, join 'em."

The other night we each pulled up to the house at four o'clock in the morning. I was coming from Oliver's and she was getting home from work. I felt sheepish about creeping in in the middle of the night. I hadn't told Nona that I was dating, and I really didn't want to hear Ivy's taunts.

But she just grinned at me a little as we walked up the path, and she didn't say a thing.

The next evening at dinner, Nona kept shooting strange looks at me.

Finally, I couldn't take it anymore. "What?!"

"Nothing," she said, pursing her lips in a vain attempt to suppress a grin.

"Then, why are you gawking at me?"

"I'm not gawking." She took a bite of salad.

I rolled my eyes.

Her grin broke through. "Okay, I'm gawking. So, when are you going to tell me about this guy you're seeing?"

"Why do you think I'm seeing someone?" A bite of chicken breast suddenly thick in my throat.

She cocked her head to the side. "You and Stephanie are a little old for slumber parties, aren't you?"

"Leave the girl alone, Nona," Ivy said.

Nona and I both whipped around at Ivy.

She pretended not to notice our shock. "She's a grown woman, right?" she said to Nona, then to me, "Do your thing, girl."

"Thank you." I couldn't believe I was actually *thanking* Ivy. Maybe all that "A.A. homework" was really working?

"You're welcome," she said cheerfully, handing Sunny one of her sweet potato fries, which Sunny promptly ate without complaint.

Nona's mouth hung open at the two of us.

But since Nona and I were getting along better too, I answered her, "His name's Oliver. We work together."

"And you like him?"

I nodded.

"I'm so glad." Glad? She looked like she was about to explode from joy.

Suddenly the air was thick with pink cotton-candy sentiment. I actually hoped that Ivy would say something sarcastic or that Sunny would make one of her silly jokes, anything to break up the sappiness.

"Chocolate cake for dessert?" Nona offered.

Ivy and Sunny went for it, but I said no. Things were getting too sweet around here as it was.

WE QUICKLY FELL into a routine. On Sunday, Nona, Sunny, and Ivy went to church and I stayed home and read the paper. On Thursday night, I watched Sunny while Ivy and Nona went to an A.A. meeting. Sunny and I read and danced around the living room, Big Silly and Little Silly, until it was time for her to take a bath and go to bed. We listened to Mary J. Blige and some of Nona's throwback CDs. In addition to gospel, Nona was partial to Earth, Wind & Fire, Marvin Gaye, Rufus and Chaka Khan, Prince, and Stevie Wonder. When I told Oliver that Sunny and I listened to Stevie Wonder's *Innervisions* album, he bowed before me and said, "Ah, the student has surpassed the master."

You would think that all the time with Nona would have been enough for Ivy to get over her jealousy, but sometimes I noticed her staring at Nona and me like we were something shiny and expensive in a store window. Once I caught her watching Nona with such naked yearning that I was embarrassed for her. We both looked away quickly and avoided each other the rest of the day.

EVEN THOUGH SUNNY and I were getting closer (I had even learned how to give her a nebulizer), she still doted on Ivy.

But one night Ivy, who had become the official table-setter, called Sunny to the table, and instead of sitting in her usual spot next to Ivy, Sunny climbed into the chair next to me.

"You have to sit in your booster seat," Ivy said.

"I want to sit by Shay."

Loss flickered across Ivy's face.

"Just move her booster seat over." Nona spoke casually because she didn't see Ivy's expression.

Ivy stood there, frozen. Sunny picked it up and moved it next to my chair.

Ivy sat down. She was only across the table from us, but she looked like she felt a world away.

"SHAY, COME HERE!"

It was Sunday afternoon. Nona, Ivy, and Sunny had just come home from church. I was still in my pajamas in bed with the *Denver Post*. It was almost all bad news: Suicide bombers in too many places to name. There was flooding in the Northwest, tornadoes in the South, and an early blizzard in the East. And a little black girl in Colorado Springs had been missing for over a year before anybody bothered to report it. The police think her foster parents killed her.

Stephanie was still on the wedding beat. This week she reported on three couples who got married at the top of Pikes Peak, while rafting the Colorado River, and in a hot-air balloon above Steamboat Springs. I was going to the Berrys' later to watch the Broncos game. I'd have to congratulate her on turning her personal obsession into a career.

"Shay, come see!"

I got up and went into the prairie room to see what all the fuss was about.

"Look!" Nona was so excited, she hadn't even taken off her jacket. She reached into a paper sack and pulled out a framed photo the size of a vinyl album. It was the picture of the three of us that Ivy had taken the day I got my hair done.

"I always wanted a family portrait," she said giddily. "This was number one on my list of things to do to be good to myself. Wait till I tell Lois."

Nona didn't have a new sponsor yet, but she and Lois wrote each other often.

"Lord, look at us. You and Sunny look like I just spit you out," she continued.

The three of us smiled out from the photo. We did look alike. And we looked something close to happy, me with my new hair, Sunny delighted at having her picture taken, and Nona over the moon at being with us both.

Ivy went to the refrigerator. She was dressed for church in a black pantsuit and fake pearls, her hair pulled into a severe bun. "I'll get the food started. You wanted to reheat the greens, right?"

"Yeah, sure," Nona said, distractedly. "Where should we put it?"

"It's huge," I said.

"Oh, I don't think it's big enough. I want to be able to see it from every part of the room." Nona went to the bookcase and moved the picture of her, Lois, and Ivy to a lower shelf and replaced it with the family portrait. "There," she said with satisfaction. She stood back to admire it from different angles.

"What do you all think?"

"It looks okay," I said.

"It looks great!" Sunny said, also still wearing her coat.

"Ivy?"

We turned around. The refrigerator door was open and Ivy was gone.

"Hmm." Nona went and closed the refrigerator and turned right back around to gaze at the picture. "Looks good from here too."

A FEW NIGHTS LATER, I had just gotten Sunny out of the tub and was drying her off. As soon as she was in bed and Nona was home, I was going over to Oliver's to "have pizza," as we called it.

When Nona and Ivy came in from their meeting, Sunny ran and hugged Nona.

"Don't you smell good? I could just eat you up," Nona said, blowing raspberries on her neck. "Say good night to Ivy and Shay."

"I want Shay to tuck me in."

Nona raised her eyebrows playfully. "Well!" She gave Sunny to me and I took her to bed.

When I returned to the prairie room, Ivy was retrieving a long blue velvet box from her purse on the floor and handing it to Nona.

"Uh-oh. What's this?" Nona asked.

"It's to thank you," Ivy said, wriggling in her chair excitedly.

Nona opened it and revealed a thick gold necklace. "Ivy, I can't accept this."

Ivy's smile dimmed. "Why?"

"It's too expensive."

"But, you let me stay here, you gave me all those books . . ."

Nona snapped the lid closed and handed the box back to Ivy. "I told you: You don't have to pay me to help you. I *want* to. Besides, you need to be saving your money to get your own place."

Ivy looked shattered. "I guess you don't have room for me anymore."

"That's not what I'm saying," Nona said. "I—"

"No, it's okay," Ivy said. "I'll take it back." Her bruises had healed and she was dancing four or five nights a week, but when she stood, she put her hand on her back like it hurt her. "I'm going to take a hot bath."

Nona didn't jump up to help her this time.

THAT SUNDAY, Nona and Sunny went to church alone, and Ivy stayed asleep on the couch. The following Thursday, Ivy didn't show up to go to their meeting.

Ivy came home after I went to bed, and I heard them talking.

"Why did you miss the meeting?" Nona asked.

"I been doing doubles to try to get my money straight so I can move," Ivy replied coldly.

"You're treading on some really thin ice here."

"Don't worry about me. You don't see me using, do you?"

"Be careful, Ivy."

Things grew tense between them after that.

—

A COUPLE OF NIGHTS LATER Oliver was studying for a test so I hung out at home. Nona, Sunny, and I watched *American Idol*. Sunny liked the cutest boys the best, no matter how they sounded. We were going to have to keep our eyes on her.

The phone rang, Nona answered and I could tell by the look on her face it wasn't good.

"What?" I asked.

She looked at her watch. "Nothing."

But it *was* something because she kept looking at her watch and getting up to look out the window. I knew it had something to do with Ivy.

Sunny was in bed. I was sorting laundry in the prairie room. Nona was sitting at the kitchen table paying bills. Ivy walked in wearing a slip dress over a pair of jeans, no coat, and sunglasses. At 10:30 at night with frost on the ground. "Hiiiii, Nona." She bent down and hugged Nona, then walked over to hug me. "Hiiiii, Shay."

She flopped down on the chair across from Nona and grinned as if she was acting completely normal.

"Come on, Nona. Let's go do somethin'! Don't y'all get sick of just sittin' around this house all the time, like, doing nothin'? Come on, let's do somethin'. Please, can we go do somethin'!"

She sounded crazy. She'd just walked in the door and she was already talking about leaving.

Nona put her pen down and closed her checkbook. "What in the world do you think you're doing?"

"What?" Ivy asked. She wore a thick coat of foundation to cover her bad skin while she worked. It might have looked good on stage or in a dark bar, but in this light it was a chalky mask.

"Stop it," Nona said.

Ivy's shoulders drooped. She jiggled her knees like she was bouncing an invisible baby. "It was, like, just a couple of beers with a customer."

She was on something way more than a couple of beers.

"Somebody named Cherry called here three hours ago looking for you. She said you had been at the club, but you left just when you were supposed to start working."

"I went out with some friends."

"I told you if you're going to stay here, you had to stay clean. That was the deal."

"Fine. Clean. I promise. Whatever." She put her stiletto-shod feet up on the chair across from her and slouched down. The straps of her dress slid off her shoulders.

"I swear to God, Ivy, if you're not going to take your sobriety seriously, I can't help you." Nona's voice trembled.

"I said no more drinks! Dag, you sound like my mother."

Nona nodded. "Maybe that's where we went wrong. I'm not your mother. Maybe I shouldn't have tried to be your friend. I'm your sponsor. Lois warned me not to let a sponsee move in with me."

Ivy sat up and pulled her straps up. "Nona, I'm tired. God, I get tired. I'm working like a dog. I'm trying so hard. How long do I have to keep doing this before I get a break?"

"As long as it takes," Nona snapped, to my surprise. I expected her to feel sorry for Ivy, like she usually did, but I had never seen her so mad.

"You get a break when you're off parole, when you get your kids back, when you can stand on your own two feet like a grown woman and look yourself in the mirror and like what you see. Then, *maybe* you can take a break. You think this is a game we been playing?"

Ivy tilted her head to the floor.

"Answer me! You see me working my behind off around here. Do you think I have time to waste on you?"

Ivy's head jerked up. "You slipped. You told me."

"That's right. And what else did I tell you? That it scared the hell out of me and I did ninety meetings in ninety days and never looked back."

"Well, that's you, okay? Not everybody can be you."

"You don't have to be like me, but you do have to be straight if you want me to be your sponsor."

"You won't be my sponsor no more?" Ivy asked.

"I don't know, Ivy. You don't act like a person who wants a sponsor. You don't act like a person who wants to be sober."

Ivy tottered up on her heels. Her voice was hard-edged, the girlishness gone. "You know what, you fucked a nigga you met in A.A. They tell you not to even get a fucking dog and you got a baby! You ain't no better than me!"

I was going through pants pockets pulling out receipts and wadded tissues, but I stopped. This had been building for a while, and I knew it was going to be bad. I don't know how she did it, but Nona stayed composed.

When Ivy realized Nona wasn't going to respond, she got her duffel bag from the hall closet. "I knew it. You don't care nothing about me! I thought you was different."

"You're not turning this around on me. You're not a victim here. Your actions have consequences."

Ivy nodded at me. "*She* can stay, but I have to get out?"

"If you're not going to follow the rules."

"I got your fucking rules and your fucking consequences." Ivy went over to the bookcase and knocked over the picture of us. It clattered to the floor, but, remarkably, the glass didn't break.

Nona's bedroom door opened. Sunny stood blinking in the light.

"It's time for you to go," Nona said softly, sounding and looking suddenly drained.

Ivy stood there for a moment longer, then left.

"Whoa." I let out the breath I was holding.

Nona put her hand up. "Shay, please. I don't want to hear it." She picked up the photo and put it back, then went to Sunny and held her.

We heard Ivy burn rubber through the intersection as she drove away.

Nona rocked Sunny, and I loaded all the dark colors into the laundry basket. Right before I turned the washer on, I heard Nona say, "As long as it takes. What other choice do we have?"

Tell It

AFTER I LOST MY VIRGINITY, I DID NOT GO LOOKING for it. Instead I went hunting for a new dress to wear to Stephanie's wedding. I found it right away. Silver, spaghetti straps, tea-length, satin. It was elegant, sophisticated, and sexy. I found a size eight and looked at the price tag: $298. With shoes and purse and new lingerie to wear under it, it would cost almost half of what I had saved. I picked up the hanger and went into the dressing room.

As I had imagined, I slipped it over my head and it slid down my body like soft water. I looked in the mirror. It was cut low in the front and even lower in the back, showing more of my skin than anything I'd ever worn, except underwear. Maybe it would make Oliver look at me like he did the chick with the nipples.

When I got home, Nona was outside in the garden with her notebook. Denver's mercurial weather was now warm.

We didn't need coats. She stood and brushed the dirt off her hands. "What's in the bags?"

"A dress for Stephanie's wedding." I pulled it out and showed it to her.

"You look happy," she said. "I hope you are."

I nodded. I was getting there. But *she* didn't look happy. She was still grieving over Ivy. That's probably what she was doing out there with her notebook, turning Ivy over to the God box.

"I want to ask you a big favor." She studied the ground, already afraid of my answer. "I'm going to be speaking in church on Sunday about my sobriety. Will you come to hear my testimony? It would mean a lot to me."

She looked back up at me, her eyes pleading.

She was going to apologize again, like she did in Iowa four years ago. I could tell. But this time publicly. It dawned on me that I was a new woman, maybe Nona was too. Maybe the "After Shay" could give the "After Nona" a chance? I took a deep breath and said I would.

ON SUNDAY, I sat in church and thought about the Virgin Mary without feeling embarrassed for the first time. Now that I wasn't one anymore, I could face the virgin. I wanted to go to a cathedral and light a candle for her. I wanted to eat a salad dripping in extra virgin olive oil. I wished I was a Virgo.

Today, in church, even though I was nervous about what Nona was going to say, I could enjoy myself. Foot on the Rock was a small, nondescript, blond-brick building.

Inside, though, the congregation had made it their own, filling it with paintings of black Jesuses and stained-glass windows of Martin Luther King, Jr. and Rosa Parks. The pastor, Reverend McGuire, was a hoarse-voiced, powerful-looking woman in royal blue robes. The choir could sing their behinds off, and when I joined with a hundred other voices lifted up in songs in which praying and thanking were the same thing, the air in the room curved into a warm embrace.

The church secretary finished the announcements and Reverend McGuire said, "Now Sister Dixon will deliver today's testimony."

Nona sat Sunny on the pew, smiled at me, and sauntered to the pulpit, her chocolate brown dress billowing like a sail in the wind.

Here we go. I felt a trickle of sweat slide from my right armpit down my side.

"Greetings, everybody. God is good," Nona purred into the microphone.

"All the time," the room responded.

"Y'all don't know how much I need to be here this morning."

"Tell it!"

"Or maybe you do?" she egged them on, laughing. She didn't seem nervous at all.

"Amen!"

"I need to be reminded that I can say 'God is good' with complete conviction because I am living proof. Many of you know I'm a recovering alcoholic. I've been sober four years."

"Hallelujah!"

"The reason I'm sober is because of God's mercy. You see, I gave my life up to God—"

One of the women in the choir shouted "Amen!" and Nona revved up another notch.

"I gave my life up to God," she repeated louder, standing on her tiptoes to be seen over the mike. "Because I finally realized I was going to die if I didn't. I was *killing* myself with alcohol and stupidity and one day I decided I wanted to *live*."

"Thankya, Jesus!" Fans and handkerchiefs started waving in the air. Two women on the other side of the room rose and swayed back and forth like mothers rocking upset babies, like they were listening to the same lullaby. The woman in front of me leapt to her feet, and started bouncing up and down, her green-polyester-covered butt jiggling in my face.

Sunny started to climb down from the pew to start dancing too. "Sit still." I pinched the back of her yellow dress and slid over to see around Ms. Jell-O Booty.

"I asked Jesus to come into my heart—"

A skinny, white-haired man stood and called out, "Oh, Father, we thank you!"

"I invited Jesus to come into my life and my life has never been the same since. Whatever success I have I owe to God. And I just wanna thank Him today."

"Thankya, Jesus!"

Nona drew back and paused melodramatically, her gold hoops catching the light. "I want to thank Him and ask for

His help. A friend of mine needs Him. Her name is Ivy, and if you would add her to your prayers and ask God to help her find her way back home to herself, I would appreciate it. Y'all came to my rescue when I needed it and I hope you will with Ivy."

"Yes! Yes!"

"Coming back to the church I could see that I should have died a long time ago, but God had other plans for me, and her name is Sunny."

Nona curled her hands into balls and pressed them against her chest as if to keep all the love she was feeling from exploding out of her heart. "My baby girl is three now, and I strive every day to make her as proud of me as I am of her."

"All praises!"

"My other daughter, LaShay, is here today too," Nona said, pointing at me. I could feel all the eyes of the congregation on me. This was it. The apology. I wanted it and at the same time I didn't know if I was ready for it. I held my breath and waited for what the After Nona was going to say, and how the After Shay was going to respond.

"So again, I thank God and I thank all of you. God bless you."

For a few seconds all I could do was blink. That was it? That was all she had to say about me? That I was here, her "other daughter," part of her adoring audience? This is what I got for giving her another chance? What about the fact that she didn't get sober for *me*? Even after all she did, Ivy got a call for prayers. Sunny got credit for keeping

Nona alive. And I got nothing. Like always. How did I let myself get my hopes up again? What the hell was I thinking?

One of the women who had been swaying started applauding. Pretty soon everyone, except me and a few people too old to stand, was up on their feet, getting happy, shouting and dancing. The scents of hair oil, cocoa butter, baby powder, perfume, and sweat rose into the air.

I grew dizzy, and before I knew what I was doing I was standing too. I shouted, "Shay! My name is Shay, not LaShay!" Goddamn it, she could at least say my name right. Every time she said it, it sounded like "la shade," like I was the darkness over everything. And Sunshine, well, of course, she was the bright reason for Nona's new life.

A few people turned to stare.

They didn't have the right to forgive her. She hadn't wounded them! She hadn't abandoned them! They didn't know her. They didn't know what she'd done. I shouted, "You can't get anything else right, at least you get my name right!"

One by one members of the choir stopped singing and folks stopped dancing until everybody was looking at me and the room was quiet.

"What are you doing?" Nona asked.

Nona's story about her past, *our* past, had been short and sweet. Her drinking just one quick bass note and the rest all flutes and harps. "You want to tell your story, so let's tell your story! Let's tell them how you left me at home alone at night to go do God knows what! Let's tell them I wasn't asleep when you left me at home in bed! I was never asleep.

And you knew it! You knew it! Before you left, you'd tell me to be good. So you knew I wasn't asleep, or why would you say that?" We had both pretended that I was asleep when she left and, simultaneously, that she never left at all. But I was sick and tired of pretending.

"Young lady, this is neither the time nor the place," Reverend McGuire said calmly. "If you want to have a conversation with your mother, you can take this in my office."

"Where were you?" I demanded of Nona.

"What?" Nona looked like she was having a small stroke.

"When you left me alone that time for an entire week, where did you go?"

People were watching us like a reality TV show or a car wreck, but I didn't care. Let them look. Let them bear witness.

Nona inhaled and exhaled deeply, composing herself. We all waited for her answer. I could see her weighing what to say, or perhaps how to say it. I had always had my suspicions, but I wanted to hear her say it, wanted her to finally admit it to me.

"I was with a man," she said.

There was a collective gasp from the congregation.

"We went to a motel room. We stayed high for days, drinking Seagram's, even doing a little coke. He told me he loved me. One day I woke up and he was gone, so I went back home."

There it was: The truth exposed like a bone in front of us. I had thought I wanted honesty, but now I knew there was still a small part of me that had hoped she was going to say something else—she had been in detox, tried rehab, had amnesia and didn't remember she had a little girl at home—anything else but that. It turned out I would have rather heard a lie than to hear my own mother say she had chosen booze and a man over me. That week while I waited up every night wondering if she was dead or if she had left me for good, she had consciously, willingly abandoned me.

It was dead silent. Even the babies seemed to know not to cry.

Nona spoke softly, but she was still near the microphone so we could all hear her. "I was a terrible mother and a terrible person for so long I could barely stand to look at myself in the mirror. I hated myself for what I did to you."

"But you're over it now, right? You're all recovered and Miss Mental and Spiritual Health. Now I'm just supposed to forget my whole childhood?"

"That's not what I meant."

"I don't care what you meant. I don't care how you feel. Nona, you *left* me!"

"I'll be paying for it the rest of my life." Twin rivers ran from her eyes and met at the tip of her chin.

"And so will I! And you will never understand that!"

"I do understand. I hurt you—"

"*Hurt me?! Hurt me?!* You left me alone all the time! Every night! And even when you were around, you were passed out or hungover most of the time. I might as well have been an orphan."

I noticed several women shaking their heads, taking my side. Two ushers came over seemingly to drag me out, but Ms. Jell-O Booty dashed next to me and crossed her arms. They were going to have to get through her formidable self before they got to me. She nodded at me, *I got your back*. I could see in her eyes that she knew how it felt for a parent to walk away, and I wanted to hug her for standing with me.

"I'm agreeing with you, okay?" Nona said, not quiet anymore. "I blew it! I screwed up royally! And I'm sorry. How many times can I say it?" She shook her head. "You don't want to let go of this. I can't make amends unless *you* face the fact that you want to hold on to your grudge."

Women all over the church went "Mmmm hmmm" at the same time.

"Hell yes, I have a grudge! Do you know that up until very recently, I was a—" I'd be damned if I let a whole room full of strangers know I just lost my virginity. "All this time I thought I was scared of relationships. But I was scared of myself. I was terrified that I'd end up like you and fuck everything up. But I'm nothing like you! I'll never be like you!"

"Sister!" Reverend McGuire said. "You will not disrespect the Lord's house!"

The white-haired man yelled, "Honor thy father and mother!"

"I wanted to be better than my mother too," Nona said, done crying, her hands back in fists, but this time she didn't look like she wanted to keep anything held in. "I had to work hard to forgive her, and understand what she went through. The things that made her who she was."

I finally said what I had thought when we had our first blowup. "This! Is! Not! About! You! Can't you get that?"

"Lord Jesus, don't let me lose it up in here!" Nona took a

breath. "You know what, LaShay? Yeah, I called you by your name. You ain't the only one who had a hard childhood! You ain't the only one who has ever been hurt!"

Several women clapped loudly, and emboldened, Nona squared her shoulders and walked determinedly down the long aisle of the church. "But I haven't been able to blame anybody for my past since I was eighteen years old and my mother put me out. I have said to you straight up: I'm sorry! That's more than most of us ever get. You better believe my mother never admitted anything close to being wrong. Shoot, Donnajean would have eaten a bowl of rusty nails with sour milk before she would have ever said she was sorry to me! *Out loud?* And if you won't even try . . . If you can't even see . . ."

Reverend McGuire interrupted again. "Sisters, please. I know y'all have a lot to say to each other. Please go into my office. You can have your privacy there."

"You think it makes everything okay because you apologized to me a couple of times?"

"That's right!" one of my people shouted. A daughter, no doubt.

Nona stopped in front of me. "A couple of times? I'm always apologizing! There's always something I don't do right or say right. But as of right now I'm through being sorry. I'm through arguing with you. I'm done. I give up." She put her hands up, actually threw her hands up as if she were flinging me off them!

I couldn't believe it! She had the nerve to say *she* was giving up on *me*? Blood was pounding in my ears. Something inside me broke open and a feeling rushed out of me so electric the hairs on the back of my neck stood up. "Fuck you!" shot out of my mouth like lightning, and Nona recoiled as if I had slapped her.

"THAT'S IT!" Reverend McGuire shouted, her eyes blazing. "Y'all are done showing out in my church! Either you're gonna go into my office and discuss this like civilized, grown women or you're gonna leave. Right now."

Nona stared at me for a few long seconds. No headlight eyes, no chewed lips. All her features stayed as blank as a computer screen before you boot up. For once, she did not look like she was about to laugh.

"I'm so sorry," she said finally to Reverend McGuire, her voice quivering. "Come on, Sunny." She picked up their coats, took Sunny's hand, and all but ran out of the church. Sunny looked back at me. Her small face full of fear and confusion.

Everyone stared at me, buzzing with the story they would tell for weeks, if not months, while Reverend McGuire worked to quiet them down. But there was no way they'd ever get it right. They'd never know that I had changed from a frightened child into a woman right before their eyes. Because it wasn't losing my virginity that made me an adult. It was telling the truth about my feelings. It was looking Nona in the face and saying what I needed to say.

I walked out of the church thinking about the Nina Simone song that had been playing the night I pulled into town. She was wrong. You don't have to choose. A gal who's been forgotten doesn't have to forgive *or* forget.

My Baby

"NOW CAN I COME IN?" I ASKED.

"No!"

I was sitting on the floor in the hall, my back against the closed door to Oliver's bedroom. On the other side, he was up to something. A surprise. He wasn't scheduled for work today and had skipped classes. As far as I knew he had started after I left for work and had been at it all day.

I came to stay with him after the fight at church. I showed up at his house still arguing with Nona, cussing like a sailor and jabbing my finger in the air. "*You're* done? *You're* done? I'm not a fucking plate of leftover food for the fucking busboy to fucking take away! You're done with me? Well, guess what? I'm through with you too!"

He let me jab and cuss until I was hoarse, then he poured me a bowl of Lucky Charms and welcomed me into his room like he had been waiting for me.

I gave him an out. I told him Stephanie was busy with the wedding and moving into her new house, but Mr. Berry probably wouldn't mind if I stayed with him for a few weeks. "You're not going anywhere," he said.

It was chilly in the hallway. The old house was drafty, and the guys kept the thermostat turned down low. We all wore layers. I folded my knees to my chest. "You're making me nervous about what you're doing in there."

"Just don't come in."

I don't typically care for surprises, but I could smell paint fumes, and had an inkling of what he was doing. We were getting along remarkably well. I didn't even care that the place was a pit. I was having fun. We ate off paper plates and slept in a sleeping bag. It was like being away at camp. We ate junk food and stayed up half the night talking, listening to music, and making love, and slept late almost every morning. Camp for grown-ups.

Finally, he opened the door and helped me up off the floor. I still couldn't believe how young he was—he would turn twenty in June. He told me to close my eyes. I did as he said and he guided me into the bedroom.

"Okay, open 'em up."

The walls were painted a creamy sage green. The futon was now up off the ground on a frame and was draped by a black-and-white mud cloth spread. A table and reading lamp were next to the bed. The piles of clothes, shoes, and books were gone. His desk was tidy and the hardwood floor gleamed.

I looked at Oliver. Looked around the room, then

looked at him again. I realized the reason I didn't like surprises: Up until today they were always bad. "You did this by yourself?"

"You don't need to be sleeping on the floor. Look." He opened the closet. Half the rack was empty. "Now there's room for your stuff. Here." He reached up and got brand-new fluffy white towels off the shelf and handed them to me.

My eyes started to fill. It happened all the time lately. Hip-hop songs. Sitcoms. TV commercials. Grumpy customers, nice ones. The blush on a ripe Bartlett pear. I hated it. "All this is for me?"

He made an "aw-shucks" grin. "You're my baby. The walls are still kind of wet, so be careful."

"Won't you get in trouble with your landlord?"

"Not as long as I paint it white again before I move."

Oliver didn't have money to spend on futon frames and bedspreads. He must have charged this stuff or borrowed money from his mom.

I stupidly burst into tears. "This is the nicest thing anybody has ever done for me."

He took the washcloth off the top of the pile in my hand and wiped my eyes. It was so soft and fluffy it only made me blubber more.

OLIVER JUMPED UP and down on the bed wearing nothing but white sweat socks and a smile, singing at the top of his lungs. "Glory, Glory hallelujah! Her truth is marching on!"

"Will you be quiet?" Though I just finished letting out a

scream myself, which I couldn't believe I did. But I was learning: What I liked and what Oliver liked. What we both wanted and needed. And the world had opened up to me in all kinds of brand-new ways. I didn't know I could feel so good. I didn't know this good existed for *anybody*. It was like cells deep in my body suddenly came alive and started moving. I swear I could feel them doing the rumba under my skin. I felt leonine, like I finally matched my new mane. My hair had started to grow back, sparsely populating the bald areas, and each little curl next to my scalp, the new growth, looked glad to be there. They actually vibrated. My whole body vibrated. I felt awake and aware of myself in a way I never had been before. When I walked, I felt my feet on the earth. I felt breezes on the little hairs on my forearms. The roof of my mouth and the insides of my cheeks tickled.

"I want the whole world to know! 'Mine eyes have seen the glory of the coming of the Lord—' "

I grabbed his skinny ankle. "Stop it! Your roommates are going to hear you. Or somebody's going to call the police."

He kept jumping and laughing. "It's your fault for whipping it on me like that. What else can I say?"

He was right. What else was there to say? We were happy and life was good. I pulled the covers off, climbed up, and started jumping. My truth was marching on.

Tangled Up

I WAS TIRED AFTER BEING AT WORK ALL DAY, AND Oliver had a paper due so I stopped at Blackberries Ice Cream and Coffee. I parked behind a group of people standing around a car, listening to the stereo. It was only six in the evening and getting dark, but in the streetlight I could see they were already drinking out of paper bags. Their car doors were open and rap was thumping so loudly it made *my* windows shake. I walked in the shop, bought a small mocha for me and got Oliver a large latte and two scoops of espresso ice cream, and headed back to my car, the scent of weed wafting over me.

There was a girl with her back to me. She tilted her head to drink, and the tip of her long sandy ponytail reached her behind. Just when I was wondering where I knew her from, she turned around. We recognized each other at the same time.

"Oh shit," Ivy said, grinning. "Miss Thang."

She had on a short skirt and Payless-looking platforms, and so much foundation she looked like a ghost. She was obviously trying to look grown and sexy, but it had the exact opposite affect. She looked like a little girl playing dress up. "Got your hair done, now you too good to speak?" she asked. "Hold up, you always did think you was too good to speak."

"You're high."

"Aw girl, this is how we do."

I was way too tired for this. I tried to step around her, but she got in my way.

"Who that is?" A man in a do-rag asked her, while trying to hold in a mouthful of smoke.

"Her mother used to be my friend," she told him over her shoulder. "You can treat her like shit and, like, that's okay. She still gotta love you, right? 'Cause you really her daughter. Not me. Me she can kick to the curb. Even though my own mother don't do shit for me, don't care about me at all."

I noticed she was wearing a necklace that looked like the one she bought for Nona. I stepped to the other side and she met me again. I flashed to the last time we did this dance, how scared I was. But this time I wasn't afraid. Apparently losing your virginity and telling off your mother in front of her whole congregation builds courage. "Move out of my way."

"Shit, they gon' fight," Do-rag said. "Handle ya bizness, girl!"

"You and your mama can kiss my yellow ass!" Ivy pushed me on the chest.

I fell back, spilling hot coffee on my hand, dropping everything. I shoved her back. Hard. She stumbled on her high heels.

The fellas whooped. "Oh, it's on now!"

My mind started working fast. Even if I managed to win this fight, there was no telling what her friends might do. The smartest move would be to defuse things and get away as quickly as possible. I opened my car door, but Ivy yanked my arm from behind.

"I'ma show you and your mama," she muttered.

"I don't want to fight you, Ivy—"

Bam! Pain zipped from my chin, across my cheekbones, through my skull, and my mouth flooded with warm liquid. I staggered, not knowing what happened to me. I spit blood and touched my hand to my lip. It was split and my tongue hurt. I heard men shouting and laughing, but I didn't know who they were or what they were laughing about. Where was I? What was going on? My heart was racing, but my brain seemed stalled. Finally, my eyes focused, and Ivy was standing in front of me. That's when I put together what had happened: She had hit me in the mouth.

In a phrase right out of Nona's A.A. talk, I had gotten in touch with my anger, and there was no going back. The next thing I knew I was sitting on top of Ivy and she was crying angrily, blood was streaming out of that button nose, and her hazel eyes bulged with fear. I remembered the time she showed up at Nona's looking the same way and I suddenly felt ashamed. I didn't regret defending myself, but

I didn't want to be like the person who had beat her the last time. I climbed off her, and she cupped her nose. I held out my hand to help her up.

"Bald-headed bitch!" she spat, blood running between her fingers.

The fellas cracked up.

"Best get to steppin', Shorty, 'fore she get back up," Do-rag said, chuckling.

I was surprised he was letting me go. Even though I was relieved, it made me feel sorry for Ivy. Whoever this man was, he didn't care enough about her to be bothered to get into it with me. He didn't care whether she won or lost the fight, or why she was even fighting in the first place. The show had been entertaining while it lasted, and now it was over.

"I know I just told you to take your skinny ass outta here," he said, not even helping Ivy stand.

I took one last look at Ivy picking herself off the side-walk. Then I climbed in my car and drove away.

I WASHED MY FACE, changed into sweats, and got into bed. No teeth were loose, but I had bit my tongue when Ivy hit me. My arms and knees were bruised; my right wrist was throbbing, and my shoulder muscles were starting to ache.

Oliver came in and put ice cubes wrapped in fast-food napkins against my swollen lip. "How you feeling?"

"I don't know." My voice was thin and shaky. Suddenly,

everything fell in on me at once—what Nona said about the week she left me, Sunny's face when they rushed out of the church, Ivy lying on the sidewalk. Hot tears started streaming down my cheeks. Oliver sat by me and put his arm around me while I cried.

Thanksgiving

"WHAT DID YOU TELL YOUR MOTHER ABOUT ME?" I yelled over The Roots blaring out of my car speakers.

Oliver was driving us to his mother's house for Thanksgiving dinner. He liked to listen to the poet-rappers like The Roots, Tupac, Mos Def, Common, Talib Kweli, and Jill Scott.

"I told her you were staying with me till you go back to school."

"Did you tell her I was older than you?"

"Yeah."

"Great."

"She's going to like you because I like you," he said.

He turned onto a street of tasteful McMansions. In a few minutes I was going to meet not just Oliver's mother, but also his auntie and his mother's best friend. The village of women who raised him. I took a deep breath and turned off the radio. The silence after the bumping music sounded loud.

"Glory, it's cool," he encouraged. "Really."

I relaxed a little at being called Glory. "Historically, your mom has been nice to your girlfriends?"

"This is the first time she's ever met one," Oliver said casually.

"You're kidding me?"

He shrugged. "Since high school. I went with the same girl all through eleventh and twelfth grades." He parked and turned off the car.

I leaned back and closed my eyes. His mom was going to think meeting me was a big damn deal. She was probably scared to death that we were moving too fast and I was pressuring her son to settle down too soon. I heard Oliver's door shut and then mine open.

"It's time," he said, sounding like the warden talking to a prisoner on death row. I unbuckled my seat belt and followed him.

Inside, the kitchen was filled with tantalizing smells, and a cacophony of pots and pans clattering, water running, food sizzling, high-pitched exclamations, and women's laughter. Oliver and I stood in the doorway watching. The three women were busy, moving in some kind of synchronized ballet from sink to stove to fridge to table, as if they were listening to the same song. But how they could hear anything I did not know considering they were all speaking at once.

"Get me a stick of butter."

"He left her with them kids."

"Girl, you gon' make us fatter than we already are, addin' all that butter."

"Calories don't count on Thanksgiving."

"You put eggs in your dressing?"

"I told her she didn't need to be messin' with no crazy, wannabe actor fool from L.A.!"

"You know I don't tell my recipes."

"She said he almost made it on *Survivor*."

"His ass need to be on *Cheaters*!"

I wished I could pull up a chair and watch and listen all day. Even better, I wanted to join this circle of women. I was suddenly overwhelmed with a desire for Oliver's mother to like me.

"My baby's home!" A slim woman, apple-cheeked, dark-skinned, and even younger-looking than Nona with a page-boy haircut, in sleek black pants and a low-cut black blouse stopped pouring red juice into a punch bowl on the kitchen table.

Oliver grinned.

I knew his mom was young, and I of all people shouldn't have been surprised considering that people mistook Nona for my sister, but I was instantly intimidated. I raised my eyebrows at him. *That hottie is your mother?*

"Hi, Mama. Everybody, this is my friend Glory. Glory, this is my mother, Aunt Kim, and my mom's friend Tanya."

I waved timidly.

Oliver's mother sashayed over to us and reached up to put her arms around his neck. He was a good five inches taller than she was. Then she ran her hand over his fro and grimaced.

Oliver pulled away from her. "Mama!"

She shook her head and turned to me. She had Oliver's doe eyes, but the rest of his looks must have come from his father. "It's so nice to meet you," she said, her dark eyes quickly running the length of my body, taking my measure, probably asking herself what does this grown-ass woman want with *my baby*.

I remembered Oliver and me in bed last night and this morning, and tried to hide the gulp in my voice and act like I had some home-training. "Thank you for inviting me, Mrs. Toliver."

"I'm not anybody's missus. Not anymore. Call me Tracy."

"Okay. Can I help with anything?"

"You're a guest," Oliver said.

"I want to," I insisted.

"Boy, just 'cause *you* don't wanna do nothing," Tracy playfully hit Oliver on the arm. "Actually, the food's just about ready."

"Come on, I want you to meet Mike," Oliver said.

Tracy pointed into the family room. "He's in there watching football."

We stepped down one stair next to a long sofa, which had seen a lot of years of wear and tear. Across from the sofa, a fire was crackling cheerfully in the fireplace, but everybody was focused on the TV next to it.

"Mike," Oliver called.

The little boy lay on the floor facing the TV.

"Mike!"

He looked up.

"Come and meet somebody."

He jumped up and ran over to me. "I already know who you are."

"I know who you are too," I said. "You're Oliver's little brother."

"You're his girlfriend." He grinned at me.

I had never been anybody's girlfriend before. I grinned back. I wished Sunny was here. I wondered what she was up to today. Was Nona cooking a big dinner? Was a similar scene that I would never be a part of taking place in my own family's house? I shook off my melancholy, reminding myself that Sunny got the After Nona, who cooked and stayed home and cared about her. I would be stuck with the Before Nona forever. There was no changing that.

Oliver introduced me to Kim's husband, a couple of cousins, and Tanya's sons. They each shook my hand very politely before quickly turning back to the TV.

When the food was ready, everybody dished up plates buffet-style. The meal was the traditional Thanksgiving turkey, dressing, and cranberries, plus fried fish, macaroni and cheese, greens, and other soul food. Since you never know who made what, I helped myself to a little bit of everything. That way, I was sure to have something on my plate I could compliment Tracy for. I was still eager to find a way to get on her good side.

Oliver added turkey to the heap on his plate.

"Are you sure you're a vegetarian?"

"I gots to eat my mom's turkey."

All the men, except for Oliver, ate in front of the TV. He and I sat in the living room with Tracy, Tanya, and Kim.

The living room was nicer than the family room, but still lived-in and comfortable. It felt like Tracy had given the other room over to her sons and kept this one for herself. There were candles and pillows and knickknack fish carved out of wood and marble, and colorful abstract prints and African masks on the walls. Above the couch Tracy's own family portrait of her, Oliver, and Michael held a place of honor. On the end table was a picture of Tracy holding a big fish in front of her.

"Did you catch that?" I asked her, pointing to the picture.

"Here we go," Oliver said.

Tracy smiled proudly. "In Minnesota," she said. "We went there last July and spent the whole week fishing. I caught what you're eating right now."

"Wow! It's really good. You rarely hear about women fishing. You put the worms on the hooks and everything?"

Kim sucked her teeth and said, "Daddy had us baiting our own hooks and gutting fish when we were in kindergarten."

That was all it took. They told me a dozen stories about fishing with their father. Then we moved onto other small talk: the weather, getting ready for Christmas, reality TV shows, work, school.

Tracy talked easily with Oliver about his classes and the record store. She was obviously a "cool" mom, what people imagined when they thought of a young mother. She seemed to like much of the same music and TV shows as her boys, yet her and Oliver's relationship was so different than Nona's and mine. Nona and I were only fifteen years apart, but we didn't share the same experiences. We didn't have common interests. Nona had done her thing: drink. And I had done mine: study.

When I was finished eating, Oliver took my plate and asked us if we wanted some sweet potato pie. We all said yes, and Tracy, Kim, and Tanya exchanged an amused look.

As soon as Oliver left the room, they started cracking up.

"Girl, what did you do to my son? Scratch that. Too much information!"

"Well, I wanna know," Kim whooped. "That boy's nose is open so wide you could fly a jet plane up it!"

I blushed furiously.

"Since you seem to have some power over him, can you please get him to cut off all that hair? Or at least comb it?" Tracy asked.

"And lose the glasses?" Tanya added. "You can't like them, right?"

"Seriously, how did my shy, nerdy little nephew end up with somebody like you?" Kim asked.

The three women leaned in.

Somebody like me? Who did they think I was? I had been asked to leave school, was working for six bucks an hour, and until recently had been pulling my hair out. Oliver had shown *me* the ropes in bed, not vice versa. He had taken me in and held me when I was upset about Nona. He had done right by me. I needed to do right by him. "Sorry, ladies, but I'm just as big a nerd as Oliver. Bigger actually. And, for the record, he ain't that shy."

They sat back in unison and looked at one another, speechless.

Oliver walked in carrying a tray with four plates of pie, each with a perfect dollop of whipped cream on top. He looked at the four of us. "What?"

They burst out laughing again. All of a sudden these three women in their late thirties were like high-school girls. Kim fell back on the couch howling, and Tracy leaned over her. Tanya was sitting on the floor with her head back against the couch.

He looked at me. "How embarrassed should I be?"

"Uh-uh, baby, don't ever be embarrassed unless you've done something wrong," Tracy said, sitting up, wiping the tears from her eyes. "And it seems like you're doing everything right."

Oliver looked dead at me and said, "I'm trying."

Tracy, Kim, and Tanya beamed at him. *That's our boy,* their smiles said.

WE HAD TWO STOPS on Thanksgiving Day. The second was Stephanie's rehearsal dinner. As we walked into La Naranja I heard Tracy's words again. *Don't ever be embarrassed unless you've done something wrong.* I was impressed at how Oliver handled the teasing by his mother and aunties, but how could he not be confident when he had a mother who gave such good advice? Knowing he could hold his own made me feel less like I was taking a lamb to slaughter. And I had stepped up too. If we could handle those three, we could handle Stephanie.

La Naranja was packed with Greg's and Stephanie's families. I looked for Stephanie or Cleo or anyone I knew. Oliver and I stood next to the hostess stand, near a couple of girls. One had hair dyed honey-blond, and the other had long braids like Stephanie now had.

"Mama liked to have a fit when I told her I had to come over here for the rehearsal dinner today," the blond one said. "She was all, 'What kind of people have a rehearsal dinner on Thanksgiving? Don't they know people got families?!' "

"True that," the one with the braids said. "Leave it to Stephanie to bogart a national holiday!"

All of a sudden they felt our presence and turned around.

"Hi. Amber, maid of honor," the blonde said as an introduction.

"Mikki, bridesmaid number three," said the braids.

"Shay, just a friend," I responded.

"Lucky girl."

I was about to ask where Stephanie was when I spotted her two aunts sitting at a table laughing. Aunt Baby Mae and Aunt Lovie were slightly round, maple-brown sisters from Louisiana, who stepped in after their sister died to help raise Stephanie and Cleo. Aunt Baby Mae wore a black turtleneck sweater that clung to her large breasts, black slacks, and a saucy newsboy cap. Aunt Lovie had on a sparkling blue dress and a full-length fur coat.

I took Oliver's hand and led him to their table. "Why, hello there, Miss Snazzy Jazzy," Aunt Baby Mae said. "I heard you was back!"

Her older sister said, "Come give Aunt Lovie some sugar."

"She betta come give me some sugar first. I saw her first," Aunt Baby Mae said.

I went to Aunt Baby Mae, who whispered "God bless you, baby" when I bent down and kissed her powdered cheek.

Aunt Lovie batted her false eyelashes at me when I hugged her. "Now, did you ever finish school?" she asked.

"My undergrad, yes. I'm working on my master's now."

"My, my, my," Aunt Lovie said.

"Go on, Miss Snazzy Jazzy!" Aunt Baby Mae said. She noticed Oliver. "And who do we have here?"

I followed Oliver's lead and introduced him as my friend.

The aunts turned on the charm, cooing and batting eyelashes and crushing Oliver into each of their bosoms. Oliver turned a shade of red I didn't know black people, even light-skinned ones, could achieve.

"Bonus daughter!" Mr. Berry came up behind me and shook my shoulders. His form of a hug. I turned around.

He clutched his heart. "No! Don't tell me you brought a man here!"

It felt like bringing a guy home to meet my father.

"Young man, what are we going to do with women today?" he asked, shaking Oliver's hand.

Oliver didn't miss a beat. "I got some ideas."

Mr. Berry leaned back and roared. "I bet you do! Y'all go 'head and eat. Young man, you get two plates cause I know you can eat." And he was off to go shake more shoulders.

"The food's good," Aunt Baby Mae said, as she pushed her fork around the dinkiest helpings of rice and refried beans.

"Not like *our* food," Aunt Lovie whispered, wrinkling her nose at her own small plate. "We had a real dinner earlier. You come on over to the house later for some leftovers."

I was about to explain that we just ate, when Oliver said, "I could go for some beans and rice."

"You want to eat again?"

"What? That was lunch, this is dinner."

I took his hand. "We have to find the bride."

I saw Cleo first. "Where's girlfriend?" I asked.

She pointed through the door into the next dining room. Then, she leaned in to whisper to me, "I love me some sexy bowlegs."

Oliver, *sexy*?

Just then Stephanie and Greg entered the room. She saw us and glided over, already bridelike in a winter-white sweater and matching jeans.

"It's nice to finally meet the guy who's keeping my friend so . . . busy," Stephanie said. The braids were gone, replaced by long, straight, tossable, movie-star hair.

"Come with me to the bathroom," Stephanie said to me. "I have to go every five minutes."

I knew she just wanted to talk. "The buffet's over there," I showed Oliver. "Why don't you get started, and I'll see you in a minute."

He didn't need me to tell him twice. He just about sprinted for the food.

"Did y'all do it?" She blurted as soon as we were in the bathroom.

I grinned.

"Well? Spill it, girl!"

I grinned wider. "It's working for me."

She laughed and went into a stall. "I really do have to pee all the time."

I looked at myself in the mirror. My hair was still a miracle to me. I was even wearing a little plum lip gloss. I ran my tongue over my bottom lip. The swelling had gone down, but the gash hadn't healed yet. "I'm staying with him until I go back to Iowa."

She came out, washed her hands, and smiled in the mirror to check for food in between the gap in her teeth. "But you're not seriously hooking up with him, right?"

"I like him. You're the one that told me to have fun." But she was right. It was crazy for me to feel such an alarming level of affection for someone so young. I didn't even know how it happened myself. He was just supposed to pollinate and move on, like a bumblebee. Not listen to my problems with Nona. Not rename me. Not shelter me.

"Have your fun. Get your swerve on, yes. Not move in with the boy, *o-kay.*"

"Don't call him a boy."

She glanced at me and then went back to looking at herself. "Desi's going to be at the wedding," she said, finger-combing her hair.

"Oh boy . . ."

"He said he really liked you."

He did? I couldn't help it. My heart did a little flip. "He

was probably trying to be nice. How's he going to tell somebody he hated her friend?"

"No. He was genuinely hurt that you wouldn't go out with him again. I don't get you. You don't 'connect' with Desi—who is fine and gainfully employed, I might add—but you do with this little record-store b—person?"

"Let's drop it, okay?"

She put on a fresh coat of red lipstick, then offered it to me. Apparently, my gloss didn't get the Stephanie seal of approval. But I liked it and I was sticking with it. I shook my head.

She put the lipstick back in her pocket. "Well, when you make up your mind, you sure don't play. You go from nothing to living together in five seconds flat."

"I had to. I couldn't stand Nona one more day." I filled her in on our church showdown, and about fighting Ivy.

She turned around to face me. "But Nona stopped drinking and stuff. She wasn't the one out standing on the corner chugging a forty."

"So?"

"I wish my mother was around so I could fight with her." She shrugged to feign indifference, but I could tell from her voice she was serious.

"My mother left me all the time by choice. Yours *died*. She didn't do it on purpose."

"All I know is that I ended up without a mother when I was nine years old, and I would give anything, *anything*, to have her here. I'd give up getting married. I'd get fat again if I could be with her just one more time."

I shook my head. I didn't want to have a mother who

had left me. I didn't want to curse her out in a church, of all places. But that was the way things were. "You don't get it."

She raised her eyebrows. "Oh no? You think Daddy was perfect? You think he didn't do his share of dirt? I love my father, but he ain't perfect. He cheated on my mother before she died."

No! No! No! I did not want to hear this. I felt like my heart might break. All these years I thought Mr. Berry was Cliff Huxtable straight out of *The Cosby Show*. He was always there, at home every night. *He* had cheated?

"Uh-huh. Didn't know that, did you?"

I was too shocked and sad to speak.

She opened the bathroom door. "Nobody's perfect, Shay. You're a fool if you think otherwise."

I opened my mouth to say there was a humongous canyon between perfect and Nona, but she swept out before I could answer. I went back into the restaurant and sat next to Oliver.

"So, what exactly has she heard about me?" he asked, chewing a big bite of food.

I leaned against him. "All kinds of things."

My Best Friend's Wedding

"MY SPIDEY SENSE TELLS ME YOU'RE NERVOUS ABOUT seeing your mom," Oliver said.

We were on our way to Nona's to pick up Sunny to take her to Stephanie's wedding, as promised.

"Something like that."

I parked the car in front of the house. "What the . . . ?" The picket fence that lined the front of the yard was gone, except for two blackened posts. So were the thick rose-bushes that had climbed over and snaked through the fence.

"Whoa," Oliver said.

My heart started racing. "I'll be right back." I was out of the car before he could respond. I stepped through where the gate used to be and saw a heap of charred, splintered wood and, for a few yards, nothing but black soil where there used to be dried twigs and stalks. The fire had stopped halfway between the fence and the house. The house was untouched.

I exhaled the breath I was holding and continued up the path. Sunny dashed out the front door. I scooped her into my arms like a lover in an old movie, surprised at how happy I was to see her. She was wearing a black velvet dress, white tights, and black shoes, the most subdued look I had ever seen her in.

"You look beautiful. I love these," I said of the sparkly barrettes in her hair.

"You look beautiful too. I missed you."

"I missed you too," I said, my voice thick with emotion.

I carried her back to the house to get her coat. Nona was standing in the doorway in sweats and a robe. Her face was grim, and all the light had gone from her eyes. "What happened?" I asked.

"Miss Ivy burned our garden," Sunny said.

"*Ivy* did this?"

Nona pulled her bottom lip into her mouth. Her eyes watered. "In the middle of the night. While we were home. While Sunny was in bed asleep. She *poured gasoline* on my roses," she said like she still didn't believe it.

I didn't want to feel sorry for Nona. I didn't want to care about her. But after everything, love was still there, lodged like a stone in my heart.

"Was she trying to . . . ?"

"No. If she really wanted to hurt us, she would have started with the house. But, good God, she was high as a kite, and everything is so dry out here. She could have killed us. She could have killed herself. She could have burned down my neighbors' houses." She composed herself. "But thankfully I was up. I saw the flames and called 911, sprayed down the rest of the yard with the hose."

"Did you see Ivy?"

"No. The lady across the street woke up and called 911 too. She said Ivy didn't leave until she heard sirens. They caught her two blocks away. She ran her car into a telephone pole. Thankfully, nobody got hurt."

"When did all this happen?"

"Three nights ago." She kept shaking her head. "This violates her parole. Arson, DUI, possession. She's going to do real time."

Three nights ago. An icy centipede crawled up my spine. "Oh my God."

"What?"

"I saw Ivy three nights ago. We got into it."

Nona squeezed her eyes shut, swaying as if dizzy, then opened them. "You fought?" she asked mournfully.

I touched my hand to my mouth and nodded. "She said she was going to show us both. It didn't even occur to me. . . . When I left, she was . . . I got mad. I fought her back, but I tried to help her up."

"Dear Jesus," Nona said.

"I'm sorry."

"It's not your fault. She wasn't mad at you."

"This isn't your fault either. She was bad news from the beginning. I told you she was dangerous."

Nona cinched her robe closed. "Remember the night Ivy got beat up?"

"Yeah?"

"It was because she wouldn't go back to the life, like her idiot boyfriend wanted her to. But after she started using again, she couldn't stand up to him anymore. She went back out on the streets. I'm only telling you this so you'll understand that Ivy's a girl who needed a lot of help. I guess more than I could give her."

"Who's that?" Sunny asked.

Nona and I both looked behind me. Oliver was walking up the stone path.

"This must be Oliver," Nona said with a small, polite smile. "I'm so happy to meet you."

They shook hands.

"Well, you all should get going," Nona said, helping Sunny put on her coat.

"Are you going to be okay?" I asked. "You want to go to a meeting or something while Sunny's with us?"

This time her smile was genuine. "Actually, I'm meeting my new sponsor."

I was so happy to hear that, I smiled back at her.

She looked past me at the yard. "Maybe it'll be like after a forest fire. Maybe something new will grow here."

"I NOW PRONOUNCE you husband and wife. You may—"

Greg grabbed Stephanie and kissed her.

"I see you have it under control," the preacher finished. People laughed and cried and applauded all at the same time.

Stephanie and Greg turned and jumped the broom, then strutted down the aisle, followed by their bridesmaids and groomsmen. Everybody looked good in their fall colors. Greg looked relieved that he'd made it through the ceremony. Stephanie wore the satisfied look of a woman who was getting everything she wanted. She looked beautiful, not at all heavy. As she planned, with the wrap, it wasn't immediately obvious she was pregnant.

After the service, we got back in our cars and drove downtown to the Marriott for the reception. Since Stephanie wouldn't be able to go to the islands, she had brought the islands to her reception. There were tiki torches, real potted palm trees, a large tropical fish tank by the gift table, and the two bars were covered with thatched roofs. The tables were done in bright Caribbean colors, with centerpieces made of exotic red flowers, starfish, sand dollars, and seashells scattered on white sand. A pair of plastic sunglasses were on each dinner plate and plastic leis were on the chairs. When Greg and Stephanie made their entrance into the ballroom, he was wearing a red linen Mexican wedding shirt and she was wearing a red sarong and an oversize turquoise blouse that didn't quite camouflage her round belly. But now that the ceremony was over she didn't seem to mind.

The meal was a Jamaican-Mexican extravaganza: roasted red snapper, jerk chicken, beans, Spanish rice, rice made with coconut milk, fried plantains, cornbread, tortillas, fish fritters, and tamales from La Naranja. While we ate, the DJ played reggae, calypso, tejano, mariachi, and salsa. After the rum and tequila had been flowing for a while, he started adding in some R & B. The dance floor was packed.

Not too long ago I would have been miserable at a wedding reception. . . . All the couples and the dancing and the small talk. I would have felt socially incompetent. But here I was in my slinky silver dress, with my date and my sister, telling stories about the bride, and laughing just like everyone else.

The happy couple slow-danced, then came the father-daughter dance. I watched Mr. Berry, still in his tux, and Stephanie as they waltzed around the dance floor smiling and crying while a slew of relatives snapped photos like paparazzi. My mind couldn't hold the idea of him as an adulterer and the image of them happily dancing at the same time. I had always envied her for being a daddy's girl, when I wasn't anybody's girl. How could she remain so devoted to him knowing what she knew?

After Stephanie's and Mr. Berry's dance was over, Oliver tried to get me on the dance floor.

"You know I don't like to dance in public."

He stood up. "We danced at the Mercury."

Sunny jumped up and down, three plastic leis bouncing around her neck. "I wanna dance! I wanna dance!"

"You're off the hook. *For now,*" he said, and lifted Sunny in his arms and took her out to the dance floor. He was really good with her. He swung her around and twirled her under his arm and stooped down low to dance next to her when she started her unrhythmic hip shaking.

"You look like you want to go out there," a low, warm voice said.

I looked away from the dance floor. Desi was standing over the table holding his hand out.

"Me?"

He looked at the empty table, amused. "There's nobody else here."

"I have to watch my little sister." I pointed toward Oliver and Sunny.

"You can watch her from the dance floor. Besides, it's illegal not to dance while Zapp is on. You hear the song. They're gonna *make* you dance."

"I don't—"

"It's not a slow jam. There won't be any grinding." He took my hand and gently pulled me up with a disarming grin. "Nothing inappropriate. I promise."

We made our way onto the dance floor, and I did my best to mimic everybody else, hoping to at least keep the beat and not make too much of a spectacle of myself.

"There you go," Desi said.

I was barely rocking my hips, trying really hard not to move too much, when Sunny saw me and ran over to us, leaving Oliver standing there watching, all dressed up in a suit, his black eyes boring into me.

I stopped dancing and caught her when she hugged my legs. "Desi, I'm sorry. But it seems my sister just abandoned her dance partner—who's my date, actually."

Desi looked over at Oliver glaring at us. "Maybe some other time?"

Desi was the kind of man any woman my age would be thrilled to have. But Oliver was more my speed. "Sorry. I don't think so."

I took Sunny by the hand and we walked over to Oliver.

"Thought you didn't dance in public."

"Can you really call what I was doing dancing?" I joked feebly.

He folded his arms. "Looked like you were doing all right to me."

"Shay, you dance with both of us," Sunny said, swinging my hand and taking Oliver's hand.

Oliver let go of her hand. "Sorry, Sunshine. I don't think so."

"It was just dancing. I wasn't going home with the man," I said, but I felt bad. I could tell I'd hurt his feelings. "I'm sorry. Come on, dance with us?"

"You owe me," Oliver said.

"I know."

"No, I don't mean this dance. You've got to do something else."

I was intrigued, though suspicious. "Like what?"

He thought for a second, then started to nod his head. "Get a tattoo with me."

"*What?!*"

"You heard me."

"You must be crazy!"

Sunny was still swinging my arm and twirling herself around me.

"A tattoo. That's the least you can do."

I was shaking my head.

"That's right, Glory. A tattoo. A big ole one. Someplace visible."

"I'll think about a small one. Where nobody can see it."

"Nobody except me."

"Nobody except you."

The song ended and the DJ put on some hip-hop. The younger people crowded onto the dance floor. I started to turn around to go back to our table, and Oliver grabbed my arm. "Thought you said we were gonna dance?"

So we danced, all three of us. And I didn't care if people laughed at me. I was in the moment, in the music, just like when I danced at home, though not as outrageous as when I was alone. I was happy, not delusional.

I saw Stephanie dancing with Greg across the floor. She was gaping at me like she just discovered me hatching an egg. I turned around and shook my tail feather in front of Oliver like the video girls, or like video girls would do if they couldn't stay on beat, and Stephanie cracked up and gave me a thumbs-up. Oliver shook his head and laughed too.

We danced until it was time to watch Stephanie and Greg cut the cake. Stephanie had threatened to divorce Greg on the spot if he smashed cake in her face, and he must have taken her at her word, because he held a slice of choco-late cake near her lips while she took a ladylike nibble.

"You and Oliver should get married," Sunny declared. "Then I can be in your wedding. And you can have cake and we can take your picture."

Oliver and I laughed nervously.

"We're not getting married," I said.

"But we are getting tattoos," Oliver said.

THE NEXT DAY before I could chicken out, I went with Oliver to Bette's Body Art near the record store. We looked through thick binders of sample tattoos until we found the ones we wanted. He selected a sun. I chose a blue morning glory. I pulled my jeans and panties down to my thigh to reveal my right hip. When my tattoo artist, a heavily inked-and-pierced blonde, made the first nick in my skin, I started to cry, and not because of the pain. At first, I thought it was what had become my usual emotional overflow. My feelings were completely out of control lately, ever since I'd yelled at Nona. Anger, happiness, sorrow—I felt everything more deeply. The tattoo chick was kind enough to hand me a box of tissues and let me cry. Pretty soon I was wailing. I sobbed so hard she had to turn off the needle.

Finally, after my crying had slowed to hiccups and sniffles, she said, "Showing the world who you are is a soulful act."

He Slipped, But I Fell

I WAS RUNNING LATE FOR WORK, ZIPPING MY JEANS, when Oliver came into the bedroom with a cup of the sludge that he, Matt, and Will called coffee. With about half a cup of milk and three spoons of sugar, it was drinkable. But this morning I couldn't take even the smell of it. "Ugh, get that out of here."

"What?"

I pinched my nose closed. "The coffee. It smells like dirt and dog shit."

He stared at me.

"Seriously. It's disgusting."

"Are you pregnant?"

"What?!"

"I was ten when my mother was pregnant with my little brother. She used to love coffee, but stopped drinking it, even decaf, because she couldn't handle the smell. Lots of things that she had loved, all of a sudden she hated."

"In case you haven't noticed, I'm PMSing. My period's about to start any second."

He set his mug on the desk. "When's it due?"

"I don't know. Today. Tomorrow. Stop it. You're freaking me out. Why are you looking at me like that?"

"You better take a test."

I took my hand from my nose. I felt sick, and nothing was funny, but I laughed as if I could control the situation by focusing on how absurd it was. For God's sake, just six weeks ago I was a virgin!

"It slipped off."

My smile vanished. "*What* slipped off?"

"You know. The condom."

Instantly, he lost whatever grown-up veneer he'd been covered with since we started having sex. It was like I woke up out of some spell, and he was little Record Store Boy again. "You don't know how to use a condom?!" I shrieked.

"Yes, I know how to use a condom. But sometimes when you come out at the end, you know, they . . . slip off. It was only once."

I lunged at him, smacking his chest and arms like a crazy woman. "Were you trying to get me pregnant?! You want to strut around bragging about knocking up your baby mama like these other little ignorant macho fools of your generation?!"

"Quit it!" He grabbed my arms and held them to my chest. "My generation! I'm only five and a half years younger than you!"

We stood there panting. His breath smelled like coffee

and peanut butter. My stomach turned and I jerked my arms away. "I wish you would have mentioned this little malfunction when it happened."

"I'm sorry. You were already all bent out of shape about your mother. I didn't want you to get more upset."

I slumped down on the bed. "I can't be pregnant. My period's going to start any second. I can feel it." I went through the pregnancy symptoms I knew about: breast tenderness, fatigue, mood swings. I had all of them, but I had them every month right before my period started. They were the PMS dwarves. My uterus felt heavy; between my legs it felt active, like right before the blood comes, like I could feel the lining pulling away from the uterus, unused eggs about to be flushed out. My body was busy doing what it did every month. It had to be.

I rubbed my earlobe. Oliver was just a boy when his mother was pregnant. Hell, he was just a boy now! "You and your ten-year-old mother don't know what you're talking about."

He frowned. "*I* was ten. Not my mother. Just take the test and then we'll know and you won't have to be worried."

I rubbed my ear harder. This couldn't really be happening. I knew better. I knew how easy it was for a woman who doesn't want to be pregnant to get pregnant. My own words to Stephanie echoed in my mind. *Shots, patches, pills. It ain't rocket science.* I thought I was such a fucking grown-up. I'd had sex, finally told Nona off. Instead I was acting like a stupid kid wondering how this could happen, when this was the first person I had ever been with, when I was still keeping track of how many times we'd done it. Forty-one.

"You want me to buy it? You can do it at work."

"I'm not taking a pregnancy test at work!"

"After, then, but right after. It's not just you who's affected by this."

He should have thought about that when the condom was "just slipping off." I didn't say it, but he looked wounded, like he had heard it anyway.

At work, I went to the bathroom fifteen times checking for blood. Each time I came out Oliver would look up at me hopeful as a birthday balloon, then deflate when he saw the worry still on my face. These last few weeks I had felt more in touch with my own body than I ever had before; there was no way I could be pregnant and not know it. Still . . . I was exhausted and irritated, and now I wondered if my mood was a sign of PMS or a sign of exactly the opposite condition. When lunchtime rolled around, was I hungry for a burger because I was piggy or because it was a craving? Had I felt sick in the mornings? I never felt faint, but pregnant women only fainted in the movies, right?

Sunny kept running through my mind. Her questions. Her wonderfully crazy outfits. I wondered how much it must cost for her clothes and toys, and asthma medicine and doctors' appointments. And day care. Damn, day care. What did that cost? Two hundred a week or something, I bet.

It would have been nice to have some customers to distract myself, but it was a slow day even for us. I kept wiping down the same spot on the counter, trying to tell myself that it wasn't possible I could be pregnant. It wasn't possible that Oliver could diagnose me before I even noticed it myself. But it wasn't working. I decided to leave early and get the bad news over with.

As I was leaving, Oliver followed me outside. "We're in this together, all right?"

I nodded, but I didn't really believe him. It was just something people said. If I was pregnant, I would be all alone.

THE SECOND PINK LINE had the nerve to appear right away, not even taking the full three minutes it said it would on the box. The first line was a control, to illustrate that the test was working. The second line was the one that indicated a positive result. I wondered who came up with that terminology, because, to me, everything was out of control and this result was definitely negative.

I slumped to the bathroom floor. I was still there when Oliver got home. He knew by the look on my face what the test said. He sat down next to me and took my hand. "I'm sorry."

I pulled away. "I'm sorry. Everybody's sorry. Sorry doesn't change anything." I had made such a horrible, stupid mistake.

"Are we having our first fight?" he tried to joke, but I glared at him. "Whatever you want to do I'll stand with you. I'm with you one hundred and ten percent."

"Yeah? You going to carry this baby?"

He paused. "I ain't never been in jail. I'm working on a double major. I always said one of the things I wanted to show my little brother was that a real man didn't make a baby until he was ready to be a father."

"Real men know how to use a condom." I knew I was being hurtful, but I didn't care. I hated him at this moment. Hated him for getting me pregnant. Hated him for knowing that I was pregnant before I had any inkling myself. Mostly I hated him for making me forget to watch out, making me forget that the rug could be pulled out from beneath me at any moment. He slipped, but I was the one who fell.

He winced, but didn't answer my taunt. "So . . . what are you going to do?"

It was insane to even consider having a baby with Oliver. I could just picture him riding it around on his bike. At least the kid would have a built-in playmate. My look gave him his answer. For a second I wondered what it felt like to have a woman tell you she was going to abort your baby. Would he be hurt, angry, guilty, relieved? I searched his face for a reaction, but all I saw was how incredibly young he looked.

Quietly he said, "I'll go with you. And I'll pay for it."

I snorted, and leaned against the wall. "Please. You don't have any more money than I do."

"I'll get it. I'll borrow it from my mom."

I slid farther down the wall. The idea of Tracy even knowing about this, let alone paying for it, made me want to scream. "It's my problem. I'll take care of it."

"It's *our* problem, and I'm trying to step up."

"I don't need your help."

His face clouded up. Now he was pissed too. "You needed my help when you moved in here."

"I needed a place to stay. What I need now is for somebody to be an adult. And obviously nobody in here qualifies."

He unfolded his legs and stood, waiting for me to apologize, to say something, to say anything, to get him to stay.

When I didn't he shook his head. "Women call all the shots. Have the baby, a brother gotta pay support whether he wants it or not. Or if he wants it and she don't, well, that's too damn bad too. She can go get an abortion. A nigga's got no rights, tries to do the right thing, still can't fucking win!" He stomped out and tried to slam the door behind him, but it bounced back open.

I leaned over, closed and locked the door, then lay on the dirty but cool tile floor and curled into a ball, feeling sick in a way that I knew wasn't the pregnancy. It was regret, remorse, shame, and something worse, something that used to eat at me all the time and now had grown into something bigger. It wasn't Oliver I hated.

I ran my fingers through my hair. I could feel the tracks of weaved hair against my scalp. The new growth wasn't vibrating now. It felt as dead as the rest of me.

How could I screw up this badly this quickly? What the hell had I been thinking messing around with a teenager, for God's sake? Here I was with my new do and my new name, thinking I had it going on, and I had made one of the biggest, stupidest mistakes a woman could make. Worse, it was the same mistake that I had hated Nona for making.

Now I was no better than she was. If only I could go back, I would say no when Oliver asked me out. No, I'd need to go back further. I would tell Nina Simone to go back where she came from when she said I should go home. I would stay in Iowa and get my ass out of bed and go to class, keep my job. I would never come back to Denver.

Coming Clean

OLIVER AND I WERE AVOIDING EACH OTHER, WHICH
takes some doing when you work together and live together. But he was studying for finals, so when he didn't
have to work, he was at the library, or his mom's, which was
where he was now while I was lying in bed in the dark asking WWNSD? WWNSD? But Nina Simone wasn't giving
me any answers.

I wondered what Tracy thought of me now. She was
only thirteen years older than I was. She had gone to college. Even though her degree was in accounting, surely she
knew the writings of Sojourner Truth, Zora Neale Hurs-
ton, Alice Walker, Audre Lorde, bell hooks. If she had,
maybe she would be on my side. I had read them and con-
gratulated myself for being black, as if I had chosen to be,
because black women were feminists before there was a
name for it.

When there were right-to-life and pro-choice demonstrations and debates on campus, I always came down firmly on the side of a woman's right to choose. I'd seen what poor parenting could do and thought it was better to let a woman who knew she didn't want a kid to not have it. I knew I would regret not finishing school, starting out with a baby behind the eight ball. Ball? Hell, boulder was more like it. I knew what it was like out there for African American women. Add single mother to the description and doors must slam in your face faster than a lightning strike. So why couldn't I pick up the phone and make the appointment?

It was 12:12. So many times in my life—for advice, comfort, to share good news and bad—I had longed for a mother, but I never had one. Now was no different. There was no way I could tell Nona, no way I could face the told-you-so look, the how-you-like-me-now tone of voice. Oliver came to bed at 1:38, and just like I had done all those years as a child, I pretended to be asleep.

But he knew better. He turned on the light. "I'll do whatever you want to do. We can have the baby . . . We can—"

Oh my God, he wasn't going to *propose* was he?! "You said you didn't want any kids until you were ready to be a father."

"A condom came off. It doesn't have to mean so much. You don't have to be so mad at yourself and so mad at me. It was an accident. Accidents happen. It doesn't have to be the end. . . . It doesn't have to be this way." His voice was pleading.

I squeezed my eyes tight. "How could it be any different?"

"Nobody has to get their heart stomped on."

His voice was so sad. I opened my eyes. "I'm sorry, Oliver. I just want to go back to Iowa, and forget all of this."

"Including me."

"No, not you."

"But you don't want to see me anymore. When you leave, you're gone."

I didn't say anything.

"I never felt like this about anybody, and I know you never felt like this before. What happened between us is a big fucking deal. Don't act like it's not."

"That's the problem. It's too big. It's too much. You are nineteen. And I'm twenty-five—"

"I know how old we are. You knew I was younger than you when we started, so don't punish me for it. I can't change what year I was born."

"Let me finish. I'm twenty-five, almost twenty-six, and just now really starting to grow up, to come out of my shell, to do stuff girls usually do when they're sixteen."

"And?"

"How many people end up with the one they loved when they were sixteen?"

THE NEXT MORNING I said I was sick, and Matt agreed to work for me. Even though I told Oliver I wasn't going to the clinic, he assumed I was and tried to stay home with me, but I wouldn't let him. After the guys cleared out of the house, I looked up Planned Parenthood in the phone book and dialed the number.

"Planned Parenthood." A woman's voice.

I slammed the phone down. Then redialed.

"Planned Parenthood," the same woman answered patiently, probably used to this. "Hello?"

I hung up again. It was just too surreal to be making an appointment for an abortion. I always got embarrassed at my annual exams. Not just because of the humiliation of the stirrups and speculum but because I had to confirm for yet another year that I was still a virgin. The last time I had a checkup, the middle-aged nurse practitioner had patted me on the knee and said, "Good for you for sticking to your guns." And now I was pregnant? I couldn't wrap my mind around it. It just wasn't possible! From my psych classes, I knew this was denial. But being pregnant seemed as likely as being president or being on the moon.

I turned on the CD player. "House of the Rising Sun" had worked once before. I cranked it up loud and danced, shimmying and shaking, even though my heart wasn't in it. It wasn't the lyrics that got to me—they were about a woman who got her heart broken by a bad guy—it was the feeling, the energy. It was recorded live, and something was happening in that room while Nina was singing. The band, the audience, everyone was spellbound. Normally, I could feel it too, but today, I got nothing. No boost of energy, no sense of freedom, no endorphin rush. Still, I danced through the song three times just like I had before.

Then I went back into the bedroom to wait. I lay in the bed, watching the clock: 10:10, 11:22, 1:23. My fingers crept into my hair, but I quickly put both my hands under my butt. I wasn't going all the way back. I waited and waited. At 3:33 my heart clenched and I sat up in bed, holding my breath. But Nina Simone did not come. I jumped out of bed, beseeching her. "Nina Simone, I need your help. Nina Simone, come to me! Help me!" By 3:41 I felt duped, like Linus waiting for the Great Pumpkin. I recalled telling Nona I didn't need make-believe, and realized how blind I had been. I had based my decision to come back home on make-believe. I had turned all those times to Nina Simone for advice and assurance. But those days were over. I needed to talk to a real, live someone who could actually help.

STEPHANIE'S AND GREG'S new house was three blocks away from Mr. Berry's, and the only difference from the outside was that Mr. Berry's house was taupe and Stephanie's was the color of eggshells. Now that I knew about Mr. Berry's affair, I could no longer see these houses as paragons of domestic bliss. They were only houses. Happy occupants lived in some and crazy, messed-up occupants lived in others.

The only plan I could come up with was staying with Stephanie and Greg for a few days after the procedure. Then I'd head back to Iowa. I was scared that her pregnancy was going to make that difficult for both of us, but I hoped she would be able to imagine if she was pregnant by someone other than Greg, to remember when she was still single and unprepared for a child.

Pregnancy suited Stephanie. She had long braids pulled into a ponytail and her skin was clear and dewy-looking. It looked like light was radiating from her. Nona had changed drastically, and for the worst, when she was pregnant with Sunny. But the only difference I saw in Stephanie's appearance was that her breasts and belly had grown rounder, and her nose had spread wide. She looked like she carried the weight of the impending changes in her life right down the center of her body.

She hugged me and I was hit with the telltale scent of waffle cones, but I didn't say anything. She led me past the living room into the kitchen. The interior of the house didn't look anything like the Berry house or Stephanie's old apartment. Unlike her father's, Stephanie's place had been remodeled in the last few years. And she had changed her decorating style. Gone were the bright island-print and wicker furniture, fake palms, and beach photos. The living room had hardwood floors and matching studded, brown leather couch and chair, and glass tables. Beige carpet under a plastic runner led up the stairs to the bedrooms.

The kitchen also looked new with gleaming stainless steel appliances and black-and-white granite countertops. She got glasses and orange juice out of the fridge. There was a vase of bright red roses on the kitchen table. I leaned in to smell them, but they had no fragrance. I remembered the sweet-smelling bouquet of fresh-cut flowers Nona had left on my nightstand the first night I arrived in Denver.

Stephanie brought the glasses of juice to the table and sat down. She moved the vase over so the roses wouldn't block our view of each other. "So, what's up?"

"Turns out you're not the only one who's not a rocket scientist."

"Huh?"

" 'Shots, patches, pills . . . it ain't rocket science'. . . ."

Her eyes bugged out. "Your mother's pregnant again?"

I shook my head and stared at her. "Guess again."

Slowly it dawned on her. She started to grin, the little gap between her teeth as charming as ever. She was probably thrilled at the idea of serving me a crow sandwich. "You lyin'!"

"I wish."

She jumped out of her chair and grabbed me. "Oh my God, girl! Our kids are gonna grow up together!"

I was so surprised, I sat there with my arms at my side while she rocked me back and forth in her embrace, her large stomach between us. She was happy about this?! My situation was totally different from hers. She was already on the road to marriage when she got pregnant. She and the father of her child had good jobs. They could afford to buy a house with three and a half baths, a backyard, and a three-car garage. "Stephanie, I'm not keeping it."

She pulled back. "What do you mean?"

"You really don't think I could have Oliver's baby, do you?"

She slowly sat back down. "I guess I won't be taking you upstairs to see the baby's room."

I couldn't believe she said that. She was the one who told me he was too young to get serious with. How much more serious could you get than to have a baby with the man? "I'm not in any position to take care of another person. I'm in school. I'm not making any money. I don't have an apartment. If my situation were different . . ." My voice sounded high and desperate. The look on her face was giving me a sinking feeling in my stomach, but I plunged on. "This isn't easy for me. I don't want to be in this situation."

"Then, don't do it. You can stay in Denver and get a job. Your mom would help you. *I'll* help you. If all these little young girls out here can do it, surely you can."

That wasn't a choice. "No, I can't. I was hoping I could stay here a couple of days, afterward, before I go back to Iowa."

She shook her head like she wasn't believing what she was hearing. "But black women don't have abortions. We keep our babies."

My mouth dropped open. Was she insane? Women have been getting abortions since the beginning of time, including black women, and Stephanie knew it. We both knew girls in high school who had had abortions. "You know that's not true."

"Most of us do keep our babies."

"Stephanie, I can't."

"Why not?"

"I just can't."

"Then give him to me. Greg and I will raise him. Or her."

"What???"

"You could walk away. Soon as the baby comes. You're probably never coming back here anyway. You could just sign the papers and go, and never look back."

I tried one last time to make her understand. "I'm pissed at Nona, but I'm not walking away from Sunny. I plan to stay in touch with my sister. I plan to stay in touch with you. I'll be back here to visit. I couldn't just walk away. You're saying we wouldn't be friends anymore?"

"I'm saying there's something more important to think about than you and me."

She didn't want to see me anymore. I had imagined being part of her family again. But now I worried that Mr. Berry, Cleo, Aunt Lovie, and Aunt Baby Mae would feel the same way. Did this mean that I would lose them too? Is that what life was going to be for me from now on, just one loss after another from one stupid mistake? I thought about the "slipping" condom and felt that sick feeling come over me, like I had swallowed a bucket of slime.

We sat silently, the tension building even though we didn't speak. Stephanie seemed to be carrying on her own internal argument. I was thinking about how stupid I felt for even coming to her house. I had thought we were re-connecting, but now that I thought about all the misunder-standings we had about her mother and my mother, all the near-arguments, I realized we were never going to be friends again. Maybe she had changed or I had changed or maybe we were never really friends to begin with. Maybe there had been a good reason we hadn't stayed in touch when I left town.

Stephanie abruptly broke the silence. "I'm not gonna lie. I'm a Christian. I don't believe in abortion."

"What about premarital sex, you believe in that?" I snapped. "What about drinking and smoking and all the other non-Christian things you do? I smelled you when I came in here. You're still smoking while you're pregnant! Hell, you and Greg go to the *gym* on Sunday mornings, not church!"

"At least I wouldn't kill a baby," she snapped back, clutching her stomach like I was going to come after *her* fetus.

"How can you act holier-than-thou when I know for a fact Greg isn't even your first?"

"So? Oliver's not your first!"

I didn't say anything. I was sorry I had let it slip.

"You trying to tell me Oliver is the first guy you ever slept with?"

I could keep up the charade or I could tell the truth. I was scared to give someone who was already judging me more ammunition, but it seemed clear that our friendship was over. At least I could go out with some integrity. "Yes."

"What about that dude, Joseph, in high school? He went around telling everybody that you guys did it. *You* told me you did it with him. You told me there were guys in college."

"I lied." Soon as I said it, I realized that I had been lying so much and for so long it hadn't even felt like a lie. I wondered how many other things I lied about, where else I fudged the facts to suit myself. I felt coated in slime and the only way to get clean again was to tell the truth.

She narrowed her eyes at me.

"I lied. I lied about all of it. I didn't have sex until six weeks ago."

She nodded, weighing what to say to her lying, baby-killing ex-friend.

I stood up and decided to save her the trouble. "Good luck with everything."

She looked at me guardedly, searching for sarcasm in my meaning. "Same to you."

I meant what I said and I hoped she did too. I looked at the sterile roses, and knew where I needed to go, where I should have gone in the first place. I left her sitting at the table, hands on her stomach. When I started the car, Nina Simone's voice drifted out of the speakers, but I turned off the tape and drove in silence out of the cul-de-sac.

THE FENCE WAS STILL DOWN. I walked up the river rock path and sat down in a chair on the patio. The sun had almost completed its descent behind the mountains. It was freezing. I wanted it to be summer again. I wanted the white roses against the serene blue of the house. I wanted to get dizzy from the scent of flowers in bloom. I wanted the sun high in the sky singeing my skin.

I don't know how long I sat there before Nona came out, pulling her coat on as she walked up to the table. She sat down and handed me a tissue. I realized I was crying, and blew my nose.

We didn't talk. She didn't ask what was wrong. She simply sat with me while I cried. Her coat pocket seemed to have an endless reservoir of Kleenex.

When I finally stopped, she stood up. "Dinner's just about ready." Her breath was white smoke. I followed her through the orange door inside to where it was warm.

Orange Mint and Honey

I QUIT WORKING AT SHAKE IT UP. ACTUALLY, I DIDN'T officially quit, I just never went back. They mailed my last check to Nona's house. Oliver's handwriting was on the envelope. He called a few times, but I wouldn't talk to him.

After a couple of days at Nona's, I scheduled the appointment. The night before the procedure I was weepy and jittery.

After dinner, Nona put Sunny to bed and said, "I had an abortion."

"When?"

"You were three. My mother put us out. We were staying with the asshole of the moment, but I knew it wasn't going nowhere. And I was already drinking too much, getting high. I was afraid there would be something wrong with the baby. I'm sad that I was so messed up, but I'm glad I had the abortion. It would have been a disaster even if I wasn't a drunk. If that's how you feel about this, then you're doing the right thing. But if it's not how you feel . . ."

I sat down. "You think I should have it?"

"Not if you don't want to. Being a single mother is harder than almost anything else in the world."

She paused for a smart-ass comment from me. We were both surprised that I didn't seem to need to make one. She continued, "If you really don't want the child, it would be impossible. What about Oliver?"

"We've only known each other a few months. Plus, he's . . ."

"What?"

"He's the first guy I've ever been with. The only one."

"Oh, Shay."

I looked at my hands in my lap. "You can't end up with the first guy you ever slept with, right?"

"Stranger things have happened. He's in college. He's not a crackhead or a dog. You've already picked better than I ever did."

I shook my head. "I don't see it happening, and I don't want to have a kid without the father. I'm not saying that to hurt you, it's just the truth."

"I understand. I wanted you and Sunny to have fathers."

I was starting to see how sometimes we don't get what we want. It was humiliating to remember how superior I felt to Nona, how stupid I thought she was for getting pregnant with me and Sunny. But she didn't rub my nose in it.

"Do you ever think how different your life would be if

you didn't have kids? Maybe if you didn't have me you wouldn't have started drinking."

"That's not what you think, is it?" She came over and squatted down in front of me so we were face-to-face. "You're not the reason I drank. Honey, listen to me. Please believe this: I drank because I'm an alcoholic. I would have been an alcoholic whether I had kids or not. I was born that way. With my family history, I should have known better than to ever pick up a bottle."

The day after I moved back from Oliver's, tissue boxes had materialized in every room. She handed me a Kleenex from the box on the counter.

"I was self-medicating. I told you, I know something about depression and anxiety. I'm sorry to say, but they run in the family."

"So why did you have me?"

She answered immediately. "I wanted you."

"You were only fifteen. You could have gone to college. You could have done anything with your life."

She leaned in and repeated herself, "I wanted you."

I wanted to believe her so badly, but there was too much evidence to the contrary. "Then, why didn't you stop drinking?"

She started tearing up. "I'm so sorry. I'm so, so sorry."

"At church, you said you got sober because of Sunny." My voice trembled. "Why couldn't you do it for me?"

"That's what upset you so much?" she said softly to herself. "No, remember, I was in A.A. when I got pregnant. I met Sunny's father in A.A. I was already trying to get sober before I got pregnant with her. And it worked because I was finally able to admit that I was out of control. I didn't drink because of you, and there was nothing you could do to make me get sober. None of my behavior was ever your fault.

"I know it makes it no better for you, but I was so crazy back then that I actually thought I was doing right by you, leaving the house to go drink, instead of drinking in front of you."

"I might not have seen you drink, but I saw you vomiting your guts up. I saw you so hungover you couldn't lift your head off the pillow. I saw the bottles you thought you had hidden. I used to pour them out, but you'd just get more to take their place."

"I wish I would have been smart enough or strong enough to go to A.A. when you were small. I wish I could take back your entire childhood and do it over again, the right way. Give you the mother you deserved."

"But you can't."

She sat back on her heels. "No, I can't. But I can be here for you now. God willing, I'll be here for you the rest of my life, if you let me."

I didn't answer.

She handed me a notebook and a pen. "Why don't you go outside?"

I didn't know if I trusted the God box thing. After all, I had "turned over" my virginity and look where it got me. But I was desperate so I put on my coat, grabbed the flashlight, and went outside. I picked up a garden spade and chose one of the bare flower beds that hadn't been burned in the fire. I started to dig a hole hoping that I'd know what to write by the time I was done. A flash of white caught my eye. I pulled out a bit of paper with just one word written on it: *Shay*. I moved the dirt around some more and found another paper with my name. I started digging through the dirt with my hands like a dog searching for a bone, and found other papers with my name on them.

When I was done, I had twenty-nine dirty scraps in front of me. Were they twenty-nine apologies? Twenty-nine blessings? How many other slips of paper in this yard had my name on them? For a long time, I sat with the papers spread out in front of me like the pieces of a jigsaw puzzle. Then I wrote "Nona" on the back of them and returned them to the ground. Whatever she wished for me, I wished for her too.

When I came back inside, she poured us each a cup of tea and we sat at the table.

"A couple of years ago, when Sunny was a baby, I was taking her for a walk in her stroller. I stopped to look at a beautiful front-yard garden. The owner, an older white lady, came out. Plant people recognize other plant people like addicts recognize other addicts. She didn't say hello or tell me her name, just introduced me to the plants like they were her children."

I remembered Nona doing the same with me in her own garden.

"In the corner, near the house, there looked to be a sea of blue mist spirea or peppermint, and I asked which it was. It was orange mint. 'It takes over like a marauding army. I cut it back and cut it back and look at it,' she said. Then, to show me why she didn't get rid of it altogether, she walked over and pulled off some leaves and brought them to me to smell. She said, 'In Africa, they make a wonderful tea with it.'

"I closed my eyes and inhaled. The mint smelled like a just-sliced orange, but not as strong. It was a more relaxing kind of scent. I put a leaf in my mouth. The taste was a mixture of orange peel and grass, and it made me smile. When I opened my eyes, she was grinning at me, happy to see somebody else could appreciate her problem child. 'Come back with a shovel and take as much as you want,' she told me. 'But I warn you: You'll never be able to control it.'

"She was right. I planted the mint next to the shed and it has spread all the way over to trouble the lilacs. But I like it. It's my reminder that we're not always in control.

"Whatever you decide, I will stand by you, and help you as much as I can." She handed me the plastic teddy bear of honey. "Just know this: It's always possible to add sweet to the bitter."

"Thanks, Momo." My childhood name for her slipped from my lips like a song that had been on the tip of my tongue all along.

A slow smile spread across her face.

I squeezed honey into my tea, and drank it down, letting the sweet and the bitter wash over me.

THE NEXT MORNING she took off from work and drove me to the clinic. She was waiting for me when I came back to the waiting room. Before I could say anything, she took my hand. I will remember until the day I die what I saw in her eyes. They said, *Forgive me and forgive yourself.* How many times had she looked at me that way? Maybe hundreds, but this time I could see it, I could feel it. She drove me home, holding my hand all the way, not letting go once.

No More Blues

ON CHRISTMAS EVE, I WAS LYING IN BED THINKING about Jesus' poor mother. Of course, Mary had more reason than I to be shocked at her condition, but still I could relate. It's more than a trip when one day you're a virgin and pretty much the next day you're pregnant.

I wondered what Nina Simone thought about that. She hadn't come to me that day at Oliver's house, but somehow I thought things were working out the way she planned.

I drifted off. At 10:24 P.M. I opened my eyes and saw her silhouette in the doorway, illuminated by the lamplight coming from the next room. I scooted over to make space. I was no longer surprised by these nighttime visits. Momo climbed in beside me. When the itchy hours started now, instead of going outside, she'd come to my room. We talked for hours, sometimes until daylight. More important, we *listened* to each other.

"How are you feeling?" she asked.

"A little shaky." I placed my hands on my still-flat stomach. Actually, I felt like one of Matt's jokes. Girl walks into an abortion clinic . . . and comes out still pregnant. *Ba dum bum.* Some punch line. I had changed my mind. Not because of any arguments for or against reproductive rights. Not because of the two half-assed protestors outside the clinic. Momo had given them one look that said, *Back the fuck off* and they left us alone.

I changed my mind because I could suddenly see with searing clarity that I had spent my entire life thinking about what I *didn't* want, and what kind of person I *didn't* want to be, instead of what I *did* want for myself. Forget about comparing myself to my mother. Forget about WWNSD. I asked myself out loud, "What do *you* want?" The answers must have been there waiting to be summoned all along because they tumbled forth as quickly as my tears. Instead of pretending to be a grown-up, I actually wanted to *grow up*. I wanted to be more than just not-Nona. I wanted to be *myself,* whoever that might be. I wanted to stop being angry and resentful all the time. I wanted to be part of a family with my mother and my sister. And I wanted to believe that she was right: that I could add sweet to the bitter, that maybe I didn't have to end up broke and depressed and driven to drink because I'd be a single mother. I wasn't an ignorant teenager. I would have a master's degree and a viable career and a supportive family and a good relationship with my baby's father, if Oliver still wanted that.

"You ever think about him?"

"Oliver?" I yawned.

"Your dad."

Now I was awake. She had never talked about my father before, unless it was to call him a dog during a drunken fit.

"Sometimes," I admitted. Anthony Thomas. A man barely an adult who wooed a teenaged girl and then left her when she got pregnant. He joined the Marines and went to Japan, halfway around the world, to avoid being my father. Even after we left Kansas City and moved to Denver, I used to look for him on the bus, walking down the street to the grocery store, in the mall, at the movies. All I knew was I was looking for a tall, coffee-brown man. My features were too much like my mother's to expect that I would find my face on a man's body. But that didn't stop me from looking.

"If you wanted to, you could probably find him."

I sat up. "You know where he is?"

"No, but his mother is probably still in Kansas City. You could start with her."

My grandmother. "What's her name?"

"Well, that's where it would get tricky. I only called her Mrs. Thomas. I never knew her first name. But I have her old address."

"Did you love him?" I asked.

"I loved him as hard as a fourteen-year-old girl could." She laughed. "He wanted to be Bootsy Collins. I think I got pregnant with you while we were listening to 'Munchies for Your Love.' Bootsy's Rubber Band. Lord, I haven't thought about that in years."

I imagined my mother as a young girl on a couch with an older boy, at nineteen an adult actually—these days they would prosecute him for statutory rape—with his arms wrapped around her, listening to Bootsy. I could picture her melting at the flattery. I tried to imagine myself at her age, having sex or just being alone in a basement with a boy. When I was fourteen, I was too shy to even smile back at Marquis Jackson. Then I saw my twenty-five-year-old self in bed with Oliver, sunlight coming through the blinds and creating lines on his naked back.

"MOST OF THE TIME if a girl is going to have a dude's baby it's because she loves him," Oliver said hesitantly, pushing his glasses back on his nose.

We were back at the Mercury Café. As soon as he slid into the booth across from me I felt a surprising urge to touch him, to peel off his sweater and see the sun tattooed on his shoulder. My feelings were possessive, almost primal, like my DNA remembered his DNA, and I was taken aback. I thought about our DNA mingling in my body, and it hit me again: I was having Oliver's baby.

He searched my face for the answer to his question.

Who would have thought that walking through those red velvet curtains and up those long steps into the dance hall would ever lead me here? It sounded crazy to say I was ready to have a kid, but not ready to be in a relationship with the father, but it was true. Maybe if Oliver was twenty-five and done with school. Maybe if he had a car and a job that paid more than minimum wage. But I just couldn't see living with Oliver and wiping the kid's behind with Taco Bell napkins. "I care about you so much. . . ."

He tried to smile and held up his hand to stop me. "It's all good."

"I'm going back to Iowa to write my thesis. I'll have the baby there, then come home. I'm going to stay with my mother and Sunny for a while. I don't want to put any financial burden on you."

"They always say that at first," he snapped. "But one day you're gonna come home tired from work to a dirty house and a screaming kid who's outgrown all his clothes, and suddenly putting a financial burden on me is gonna sound like a damn good idea."

I knew he wasn't mad. He was hurt.

He slumped back in the booth. "Don't worry, I'll do my part."

The waitress came to the table. "Do you know what you want?"

I burst out laughing at her question, freaking out Oliver and the waitress.

"I'll come back," she murmured, slinking away.

"This changes my life too, all right?" he said. "It's not all about you."

I collected myself. "You're right." It was the same thing I had once said to my mother. I wondered if everything we did didn't somehow affect someone else. But one thing was for sure: Whatever Oliver and I did from now on was definitely going to affect the baby.

"I want my child to know me," he said. "I don't want to be just some dude who deposited his little donation to the gene pool and moved on. If I'm going to be a father, I want to really be a father."

A baby could do much worse than to have Oliver for a dad. A woman could do much worse than to have him as the father of her child. "I want that too."

The waitress returned, and this time we ordered. After she was gone, Oliver reached in his pocket. "I brought you this. It's for your drive back." He put a cassette tape on the table. "No more blues, all right?"

I reached for the tape, and put my hand over his hand. "All right."

Rebuilding

I POUNDED THE NAIL INTO THE WOODEN SLAT WITH
satisfying thuds. Steve and some of Momo's other A.A.
buddies and I were helping her rebuild her fence. We were a
mini Habitat for Humanity, in jeans and sweatshirts and
bandannas (this time just to keep dirt and sawdust out of my
hair), working in tandem on an unusually warm January
day.

It was strange, great but strange, not to have to do
everything myself. For the first time ever, I had help.
Momo reserved my dorm room and was putting together a
care package for me with enough toiletries and snacks to
last the semester. Semester. How I used to measure time.
Now it would be in trimesters.

I wasn't going to work, so I could make up a couple of
classes and finish my thesis. It would cost me more in student loans, but I knew now that I had limits: I couldn't take
a heavy class load, write a thesis, work, *and* be pregnant and

not end up with bald patches again. I also read the book about adult children of alcoholics. When Momo first gave the book to me, I thought she was trying to make me read something that was going to explain how alcoholism is a disease, and be all like "You wouldn't hate a diabetic, would you?" That it would be about *her*. But instead I saw *myself* all over the place. No matter how many pages I skipped over, no matter where my eyes landed, it was like looking in a mirror, and I knew I had "issues," as Momo would say. So I also made an appointment to see a counselor when I got back to campus.

"What do you think, Nona? It's coming along, isn't it?" asked Shirley, Momo's new sponsor. She had shoulder-length, silver dreadlocks, a serene face, and perfect posture. Nona and I both stood a little straighter in her presence.

"The Lord gives and the Lord takes away and sometimes the Lord gives again," Momo said, handing me a bottle of water.

We smiled at each other.

"I'm glad it's going so quickly, because I'm supposed to see Ivy tomorrow," Nona said.

"You're supposed to what?"

"She's got thirty days clean now. She has a sponsor. She wants to make amends."

I was stunned. Ivy had betrayed all of her trust, had endangered her and Sunny's lives, and yet she was willing to give her another chance.

She anticipated my thoughts. "Ivy's got something strong and good in her. She just doesn't know it yet. But my concern is not what Ivy will do with my forgiveness. I'm forgiving her for myself. To set *myself* free."

I thought about how much Ivy wanted Momo to be her mother, and how much Momo looked up to Lois, and it came to me then that the connection Stephanie and I shared was that we both grew up missing our mothers. All those women singers I loved so much, they weren't just role models, they were the mothers I never had. They had comforted me, educated me, and lifted me up high enough over my life to know that I could be something more than just an alcoholic's daughter. They sustained me. And I would always be grateful. But I knew now what Nina Simone had known when she told me to go home: that there was a vast difference between what my spirit-mothers or play mamas, or whatever you wanted to call them, could give me compared with what a flesh-and-blood, present, willing mother could offer.

The soil still smelled faintly of gasoline. "You going to plant roses again?" I asked.

"I was thinking morning glories," Momo answered.

THE NEXT MORNING, Momo, Sunny, and I got up early to have breakfast before I got on the road. I was stiff from working on the fence, and my breasts were swollen and painfully tender. Momo made her pancakes. But because I still couldn't handle the smells, no burned bacon or coffee. Instead she topped them with homemade blueberry compote. While she cooked and we ate, Take 6 sang, Sunny chattered, and I felt something very much like happiness.

After breakfast and a quick trip to the bathroom (the drive back to Iowa was going to take a lot longer than the drive here, with all the restroom breaks), they walked me to the gate, the two of them with coats over their pajamas. When I had arrived five months ago (only five months!), Momo had been the one with tears in her eyes. This time she was dry-eyed and I was the one who cried.

"God, am I ever going to stop blubbering?"

"Never again," she joked, smiling at me. She pressed something into my hand.

It was an A.A. chip, different from Ivy's, black with a sparkly blue triangle in the center and "IV" in a circle in the middle of the triangle. But like Ivy's it said, *To thine own self be true.*

"Lois gave it to me for my fourth birthday. I want you to hold on to it. By the time you come back, I'll have my five-year chip."

She was making a promise, a promise that I knew I could trust. I slipped the coin into my pocket. "Thanks."

We hugged. "No, thank *you.* To be able to help you, to have something to give you, is an answer to a prayer," she said into my neck, squeezing me tighter.

"Ow!" I pulled away and put my hands to my chest.

She laughed. "I was the same way when I was pregnant with you. My breasts felt like hot-water bottles filled with pins and needles."

"Yes!"

"They'll stop hurting so much in a couple of months."

I hugged Sunny again. "See you later, crocodile."

"See you later, *alligator,*" she corrected.

The idea that she was going to turn four before I saw her again broke my heart a little. "I'll be back before you know it."

"I'll be back before you snow it," she answered.

"We'll have to keep working on the rhyming thing."

I got in my car and drove down the street, looking back in the rearview mirror at what I was leaving behind and what I was taking with me at the same time. I turned on the stereo and put in the tape Oliver gave me. His voice came through the speakers:

"So, this is me, Oliver. I made this tape for you. Picked some good tunes, with some good messages for you. Hope you like it. First up is 'Free Like We Want 2 B' by Ziggy Marley and the Melody Makers. Be free, Glory, but keep in touch, all right? You never know, one of these days a younger man just might sound good to ya."

I laughed and turned the reggae up loud. By the time I was on I-76 the sky had changed from lavender to pink to orange. I rewound the tape. The Melody Makers and I sang about being free, and I headed east into the rising sun.

NONA'S ORANGE MINT TEA

—

Orange mint is easy to grow, but (like all mints) is very invasive. Introduce it in your garden at your own risk! For the best flavor, harvest small leaves on low shoots. This recipe is adapted from a recipe at www.blossomfarm.com.

2 cups dried orange mint (or other garden mint) leaves
8 teaspoons orange pekoe (black) tea
2 tablespoons dried orange peel
1 tablespoon dried lemon peel
1 teaspoon ground cloves

Mix all ingredients in a bowl. Place one tablespoon of mixture into a tea ball. (If you don't have a tea ball, simply place a tablespoon of loose tea in a cup and strain it after it has steeped.) Store in an airtight container for a taste of summer any time of year.

Pour boiling water over the tea ball (or loose tea) and steep for 4 to 5 minutes. Sweeten with honey.

If you don't have a garden, you can still make a wonderful orange mint tea: Steep one peppermint tea bag in a cup for 1 to 2 minutes. Steep one orange tea bag (Tazo Wild Sweet Orange, Celestial Seasonings Tangerine Orange Zinger or Bigelow Constant Comment) for 4 to 5 minutes in a large mug (leaving room to add peppermint tea). Pour ½ cup of peppermint tea into the orange tea. Sweeten with honey.

Serve both recipes hot or over ice.

ORANGE MINT AND HONEY
BUTTER COOKIES

—

Here's a recipe for the cookies Nona serves Shay and Sunny at the beginning of the story. These rich shortbread–style cookies have a lovely orange flavor. The speckles of mint add a hint of interest for the taste buds and the eyes.

Yield: 2 DOZEN COOKIES

1 ½ sticks softened butter

⅓ cup sugar

⅓ cup orange blossom honey (or any other honey)

1 large egg, beaten lightly

1 teaspoon vanilla extract

2 teaspoons orange extract

2 cups unbleached flour, sifted

1 teaspoon baking powder

¼ teaspoon salt

3 tablespoons minced fresh orange mint leaves
(or other mint leaves)

1. Cream the butter, sugar, and honey until light and fluffy. Add the egg and vanilla and orange extracts.

2. Add the dry ingredients and mint. Beat the mixture until combined.

3. Form into a log and wrap in plastic. Chill in refrigerator for 1 hour or in freezer just until firm, about 20 minutes.

4. Preheat oven to 350 degrees. Slice the dough into rounds about ¼-inch thick and arrange them on baking sheets*. Bake 10 to 12 minutes or until the bottoms and edges turn gold. Cool on rack.

*A tip from *The Joy of Cooking:* Put the cookie sheets in the freezer before you put the sliced dough on them. The cookies will hold their shape better.

ACKNOWLEDGMENTS

I THANK MY FAMILY FOR THEIR LOVE AND SUPPORT, especially my beloved grandfather William Oliver Melton, who passed away shortly before publication of this book. (Yes, Oliver Toliver is his namesake.) All this magical music here is Papa speaking through me. Did you hear what I said?

I thank the too-many-to-name relatives, friends, acquaintances, and co-workers who regularly asked me "How's the book?" Now, you can tell me.

I also feel deep gratitude for the following people and organizations: Marisol and Rob Simon for seeing the perfect title inside my story; my agent, Victoria Sanders and her editorial director, Benee Knauer, for believing in this book and in me; Melody Guy for being a supportive editor and a genuinely nice person; Signe Pike, Shona McCarthy, Kate Blum, and all the folks at Random House for their hard work on my behalf; Kelli Martin for her insightful and entertaining Reader's Guide; my reader- and writer-friends

Diane, Maryann, Tanya, Leslie, Ru, Kieran, Cynthia, Karen, Debby, Lois, Val, Marion, Janet, Wuanda, Akasha, Elaine, Gayle, Trina, Tracy, Jan, Heather, Elizabeth, and Constance for ideas, laughs, and encouragement; writing teachers Bill Henderson (Lighthouse Writers) and Venise Berry (University of Iowa) for helping me tell this story; the American Animal Hospital Association for being such a great place to work; and Lighthouse Writers, the Denver Public Library, and Tattered Cover Book Store (all the great indies in Denver!) for making Denver such a wonderful environment for writers and readers. I would like to thank Marilyn Eudaly for getting a good photo of me.

This book is about mothers and daughters so I end by honoring and thanking my mother. I always said she belonged in a book. None of these characters are based on her, but she lives in me and in these pages.

Orange Mint and Honey

Carleen Brice

. . .

A READER'S GUIDE

A Conversation with Carleen Brice

. . .

Kelli Martin is an editor and writer.
A Williams College graduate,
she lives with her husband in Brooklyn, New York.

Kelli Martin: Carleen, let me start out by saying that this is a mesmerizing, powerful novel. I had to stop myself from racing through the pages. It is filled with meaningful layers and symbolism, yet it is so accessible and moving and heartwarming. Shay and Nona and Sunny and Oliver stayed with me long after I had turned the last page.

Now let's begin with *Orange Mint and Honey*'s moment of creation. I read that you knew you were ready to write this story when you heard the voice of Nona, Shay's mother. Often, we read that it's the protagonist's voice that the author hears first. Why do you think it was Nona who you heard first and who moved you to write this novel, rather than Shay?

Carleen Brice: I tried to write this story years ago, but it was too one-sided. I was too young. I think as I got older I related more to Nona's character, and that was really important to me—to make sure that she was a real, three-dimensional person. Shay's voice was already in me for a long time, but I couldn't write the story until Nona came to me.

KM: What classic and contemporary novels, memoirs, or poetry did you have in mind or use for inspiration when you conceived and wrote *Orange Mint and Honey*?

CB: I didn't really have anything in mind when I started. But Alice Walker's essay "In Search of Our Mothers' Gardens" probably was in my mind from the beginning. Such a great metaphor for the unsung contributions of the women who came before.

KM: Carleen, you write some of the truest, most raw and powerful scenes: Shay losing her virginity, Shay and Nona's confrontational showdown in the church. Is this something you had to work at—making these parts ring so emotionally true? Or is this an element of your writing that comes naturally, almost easily, to you? Did you have to dig deep into your own life to capture the requisite emotion or is it more your creative imagination inhabiting someone else's life? Or both?!

CB: The easiest scenes for me to write are the highly emotional ones. I can just put myself there and feel what the characters are feeling. Sometimes as I'm writing I'm speaking the words out loud as the characters would, almost like I'm reading a script in my head as I type. Those scenes pour out, but they are exhausting! Especially a scene in which I have to put myself into the minds of both people, to keep track of how both people would naturally feel.

KM: Gardens figure prominently in *Orange Mint and Honey,* from therapy to solace to peace to wishing well to healthy addiction to site for growth. Do you share the characters' love of gardens? If so, what drew you to fall in love with them in the first place and how do they figure in your life now? Why do you see them as healing?

CB: I do have a love of gardens. Until a few years ago, I was always just a container gardener, but Denver has been in a long-term drought, so my husband and I got rid of the front lawn and started planting low-water plants. (It's called a "xeriscape garden.") I worked on our yard as I wrote about Nona's yard, and just sort of turned into her. I even use Nona's "God box" concept (and it works!!).

Gardening is healing (and addictive) because it works on you on so many different levels. Physically, it's movement, so you get endorphins. Psychologically, it's rewarding to have a vision in your mind and see it come to fruition in your yard. And since it never turns out quite like you envision, it's spiritual, because it helps you see there are forces at work in the universe far bigger than we are. And just the beauty of flowers is healing, the colors and the scents. There's just something magical about the whole experience.

KM: To cope with her emotions and the stress in her life, Shay pulls her hair. Why did you use trichotillomania to show her anxiety?

CB: I wanted a visual way to show that her childhood still affected her. It's one thing for a character to *say* she's been hurt or traumatized, but it takes it to a different level to show what that really means. I have a good friend who suffers from this form of OCD and she let me use it in this story.

KM: Which character was most natural to write and why? Which was most challenging to write? Were you surprised by which character(s) became your favorites or least liked?

CB: I was surprised by how much I liked Oliver. Originally, he was just this geek, but he turned into such a wonderful person. I absolutely love him. Love, love, love him! I didn't have any young guys read for me, but Oliver is a combination of the good boyfriends I had (not many) when I was young, and my husband, and my brothers and my nephews. And . . . a guy who used to work at my video store. Every time I went in, I just wanted to pinch his cheek.

Ivy was the most challenging character to write. I empathized with her, but at the same time I knew she wasn't going to get her act together, which was important to show: Not everybody recovers. That's life. But she was so manipulative and hostile that it was hard to remember her humanity, and that underneath it all she was a lost girl just like Shay. They are kind of two sides of the same coin.

KM: Nina Simone is a provocative choice for a character. Why her and what do you think her role is? What impact has she had on your own life and love of music? What other classic and contemporary singers do you love?

CB: Nina Simone is the herald who sets Shay on her path, and she's a straight-shooting guardian angel. She's like Glinda the Good Witch, only with more sass and more soul. Why her? Because she's the one who came to me. And I instantly loved the idea because she was such a larger-than-life character in real life.

I love all the singers I mention in the book (including Bootsy Collins!). I like old-school R & B and neo soul. I'm a huge Prince fan (as was Nona), and I love Erykah Badu and Jill Scott. I just saw Corinne Bailey Rae and John Legend in concert, and will definitely keep my eyes and ears on both of them.

KM: Was it a deliberate choice to make Shay a virgin? We'd love to know why.

CB: It was not a deliberate choice at all. True story: I was washing dishes, thinking about the story and realized *Oh my God! She's a virgin!* You would think that since she's a character that I made up I would know such a thing, but I was a good chunk into the first draft before I discovered her secret. And, of course, that dramatically affected the direction of the plot. It's like that old line about if you show a gun in the first act, somebody better shoot it before the play is over. Well, if a twenty-five-year-old is a virgin (and doesn't want to be) . . .

KM: You do an extraordinary job, Carleen, of exploring and evoking how hurt Shay has been by her mother's alcoholism. In fact, Shay tempers her begrudging love for Nona with constant reminders (self talk) about her mother's mistakes. It's an amazing way for the reader to learn about both women and about the past. Was this balance deliberate? If so, why did you want to explore that?

CB: This is the root of the book, that we can love someone and hate them at the same time. Especially a parent. The mother–daughter relationship can be so complicated in the best of circumstances, and when you add an issue like alcoholism it compounds it so much. I wanted to make it clear that both women have very complex emotions.

KM: You did a wonderful job making sure Nona came across as sympathetic and human, not a one-dimensional bad guy. What research did you do to accomplish this? Do you think Nona deserves the punishment Shay gives her?

CB: I read a lot about recovering women alcoholics. One of the common characteristics is deep guilt for what their drinking did to their children, and women typically have a very hard time forgiving themselves for it. Our society is very, very hard on mothers who don't live up to almost impossible standards. And when you take a woman like Nona, who really did do bad things, I could see how she wouldn't be able to forgive herself. But it's actually an important part of recovery to let the past go, and stop torturing yourself, and I wanted that for her.

Nona does deserve what she gets from Shay. But I agree with Nona that, after a while, it's obvious that Shay doesn't want to let Nona make amends. To me, that's one of the interesting aspects of forgiveness. The person who is wounded must be willing to accept the apology (when it's sincere) and if she won't, then there's nothing the person who caused the harm can do. Nona's efforts are sincere, so I'm glad when Shay finally gives her a chance. To me, that's what forgiveness is: just the willingness to loosen one's grip on the grudge and see what happens.

KM: The mother-daughter church showdown is out of sight! Why did you choose the church as the locale for this necessary confrontation? Why did you write it with some of the women taking Shay's side and some taking Nona's side?

CB: Thank you! It was very important to me that Nona be able to air her side of the story, and I needed a way for her to also show that she was fed up with trying so hard. The church was a natural place to do that. I'm not a regular churchgoer, but one of the things I love about the idea of church is that it should be a place of truth, a place to be stripped bare, and a place to be real. That's when healing and forgiveness can really happen.

I wrote some of the congregation taking Shay's side and some taking Nona's side because I saw that happening with readers. In one of my critique groups, the women who were daughters, but not mothers, took Shay's side and the women who had kids took Nona's side. As the writer, it was fun to see that happening, so I decided to put it in the book. I think it makes it a much better scene. Thank God for writers' groups!

KM: About your writing process: Do you have a specific place or time of day when you craft your work? Do you work from an outline where the entire book is laid out from beginning to end or do you write free-form, from what unfolds organically from your mind?

CB: I have a home office and I have a laptop. So sometimes I work in my office, sometimes in the kitchen, sometimes on the patio or in a coffee shop. I prefer to write first thing in the morning, but I write at night, whenever. All the time!

I kind of write and outline at the same time, going act by act. The middle is usually the hardest part for me, so I need to have lots of ideas going into the middle or else I get in trouble.

KM: What are you working on next?

CB: My next novel is about two sisters. The two sisters, one biracial and one white (they have the same mother, but different fathers), were separated by adoption. The biracial sister was adopted and raised by a black family. The white sister was kept and raised by their grandmother. The story explores race and identity and what makes a family.

KM: Thank you so much for taking time to chat with us, Carleen. *Orange Mint and Honey* is a love story and a family drama full of hope and humor—and so much powerful, raw emotion. I think I speak for all of your fans when I say that we can't *wait* to see more novels from you in the future.

Reading Group Questions and Topics for Discussion

. . .

1. Forgiveness is a central theme in the novel. Explore the ways in which Shay, Nona, Stephanie, Lois, Ivy, and Oliver take steps to forgive or not forgive one another. How does each person redeem (or not) him- or herself?

2. What do you think the author's perspective is on forgiveness? In your own life, what paths to forgiveness have you taken? Do you think the past ever ceases to matter, when it comes to matters of forgiveness and redemption?

3. In what ways does Shay show her love *and* hate for her mother? Do you feel more sympathetic toward or side with either of the two women more than the other? Why?

4. At what point in the novel does Shay stop constantly recounting her mother's past? In what ways does Shay finally start to open up to Nona?

5. Motherhood is a pivotal theme in Carleen's debut novel: There are many mothers and daughters, surrogate mothers, and surrogate daughters in *Orange Mint and Honey*. Dis-

cuss the roles of motherhood—and daughterhood—each of the main women characters play. What makes a woman a mother?

6. Throughout the novel, Shay is on the cusp of womanhood. At what point(s) does she decide and actually begin to grow up and embrace her future? Pinpoint in your own lives a moment or experience in which you started to become an adult woman.

7. There are several sisters and surrogate-sister relationships in *Orange Mint and Honey:* Shay and Sunny, Lois and Nona, Ivy and Shay. Explore each dynamic and how they are sisters to each other.

8. Throughout the novel, Shay is determined to make Nona "pay" for her past mistakes as a mother. At a gathering of recovering alcoholics Shay thinks: "Where were the signs of the wrong choices they had made? Years of drinking should have ravaged these women. I wanted scars." And "It was all I could do not to run back into the kitchen and let her have it, but she wanted it too much. Silence was how I could make her pay."

Do you think Nona deserves Shay's punishment? Why or why not? In your own life or in society as a whole, explore the various degrees of "mistakes" that mothers are allowed or not allowed to make. What are their consequences?

9. What do you think Nina Simone's role in the story is? Why does Shay admire Nina so much? Explore the role music plays in *Orange Mint and Honey*.

10. Why do you think Shay pulls her hair (a condition known as trichotillomania)? In what ways does your body show its stress and overwhelming emotions?

11. Part of Nona's recovery is working in the garden. What role does the garden play in Nona's and Shay's lives? In your own lives, is there a similar space that you see as healing?

12. Oliver is a powerful force in Shay's life. What part did he play in her maturing and becoming a woman? Why do you think she decided not to continue her relationship with him? Do you think she *could* have—or should have—continued to be with him?

13. When Shay returns home, she sees that Stephanie's home and her personal style are extremely different than what they used to be. What is the significance of this? Discuss one of your close friendships that may have shifted after the two of you had been close in childhood or college. Why do you think that shift occurred?

14. After being in a relationship with Oliver and after yelling at Nona in church, Shay's feelings had become "completely out of control" and an "emotional overflow." Why do you think this happened and why is it significant? Dis-

cuss a time in your own life when you have felt and done the same.

15. Shay tries so hard to not be like her mother. Throughout the novel, in what ways are Shay and Nona different, and in what ways do their choices and personalities become more similar? What about for you and your own mother or mother figure?

CARLEEN BRICE has edited and authored nonfiction books, but this is her first novel. She also has written for various publications including *Mademoiselle,* the *Chicago Tribune, The Denver Post,* and BET.com. She lives in Denver, where she and her musician husband spend their free time growing lots of drought-tolerant plants and letting their two cats in and out of the house. You can visit her online at www.carleenbrice.com and http://pajama gardener.blogspot.com, where she blogs about writing, gardening, and other topics that strike her mind or boggle her fancy.